Tonya

Books by Gregory Boyington

BAA BAA BLACK SHEEP

Tonya

by

COL. GREGORY "PAPPY" BOYINGTON

THE **BOBBS-MERRILL** COMPANY, INC.
A SUBSIDIARY OF HOWARD W. SAMS & CO., INC.
Publishers · INDIANAPOLIS · NEW YORK

This book is a work of fiction, and
any resemblance between its characters
and real persons living or dead is coin-
cidental.

I DEDICATE THIS BOOK TO MY INSPIRATION—
MY BELOVED WIFE, JO.

MAY ALL THE WOMEN OF THE WORLD PROFIT BY IT
AND THE MEN TAKE CARE!

CONTENTS

Tonya

1 · The Battling Brownfields

BY THE END OF 1941, almost anything Russian was assumed to be an asset—if one could believe what one read. But Russell Bush momentarily lost track of any such assumption, as he supported the upper part of his naked body on one elbow. He had recoiled to this position in surprise. He realized that the shapely form, presently pinned down by the pressure from his thighs, had slept with other men. But then he, too, had slept with other women.

For a moment he wondered whether passion could have distorted what he had heard. Never before in his experience had the ultimate moment been climaxed by the cry of another man's name: "Jacques—Jacques—Jacques!"

Russell waited. He was not trying to be polite, or patient. Through the windows the moonlight dimly outlined heaving well-formed breasts, as the pulsing in the slender throat subsided. There wasn't sufficient light to show the green of the woman's large eyes set off by her fine auburn hair. Only her soft white skin.

The Burma night was soundless.

"Just who in the hell is Jacques, Toni?" Russell's deep voice shattered the silence like glass.

"What difference does it make, Rusty?" Tonya teased. Her voice had a faintly hissing accent, provokingly hard to identify, but delightful nevertheless.

"You know I'm married," she said. "You've never been really interested in me—except for the night."

"Well . . ." He realized any advantage he might have had over Tonya was gone. "Sure I'm interested in you, Toni. But who—?"

"Maybe you won't care for me as much, but I feel like talking tonight."

"Be my guest, you gorgeous rascal."

Rusty rolled over on his back, barely listening as Tonya talked on. He anticipated getting a few polite catnaps before dawn arrived, and time to sneak back to his own quarters.

"I've kept my background my own business," Tonya reminisced. "When people ask me, 'What is your accent?' I say, 'Just an American, that's all.'"

Tonya's voice droned on and on. Gradually Russell learned that back in Russia her "papá" had been a mining engineer who worked for the Czar—until the Revolution. Though not technically an aristocrat, he was regarded with suspicion, as was any educated person at that time. Sooner or later the family would have been in danger. So, in 1920, he had taken his family to Mexico. Tonya kept insisting that she really couldn't remember any of this because by the time they arrived in Mexico City she was only three.

The Berovsky family found Mexico a sanctuary for victims fleeing from governmental upheavals and for revolutionists as well. And for Americans, who liked what the United States had to offer, but had larceny in their hearts.

By the time Tonya was in high school, she was able to converse and write in three languages. Two came quite automatically—the Russian and the Mexican—but she made a special effort for the English. The customs, mannerisms and actions of the Americans she met had fascinated her. Tonya knew she was going to marry an American and wind up in the United States some day.

Rusty stifled a yawn.

By Tonya's second year in the University of Mexico, her mother frequently made inquiries regarding her daughter's plans, if any, for marrying one of the local young men. Tonya made her answers short and sweet: "Quique, Paco, Carlos, Juan—all of them—peons!" Invariably after such questioning she left the house in a huff with disgust written on her face.

Tonya had no trouble in handling her father. Whenever he questioned any part of her behavior, she would give a little shrug and look down at the vee in her bosom. If they were outdoors she would whirl rapidly, ballooning up a full skirt until her short panties showed. Her father would caution: "Tonya, you must not do this. Your legs are shapely, but the streets are no place for ballet."

Perhaps the local fellows weren't for Tonya. But her

younger sister Kira had decided not to let any good bets go by, and had left school in her junior year to marry the son of a German immigrant.

A familiar movement in Tonya's body as she talked now about sex prodded Rusty from his dozing.

"I had seen her husband Carl many times," she went on, "but, for some reason, I never really noticed him—not until their wedding."

"Good God, you're not trying to tell me you made your sister's husband!" Rusty exclaimed.

"Why not?" Tonya turned and kissed him on the shoulder. "I've told you before, I'm a nymphomaniac. I can't help it."

"I know. But there ought to be a limit to everything." He spoke with finality. "How did you manage without your sister catching on?"

"That was easy. Kira always went to Mass and came home at a certain time. But one day, the whole family came home earlier for some reason or another, and caught both of us without a stitch on. You should have been there—half of my family screaming in Russian, and the other half in Mexican."

"I'm real sorry I had to miss that," he laughed.

"Shh—I think I hear something," Tonya cautioned.

"Just the guard being relieved," Rusty reassured her after a pause. "No need for alarm."

The guard procedure sounded familiar enough to ex-Marine, Russell Bush, even if he couldn't understand the commands of the detachment of Gurkhas that protected, professionally, the airstrip and the one-story, thatch-roofed buildings.

"They startled me, but I like their protection." Tonya sighed. "I don't trust these Burmese."

"Great as they are," Rusty said sarcastically, "they're no damn good to me."

Tonya's eyebrows arched into a puzzled expression, but she said nothing.

"I don't believe a whole army of Gurkhas," he went on, "could possibly understand the only warning I need is when and if one certain party, a bird who calls himself Lieutenant Colonel August Brownfield, is arriving."

"Oh, Auggie!" Tonya said disgustedly.

The last legitimate rank August Brownfield had held was First Lieutenant, United States Army Air Corps. He had held it from the time he managed to graduate from West Point with a regular commission in 1927, until June of 1936.

After serving a mandatory two years with the gravel-crunchers, he transferred to the Air Corps, not because he had guts or loved flying, but because Auggie always had to have more money. (The services gave an additional half pay for wings.) Spending money made up for his lack of self-confidence. He was aware that his abilities were sadly limited.

During the Depression Thirties, a first louie getting flight pay, and with no income tax or wife, was considered pretty well off. That was not the case with August, even though all his drinks were for free while he was on the base, because he was manager of the Officers' Club at Kelly Field. In a matter of months the club became a non-profit organization—not that it was intended that way.

Auggie was called into the C.O.'s office. Next came a preliminary investigation for a general court-martial. Since regular officers are usually given a choice at times like these, Brownfield did what all smart people who are guilty do—he resigned.

Fortunately Auggie had entertained a few of the right people, and had a knack for impressing anyone who didn't know him very well. According to Auggie, his personal connections with the heads of foreign governments were plentiful. So Don Dodds, the president of Westlake Aircraft Company in Los Angeles, hired him as the company's first foreign salesman, and gave him practically an unlimited expense account.

Auggie stuffed a fat cash advance into his wallet, and smiled reassuringly at the president of Westlake. As they shook hands Auggie said: "I know my friend the President of Mexico will buy three transports, and probably three pursuit squadrons. But the big market is China. China is going to be in the market for unlimited numbers of planes of all categories to fight the Japs."

"That's very interesting," the president of Westlake said. "But you go to Mexico first." Westlake, he implied, would be more than happy with a firm order for three transports. It would be expensive to shoot for the moon first.

Life at the Hotel Reforma in Mexico City was made to order for August Brownfield. He even sold one plushed-up transport to Mexico's President, after he had finally located the proper person to take ten per cent of the sale price.

For nearly a year after this stroke of good fortune, Auggie continued living the life of Riley. It was then that he met Tonya. But finally his wires to Westlake's president for more expense money brought an ultimatum in the form of a telegram. Its arrival marked the first of many occasions to follow when Tonya saw Brownfield's blandly handsome face turn red with rage.

She read the message over his shoulder:

RETURN LOS ANGELES STOP IMPERATIVE
YOU SAIL FAR EAST STOP ALL FUTURE
EXPENSES REIMBURSED AFTER SALES
DON DODDS

It was then that August and Tonya had really got together. Each needed the other desperately. To her, August was a rich American—and marriage. To him, Tonya

17

was a necessary contact for getting enough money to return to Los Angeles and pacify Westlake.

Auggie said an American magazine wanted a picture of Leon Trotsky. Tonya revealed that Trotsky was a friend of her father. Eager to be helpful, she encouraged her father's friend to walk to the gate of his garden which bordered the street. At the last minute Tonya realized this was nothing but a ruse to assassinate the revolutionist. She let out a piercing scream. The plot failed.

Suddenly Tonya realized how much she needed to marry an American.

The boldest deal August had ever undertaken had collapsed—and the other half of the money was gone. Originally, he had planned to travel alone. Now, discretion told him it would be far safer to hurry and take two with the half already collected.

An attractive young wife with a cute hissing accent might have been the deciding factor. At any rate, Don Dodds either had a change of heart, or he was convinced all over again.

From 1937 to 1941, every major city up and down the Far East Coast, from Hong Kong to Soerabaja, Java, had been blessed with the presence of the "Battling Brownfields," as they were soon and appropriately titled. For even though they seemed to be lovebirds when they appeared at any social function, and Auggie proudly introduced his beautiful wife, most of the others present had heard the shouts of "You did too!" and "I most certainly did not!" as the Brownfields were dressing for the occasion. Auggie's diffidence was not helped in the slightest by marriage to Tonya. Now even he doubted his virility.

At Hanoi, French Indo China, Auggie had presented his young wife to a member of the Gendarme stationed at the Citadel.

"Captain Jacques Le Blanc, may I present Mrs. Brownfield."

"*Enchanté, M'sieu Capitain,*" greeted Tonya, taking in the wiry Frenchman's good looks.

"Ahh—*Madame parle Français,*" he said, his eyes brightening at the warmth of her glance.

"*Un peu,*" she smiled. "*Je comprends bien. Il faut que je trouve quelqu' un qui parle Français.*" She looked at him with one eyebrow raised in obvious question.

As Auggie stepped aside to greet a passer-by, Jacques smiled knowingly at Tonya and replied, "One so lovely should never be lonely. I will be happy to spend my spare time conversing with you——" As Tonya moved closer he took a quick breath and added, "To help your French."

"*Bon, ce soir.*" Tonya raised her eyes to his in promise, then turned to join her husband.

19

TONYA

"*A bientot*," Jacques said, as his eyes followed Tonya's departure.

That night, and many nights to follow, Jacques was an invited guest in Tonya's boudoir, entering via the window. Conversations were always low, and in French, but not of the drawing room variety. They practiced the technique of French amour. Unknowingly, Auggie had been sleeping in his own bedroom at the opposite end of the house—most of the time.

"Do you mind the window, darling?"

"*Ma chérie*, the window is nothing," he replied. "Mountains or wars cannot stop me from having you."

"Yes, yes," she panted, "being together has brought every part of my body alive. Some I didn't know existed."

"*Rien n'importe si tu es à moi!*"

"You're so deep, I'm getting weak, make me yours! Take me—take me!" came her breathless cry.

"*Ma chérie—ma chérie—tu es magnifique!*" He pressed his lips hard upon hers, muffling further words.

Tonya writhed, turning her head from side to side, as if in agony, and in a much louder voice cried out, "Jacques—Jacques—Jacques!"

At the sound of Auggie's incessant pounding on the door Tonya and Jacques attempted to suppress their heavy breathing, until certain it could not be overheard. They waited. It was an eternity. The pounding of their hearts resisted any such control, and got louder and louder and louder.

20

"Let me in. Unlock this god-damn door," Auggie screamed, his voice becoming almost a shriek as he added, "There's somebody in there, and I know who it is!"

"You haven't time to dress, Jacques," Tonya whispered during the clatter, "and you can't leave naked. You must hide here." Then for Auggie's benefit she faked a sleepy voice saying, "What on earth is it now? Hold on a minute, I'm getting my robe!"

Perhaps Jacques had foresight, or maybe he had been in similar circumstances previously. Before Tonya could finish her conversation, Jacques and his clothing were on the floor, tucked in tight at the foot of the bed. The bed-spread draped over him loosely, covering everything underneath in large, unassuming folds.

The lights were on as red-faced Auggie stormed past his wife to the window and peered into the darkness.

"Can't a person have a little fresh air," she asked indignantly, "or a little sleep for that matter?"

"I know that Frog has been here," Auggie howled. "He didn't have time to dress!"

He quieted down, more or less talking to himself. "Oh, here you are!" he repeated in advance each time he looked anywhere: the bathroom, the closets, under the bed and even in the dresser drawers before he was through. Completely baffled, Auggie decided to call it a night and started out of the room. He stopped at the door with a look of desperation, as if he wanted to say, "I know he's here—but where?"

In silence Tonya smiled smugly, thinking, "You searched everywhere, stupid—everywhere except where a Frenchman would hide."

Rusty Bush was not too unhappy when his bed partner finally finished talking. He knew better than to be jealous of Tonya. Anything that hadn't been said about Auggie could be easily assumed. Now that her exclamation of "Jacques" had been accounted for, he took it more as flattery than anything else.

Anything connected with endurance, Rusty did better than anyone else and more often—including drinking. Handsome in a Neanderthal way, he had an animal-like sense that warned him about people and situations capable of bringing harm.

Tonya rolled over and rested a soft cheek on Rusty's chest. The pressure of her firm breasts felt hard, even against his well-muscled abdomen. Her fingers rubbed his short-cropped hair. Then a circular movement by her hand across his skin, including the fronts of his thighs and his lower belly, made him realize that he was being invited.

"Better be careful, Toni," he warned, "you're waking up the dead."

"Oh, darling—darling—darling."

"That's much better," Rusty approved, recalling "Jacques."

"At least, much safer," she answered coyly.

This night was reminiscent of a few others as far as August Brownfield was concerned. He was red-faced and angry. He shouted. He banged upon a locked door. And he entered and searched with the same discouragement as a desert prospector searching in the heat for the "Lost Dutchman's Mine."

"Why can't you let me sleep? You know what a day I have tomorrow," Auggie screamed as if it were already ruined. "We have that important meeting with Paul Eddy. If things aren't right, our Lend-Lease may be cut off. Even the Empress may fly down. The old man expects me to have a clear head and keep everything under control."

"Then why don't you try sleeping?" Tonya said. "If Francis Stud wanted you to do anything but stand around, he would have told me."

Before he lost any more prestige Auggie stormed out and slammed the door behind him. The spread over the foot of the bed flew up, and Rusty proceeded to dress for the trip to his quarters. There wasn't enough darkness left to bother, really. In an effort to get away, he finally had to pull first one arm, then another from around his neck.

"Promise you'll see me tomorrow," Tonya pouted.

"I've already told you—if I can," he said with irritation. "Say, by the way, just how close to Colonel Francis Stud are you?"

"If you don't promise," she threatened, releasing her grip but still pouting, "I'll tell the colonel that you kissed me."

"Go ahead." But his tone changed as he stepped through the doorway and winked over his shoulder, "But puh—leese don't tell him where!"

2 · Top Level Dilemma

A PADDLE-BLADE FAN rotated clumsily overhead. The monsoons were over, and it was beginning to get hot in Central Burma as early as ten in the morning. Any breeze was welcome. The people in the Paygoo clubhouse, benefiting by the meager airflow from the fan, were designated as members of the Flying Sharks staff. Usually, they did nothing. Now they were waiting.

The working members of the Flying Sharks were on the nearby R.A.F. airfield doing what they did everyday—working on planes.

Colonel Francis Stud had been north for nearly two weeks. Everyone was anxious for his return, and perhaps some important news from the Empress. The reports said he would be arriving that morning. They also said Paul Eddy would be arriving from Rangoon some time that day.

Paul Eddy was not generally well known. He didn't have to be—to be important to this group. The red carpet was rolled out, in any event.

TONYA

The Brownfields had never met Paul Eddy.

"I understand this Eddy is a pretty dapper gent. Really goes for the dames," Auggie spoke up.

"Oh?" Tonya replied, showing little interest.

The three pilots present were the Flying Sharks squadron commanders, chosen from the first detachment that arrived in Burma. To anyone who knew anything about flying, it was obvious that Tonya had been instrumental in their selections. For what they lacked in flying ability, they more than made up for in sex appeal.

"Everything will be okay, if he stays out of Stud's territory," one of the pilots mumbled with a knowing glance at Tonya, as if he had heard her saying to herself: "Things are looking up. Maybe a new playmate tonight. I hope the god-damn boy changed my bed sheets this morning!"

Tonya scuffed a shoe in impatience. "There's absolutely nothing worse than waiting. Especially in a sticky place like Paygoo."

Still she realized that waiting was important. She knew, and she knew that everyone knew, the rumor that Auggie had been the only Asiatic bum turned down when he applied for a position with the Sharks. Outside of the pilots, the entire staff were already in the Far East prior to 1941, doing business of some kind—God knows what. Auggie had once served under Stud in the Air Corps. And once had been quite enough. However, Francis Stud decided Auggie should have another chance—after he met Tonya. He had made August Brownfield his executive officer.

"Eddy certainly came up fast," said Doc Ward, the round little Flight Surgeon. "Eight years ago he was in college, with only one threadbare suit to his name. More often than not," he went on reflectively, "it's more profitable for a man not to share the limelight. Then a change in his character is less noticeable."

"Do you think this Eddy person will show up?" Tonya asked a little anxiously. After all, she was thinking, there hadn't been anything new with pants on for some time.

"Unless I miss my guess," the surgeon predicted, "it will be late afternoon. Paul Eddy is not one to leave the cool of Rangoon in the heat of the day."

Tonya got to her feet, stretching languidly. "I'm tired of waiting around here," she announced, "I'm going home."

One of the three squadron leaders leaped up. "I'll drive you over, Mrs. Brownfield. I've got a jeep just outside."

Tonya smiled at him gratefully and took his arm. She was not going to miss being on hand the moment either Stud or Eddy arrived.

Out on the Paygoo airstrip, the hot air hung motionless. The direct sun made it impossible to handle any metal parts. Almost the only movement was the forced breathing of members of the Flying Sharks. Here and there, a black tarpaulin stretched over a plane, the four corners supported by poles standing at odd angles, and sagged in the middle. Underneath a crew might be working.

As he walked slowly in loose gravel bordering the macadam strip, Rusty Bush was deep in thought, his tropical pith helmet pushed back on his head at a jaunty angle, though with his beetle-browed countenance and deep-set eyes, he didn't really need a hat at all. Rusty altered his direction without moving any faster, as he saw Chuck Reynolds, the line chief, motioning to him from under the tarp.

"Any new scuttlebutt?" The muscular line chief wiped tobacco juice from his unshaven chin with a hairy forearm. Chuck had acquired his job because no one else wanted to stand up to him. In a Utopian air force, without rank or discipline, knowing how to take care of oneself helps.

"Why ask me? I'm not in charge."

"Oh, I dunno'." Chuck returned to his work so that he wouldn't have to face Rusty. "Just figured you might of talked to someone who did, that's all. Somehow, after Brownfield made all that commotion last night, I couldn't get back to sleep till you sacked in."

Rusty changed the subject abruptly. "Will you guys ever finish these damn P-40's so I can fly? The third detachment of pilots are arriving soon."

Rusty had arrived in the second detachment, but Chuck had come over with the first, in March of 1941.

"Don't tell me your troubles—you ex-officers have it easy. That lying FEAMCO Rep said us mechs would be supervisors. The slopeheads would do all the work. Even told us to take warm clothes because it's cold in China. What a laugh! I've been in Burma nearly a year."

"Did Lafayette Escadrille Oldfield recruit you, Chuck?"

"One and the same. I was a tech sergeant at Selfridge Field when he got me. We called him 'Pruneface.'"

"Okay, Pruneface, then, told us the slopeheads were building hot stuff to fly at Toyling. How come nothing but P-40's?"

"Hell, in order to get something they wanted, like butter, the British had to take so many P-40's. The Limeys didn't give a damn about the planes, but they sure raised hell if anyone tried to get a pound of butter or a pack of American cigarettes designated to them. Stud got tired waiting for planes so he made up his own cablegram and we gave it to the Rangoon port authorities and they turned the planes over to us."

"God, no wonder forty of the first arrivals went back home. Nothing to fly, plus Brownfield." Rusty shook his head. "That's tough to take."

"Those six guys who spun in didn't help any either. Say, what makes these planes spin end over end—and so hard to get out?"

"Jesus Christ, man, you don't have to be an engineer to figure that out!"

"What do you mean, Rusty?"

29

"This model wasn't designed for all that load—guns, ammunition, and self-sealed tanks. And if you think that hunk of armor plate you're sweating over isn't a few feet from the C.G.—you're crazy!"

Suddenly Chuck pointed over Rusty's shoulder. "Say," he teased, "look who's coming in the jeep. And I don't think she's coming to see me!"

Rusty flushed as he turned to see Squadron Leader Robert Sanderson III, driving Tonya. "Wonder what they're doing away from the clubhouse fan."

From the approaching jeep Tonya called in a possessive tone, "Rusty, come here." His faint flush turned to beet red in front of the burly mechanic. "Oh, hello, Reynolds," she added as an afterthought. Chuck was an ex-enlisted man and could never be of any use to her.

"Hi, Toni—hi, Sandy." To avoid any further remarks from Chuck, Rusty walked out to meet the two as they alighted from the jeep. "What brings you out in the heat of the day?"

"Colonel Stud will be landing in a few minutes in the Beech," Sandy said. "Looks like him coming now—it's a twin."

By the time the Twin Beech had landed and rolled to a stop, the entire staff was lined up on the hot strip. Francis Stud alighted from the plane, followed closely by an insipid-looking newsman Rusty recognized as Gilbert Withcomb.

The colonel looked dapper in his uniform with its Chinese colonel's insignia. With a half smile, he shook a few proffered hands, among them August Brownfield's.

"It's wonderful to have you back, Colonel," Auggie palavered. "I have everything in order, sir."

"Thanks, Brownfield, I'd like to have the personnel gather in the clubhouse, say, in thirty minutes."

"Yes sir." With a sharp salute, Auggie jumped into his jeep and started driving about the area like an ant on a red hot stove, ordering each man officiously, "You'll report to the clubhouse at exactly 1100. Failure to do so will result in a court-martial."

"Where in hell does he get this court-martial crap?" a crewman snarled after Auggie had departed. "We're civilians, not servicemen, under a year's contract like any other employee."

"The bastard hates everybody, including himself," another crewman observed. "Must have nightmares of facing general courts in his brilliant past."

The group dispersed and headed for the clubhouse. The majority walked, for transportation was limited. Stud sat beside Tonya in the back seat while Robert Sanderson III drove. The colonel allowed sufficient time for the jeep to kick up a camouflage of dust, before he reached for Tonya's hand.

"Tell me, how has our little Group Historian been?"

"Lonesome. I've missed you!" Tonya rubbed a bare

knee against the finely creased khaki trousers. "When you assigned me Historian of the Group, you said I would have to travel with you. Instead, you take that character Withcomb."

"Now, now, what is this, professional jealousy?" Stud consoled. "Withcomb won't be here forever. You'll have enough material to write a whole book if you want."

"It isn't that."

"He tries to be nice to you. What is it then?"

"The guy's a real creep. I can't stand anyone who shoots birds in trees with a shotgun," Tonya said emphatically. Then in a warmer tone, "You haven't told me about Kunking yet."

"It's almost 1100. Think you can wait till then?"

Waiting for the colonel at the clubhouse, the group speculated with griping remarks on what the meeting might cover.

Promptly at 1100 Auggie called, "At-ten-shun!"

Francis Stud entered.

"At ease, gentlemen," Stud began. "From time to time we will gather for a critique. On these occasions, I will keep you posted on the most recent developments affecting the Group, mostly for the benefit of the recent arrivals. I will explain progress of the Group to date, and the plans for the future. As I understand, rumor and your imaginations are running away with you.

"A cablegram came last night which may alter our plans

slightly. The third detachment of pilots, due in here any day now, will be the last. Up until now I have permitted members of the Flying Sharks to return to the States if they weren't satisfied. However, in the future, all members will be frozen out here until they complete their contract. This is the only way I can handle the situation now."

A few of the members had questions at this point.

"We will omit any questions. I'm certain everything will be perfectly clear after I've finished."

It was obvious the man with the deep-lined face was going to have things his way. This was his party. Anything or anyone who chose to cross his path would be smashed. After breaking loose from his doldrums in 1935 to 1940, Francis Stud was damned if anyone was going to push him back into oblivion again.

"Now then, to continue without further interruptions, the only reason we are in Burma is to train and equip our aircraft. The terrain and climate is far better suited for this purpose than China. Besides, I don't need to remind you that China and Japan are at war, while Burma is not. The Japanese have flown over Burma on occasion, but they have left us alone.

"The Chinese leaders are far more anxious to get us into China than you are to go, believe me. China has everything at stake in this Group. Helpless men, women and children are being bombed daily, so don't think I find it easy to remain here.

"The Battle of Britain taught us the necessity of placing armor plate behind the pilots, and installing self-sealing fuel tanks. All this modification takes time, but it will pay off in the end. With a little delay now, we will be far more valuable to China with a more durable air force.

"Our foe is not of the same school of thought, because the Japanese, to date, have not gone in for protective tanks or armor. Let's hope they don't.

"Don't worry. When we are ready, we will paint on our Chinese insignia and fly into China for business. So, unless you hear otherwise through my staff, continue training and get in all the time you can.

"That is all. Group dismissed!"

As the group was breaking up for lunch, Robert Sanderson III observed, "The old man is certainly an impressive speaker."

"I hope to shout," Chuck Reynolds agreed. "We wind up blaming our own imaginations for everything."

"For a minute I forgot my bar bills, and getting straight with the commandant of the Marine Corps," Rusty sighed. "Like listening to John Philip Sousa's band."

The Brownfields, and a few of the staff were en route to the colonel's quarters before anyone spoke.

"Are you satisfied, Auggie?" Francis grinned to his self-made executive officer. Auggie had been annoying the colonel with repeated wires advising that the troops were getting out of hand.

"For the time being," conceded the watery-eyed, over-weight exec. "I'll know better after Paul Eddy arrives. Must be awfully important, or he wouldn't be coming way out here. Shall I send a wire to see when he's coming?"

"No, that won't be necessary," Stud decided. "I'd suggest taking our usual nap after lunch, so we can all be fresh for a meeting to discuss matters when he does arrive."

3 · A Pledge of Allegiance

A FEW YEARS BEFORE, a meeting of even greater importance was pending. In the White House in Washington, D.C., the President of the United States and the Chinese Ambassador were also waiting for none other than this same Paul Eddy, whom the President's secretary had summoned by telephone.

While taking a business administration course at Miami University in 1931, Paul had made the acquaintance of Jack Ryan, a power in the Democratic Party. The Democrats were going all out for a New Deal in 1932. Their method of approach was a small amount of expense money, coupled with a promise of a secure future. Presently big Jack Ryan had hired himself a boy. Paul was one of the more fortunate during those depression days; he owned a coat to match his trousers. With what few clothes he possessed, he managed to present an immaculate appearance at all times. It became a trademark.

A nice appearance wasn't all Paul could offer. He was

clever, and he had a pleasing personality. Though he had not the faintest trace of a southern accent, he was given credit for a tremendous amount of votes in that area. Ryan had placed Paul in an adequate position in Washington—until something better came along. With a second term for the New Dealers, the opportunity came in the form of the aforementioned telephone call. Paul was in the winner's circle at last.

Ambassador from China, Sam Choy, was completely at ease in the White House. Sam was polished, and quite a gourmet. He was versed on all subjects—art, sports, politics, women, history, war—you name it; he knew it. Delightful company. No one ever questioned—or could question, for that manner—that Sam was the greatest friend anyone, even the President of the United States, could have.

"I trust you feel better today," Sam inquired with a toothy smile as he sat beside the President's huge desk. "You should, you look like a million bucks."

"Thanks, Sam, but my back is driving me mad. Sometimes I wonder if it's worth it all." The President gratefully acknowledged, trying to force a smile.

The secretary interrupted these amenities by introducing the most recent arrival. He was offered a chair.

"You come most highly recommended, Mr. Eddy," Sam Choy spoke smoothly as he sized up Paul. Apparently he approved of the expensively tailored brown gabardine suit with all the accessories to match. "I would consider it an honor to work under you. Both the United States and China will be proud of you."

"Paul," the Chief Executive broke in before Eddy could say thanks, "you have been considered to head a project for aiding China. Over five hundred million human beings there are in desperate need of help. Almost a fourth of the earth's population. They need hospitals, schools, education, just about everything I could name. They even need religion—Christian religion."

"I would be happy to do everything I can," Paul said, smiling agreeably, "but I'm afraid that preaching religion is not one of my talents, Mr. President."

"I wouldn't expect you to." He laughed, then became serious. "Although poor now, China has prospects of being our greatest ally in the future."

"Only too true!" intervened Sam. "We love the United States, and will stand by them forever. Your big threat is Japan. Chinese hate Japanese, and if you help us, you are helping yourselves."

"And how do you propose to do this?" Paul asked.

"The United States has to grow up and take its position in the world," the President spoke with decision. "The public has to be educated slowly. It is difficult to arrange everything through Congress. Because of the time element, the usefulness and strategy of Congress are practically nil. Tell him what you suggested, Sam."

"In order to best suit the situation at hand," Sam suggested, "we should have something which brings quick results. China wants to do her share. We don't want charity, and you should know exactly where what money we do get goes."

"Those are almost the exact words the Empress used when she stayed with us six months ago," the President interceded. "Anything Mr. Choy says, you can rest assured she will be in complete accord with."

"He's forgetting just one unfortunate incident during her stay at the White House," Sam laughed jovially. "She raised the roof and threatened to leave because there were no silk sheets!"

The three men laughed together.

"It is a certainty America will eventually be in the war," the President stated. "Our people will never believe this. They are like ostriches with their heads in the sand. We have to prepare for their benefit. For example, where would we be today if the Navy and Air Corps were training fifty pilots instead of one thousand? This mass production of aviation cadets has been operating only one year, but I started working on it eight years ago—four years before I became President."

"Yet," Sam questioned, "how can this best be handled so that our press friends won't misunderstand by getting information prematurely?"

Paul Eddy now had the necessary information for a

complete solution. He spoke with authority. "Well, gentlemen, I think I have it. Let's set up a corporation in New York City to handle this . . ."

"I follow you," Sam interrupted, his eyes lighting up. "Sort of a dummy corporation?"

"Call it what you will." The President raised a hand to silence Sam.

"This corporation," Paul continued, "will advertise for the necessary personnel to help build aircraft factories overseas. We will offer enticing wages and superb living conditions at small expense. I will set these up, and when the Chinese have sufficient know-how, they can take over. The money for the operation can be accounted and paid for by Lend-Lease money right here in the States."

The President nodded. "Once established, and with some results coming in, it will be fairly easy to step up the allotments to China."

"This is wonderful, gentlemen," Sam added, as he noticed the meeting was about to terminate. "But you realize China is very poor, and it will take a long time . . ."

"All right, all right." The President raised his hands to conclude the meeting. "Please don't worry. We will call this Lend-Lease for friendship!"

Six months after leaving the meeting, Paul Eddy hadn't so much as set foot in the Far East. He had not been idle, however.

On the fortieth floor of a Rockefeller Plaza Building in

A PLEDGE OF ALLEGIANCE

New York City was a swanky set of offices. The glass door leading into the suite had some fancy lettering: "FEAMCO." In case anyone inquired, he was told this stood for Far Eastern Aircraft Manufacturing Corporation. There was no stock for sale.

In a large corner room, the president of FEAMCO had a private office—the only space available with windows on both sides. It had mahogany paneled walls, and was luxuriously furnished. One entire wall consisted of sliding doors. Behind them hung forty hand-tailored suits patiently waiting for Paul Eddy to pick the lucky one for that day.

Two sites were selected for aircraft plants; one in India, one in China. A location in India presented no problem; boats docked at Calcutta. China was different. Upon leaving Lashio, the most northern city in Burma, the FEAMCO employees found the roads of China's interior too primitive for their soft American posteriors. They settled for Toyling, the first village across the border.

For convenience, natives of the village lived beside the Chen River, which wound down a peaceful valley. Walking was easy there, and the river furnished a supply of water for their meager rice paddies. The employees of

FEAMCO, however, were different. They chose a hilltop overlooking the beautiful valley. Tons of earth and rock had to be leveled from the top to accommodate the American Hostel. When completed, it had plate glass windows on all sides, and could well be the envy of any country club in the world.

The next project was to build an airstrip so that supplies could be flown in easily. Many of the foods coming from home would perish on the road. Due to urgency, this project was accomplished the easy way; a few of the town's rice paddies were drained, filled in, and leveled off. The Chinese did not protest. Judging by their immobile faces, this was like any ordinary famine, or any war lord's demand.

After living quarters and transportation were established, the aircraft factory came next. During the construction, a portion would be partially completed when it was discovered a part was missing. First there was a search. Then all work stopped completely, and everyone retired to the hostel while a new part was ordered from home.

Days of loafing and drinking can become monotonous. After an appreciable wait, when it became apparent that the missing part was not coming, another section of the factory would be started. This routine repeated itself, until months later the construction resembled a motion picture set. Hope for ever running a complete assembly line had long since vanished.

Even so, all this was good enough for the president of FEAMCO. Wonderful photographs of progress could be taken at the plant—provided the camera angle was right. In fact, everything was going fine until Sam Choy received a cable from the Empress: "Come home at once. We must have words."

When Sam Choy arrived, the Empress was doing something she seldom did, discussing business with her husband, the General. At best, he was difficult to talk with.

As one of the Tung family, the Empress figured the half billion people and the ground they stood on was her oyster. Although the family agreed in principle, each wanted the oyster for herself. Each sister had married for convenience, and each controlled one-third of China.

Of the three, the Empress was the one with connections in the United States. The family had sent her to Brentwood in New York, the most exclusive girls' school in America. Teachers, schoolmates and their parents alike were enchanted by her Oriental daintiness. "Isn't she the cutest little thing!" they would say. "Just like a China doll. She couldn't think an unpleasant thought, let alone hurt a fly." The Empress loved these impressions she made. She found they could be put to good use.

At the capital, Kunking, Sam breathlessly addressed the General and the Empress. He gave the impression of having run all the way from Washington. Walking up one hundred fourteen stone steps to enter the palace had done the trick. He counted every step.

43

"Humph, humph," was all the General said. On other occasions, someone had interpreted these sounds into several lengthy paragraphs.

"I thought you said you could handle this Eddy," the Empress stopped Sam in his tracks. "The way things are going, we aren't getting a drop of Lend-Lease. Eddy is the fat one."

"Please, Your Highness, practice the patience of our most honorable ancestors." Sam's voice was like oil. "This will take time."

"Don't you try to soft pedal me, Sam Choy. Someone is bound to check on something like Toyling. And who gets the blame? Eddy? No! I do! And for what?"

"Humph," grunted the General. For all Sam knew, he could have been agreeing with the Empress, or he could have meant something else.

"What does the General mean?" Sam was too smart to chance guessing.

"An idea comes to mind," she mused.

Sam waited patiently for the Empress to voice her husband's thoughts, or to provide a solution.

The channel into which the General's thoughts were grooved cost her little effort to interpret: "Talk the United States into sending war materials to fight the Japanese. Any kind of supplies that are salable. By playing one of your brothers-in-law against the other, I can get top price."

Sam got the point. He knew the Empress had married

the General for only two reasons: she needed a front man, and he had ability for dealing with the other war lords.

"We need a setup where results cannot be checked. Nor waste questioned." The Empress spoke haltingly, almost as if in severe pain. Both her hands were clenched and pressed tightly against her temples. "Why can't I think of a solution?"

"Please," Sam pleaded, "whatever we do, we must not deviate from our original plan too much. The President favors anything pertaining to aviation." He feared the Empress was overtaxing her mind, and wanted no part of it. He remembered their last session all too well. "Please rest a while."

The suggestion was accepted. She reclined on the sofa, shading her eyes with a forearm.

The General's expression did not change. He rose slowly and strolled out to the balcony to gaze into the horizon.

Attentively Sam sat close by, waiting for the Empress to regain her composure.

As the Empress relaxed, her mind wandered back a few years. There had been a man who was physically attractive to her. It was spring; the air was warm and the meadow beneath them soft. They were near an airfield. He was talking.

TONYA

Francis Stud had been Army Air Corps from World
War I days until 1935. Although he was an excellent
pilot, the Corps did not permit men with small children
to go overseas during hostilities. The Studs had three small
children.

The Army wasn't intentionally unkind, sending bache-
lors first. The war just ended too soon to suit Francis. As
time went on, the Stud family increased to thirteen children. This necessity for occupying three sets of quarters
wherever they went could possibly have had something to
do with his separation. Regardless, he was retired as a
first lieutenant. The rejection made him bitter. He
claimed he was retired because of the Air Corps' inability
to cope with his advanced ideas.

During the mid-thirties, it was difficult to obtain work.
After nearly a year of futile searching, Francis wrote a
couple of his old friends, former sergeants who were flying the General's private plane in China. These men
talked the General and the Empress into hiring Stud at
$500 a month to organize an air training school for China.

After his arrival, he laid out elaborate plans for a training program, but after a few months it became obvious it
would take five years, or more, to train a Chinese pilot. An
outmoded fighter was being used, an old Curtis Hawk
biplane.

"What can I do to help you?" the Empress recalled asking.

46

"If only I had a Boeing P-26," Stud had replied, "it would be much faster. I could ride herd on the pilots."

The P-26 was priced $60,000 f.o.b. at a United States port.

When the Empress explained the logic of such a purchase to the General, he had answered, "Humph." Meaning, "It's not worth the price."

The Empress wanted to help Francis Stud. If being polite failed, she resorted to any means necessary to obtain her own way. This time, however, no one was hurt.

"Stoney," she said, "I think we'll buy a P-26."

She knew he would have to go along with her, but she was subtle enough to wheedle him into doing so. Both of them liked the nickname they had overheard his two pilots use, thinking it referred to his smooth-shaven head which did resemble a worn pebble. Actually his stone-like silence was the reason for the name.

"Why don't I visit my friend in Tontung for a while?" Stoney suggested. "Hong-Lo has a nice restful place."

"Excellent, excellent," the Empress agreed. "I will go to the United States and make talks and appearances again. We will take up collections."

"Right—I will pay Hong-Lo ten per cent of half we collect. No one will be the wiser. Your friend has his airplane, and we have a little gold."

The Empress went to America, Hong-Lo entertained a

visitor, and Francis Stud supervised the assembling of a P-26.

The P-26 was flown less than six hours. Three test hops of approximately one hour's duration were for familiarization. A cross-country training flight was interrupted suddenly by a patrol of I-96 Japanese fighters. All six Curtis Hawks were shot down. Students couldn't be criticized, especially with no ammunition in their guns. An old flyer suddenly lost the desire to become an ace, as the P-26 managed to limp home.

"On the whole, aces are young men who like to drink and chase women," Stud thought to himself. "And although one likes what an ace does, he must be young—for combat and drinking, at least."

But to the Empress he explained: "We have to have American pilots, many of them, both for training and flying combat. We must have the latest combat planes America can supply. Not only planes, but the personnel, matériel and all the supplies that go with them. Hundreds of thousands of dollars worth. If I had this, I would make the Rising Suns of Nippon sorry they ever learned to fly."

Figuring Stud for a cigarette-rolling dreamer, the Empress grew cold. Also she had reached a point where she no longer desired any man physically, for fear he might take over the reins. Later, on the few occasions they met briefly, it was obvious their relationship had reached an end.

Stud never flew as a pilot again. He just talked. Strategy

and tactics, supply and command, the Army terminology rattled on.

On the sofa, with her composure regained, the Empress suddenly realized that Francis Stud, rolling and licking his homemade cigarettes, might well be the solution.

"Sam, I think I have the answer . . ."

Sam was delighted. "That's great, Empress. Is there anything I can do?"

"Can you get a Washington newspaperman over here? Someone who would rather make some money than dig up a lot of dirt?"

"That's easy. A half a dozen come to mind. One, named Gilbert Withcomb, has asked me repeatedly, and I know he'd print anything for favor."

"Why Withcomb?" the Empress queried. "What makes him better than the others?"

"To begin with," Sam replied, "Gil has a stooge on the same paper, who writes his column when he's out of town. Merely as a matter of form, the stooge writes up everything Gil sends in, as is."

"You're wonderful, Sam! You feel sure we can depend on Withcomb?"

Sam smiled smugly. "Once a person has committed himself it is almost impossible to back out. He would be ruined. What is your thought?"

"I was thinking of Francis Stud, regular retired Air Corps. He's been here three years doing nothing. But he knows the proper terminology to lay out a plan for an air force. A great talker. Withcomb can build him up in Washington until even the President wants to talk to him." The authority in her voice was unmistakable. She was again in complete control of the situation.

"Holy Dragon, what an order! I never heard of Stud."

"Yes, but you will, Sammy boy," was her dismissal.

Gilbert Withcomb knew his business. Before long Francis Stud had fulfilled his life's dream. He had shot down over forty planes in China. There it was—in print. Here was a man who couldn't be stopped with proper equipment. Billy Mitchell's crucifixion was unearthed, which always made for great aviation writing, and justly so. Francis Stud's name was linked with Mitchell's. An early retirement was justified by this association. Eventually, through sympathy aroused, not only the President wanted to help Stud, the whole world did!

4 · Sex or Politics

FLIGHT SURGEON WARD's prediction was correct. A British Loadstar touched down on the Paygoo airstrip just prior to the sun touching down on the horizon. The inspection tour planned for the visitor had to be abandoned, for twilight being non-existent near the equator, darkness would follow immediately after the sun set.

An immaculate Paul Eddy, accompanied by his tired but attractive secretary, Lucy Dodson, was escorted to the clubhouse. A special table, laid with a linen cloth, was reserved a little distance from the others. In the corner next to it was a bamboo, serve-yourself bar.

Most of Stud's staff were north. Those present patiently waited, drinks in hand, for the guests to freshen up in the adjoining quarters.

Lucy found the path to dinner short but slow-going for her high heels. The grass-thatching of the club absorbed light about as rapidly as the tired generator could supply it, but the few slivers which did escape from within pierced the darkness at angles which lacked symmetry or purpose, yet served to illumine Lucy's progress.

"Wow, get a load of what's coming in the door!" Kirk Jackson, the Second Pursuit squadron commander, almost dropped his glass.

All heads turned to the low-cut cocktail dress into which a voluptuous blonde had been poured.

"Not bad, not bad at all!" Ole Nelson, commanding officer of the Third Pursuit, verified Kirk's observation.

"It isn't often," Doc Ward laughed, "but at times like this, I miss my old state-side practice."

"Rumor has it the gal lives on a liquid diet," Al Plummer, Stud's personal pilot and adjutant supplied. "Eddy brought enough booze along to last a year!"

"If I were her physician, which I am not—" Doc's eyes twinkled as he talked—"I'd say the diet puts it on in the right places. More women should try it!"

Robert Sanderson III, standing near Tonya, was not so stupid as to commit himself so openly. He could sense Tonya bristling at this masculine applause. The way Tonya was measuring up Paul Eddy could mean anything—up to a new suit!

"This competition just has to go, or the evening will be ruined," she thought to herself. Her answer came from Papa Berovsky's words: "The easiest way to a man is through his best friend." Tonya recalled Al Plummer's remark. Here was the friend.

"It must have been a grinding trip, my dear," Tonya

said to Lucy Dodson. Then turning her head to the men, she raised her voice slightly, "Can't you stop talking long enough to offer the lady a drink?"

"Thanks, I could use one. I'm dead tired," Lucy admitted. "Maybe a martini would help."

"Dearie, you'll get help all right," Tonya thought to herself, but she said aloud, "No martinis, but we have something that gives the same effect."

"Gin and tonic keeps the old malaria at bay," Doc Ward prescribed amiably.

"Better listen to the quack, honey," Kirk advised. "He's not much, but things are rough all over."

An hour later, with the formalities of dinner behind them, the group moved back to the bar.

Taking Lucy's arm, Ole offered: "There's a bottle of V.O. in my quarters, some star sapphires, Indian prayer rugs and some Gurkha knives—if you'd like to walk over and see them."

"Nice of you, Ole," Lucy begged off, "but it's too hot, and I like ice in my drinks."

"Maybe you'd like to walk down by the planes," Sandy spoke up bravely. "There's usually a little breeze on the strip at night."

"Not in these shoes. I barely made it in here!"

"Oh—oh, don't look now boys, but here comes our gay Lothario," Doc warned.

Simultaneously Lucy's admirers quickly turned their backs on the approaching figure, as if to hide her. Undaunted, Rusty penetrated the group like a homing pigeon, direct to the object of their attentions.

"Well—" he smiled at her—"where have you been all my life?"

"Rusty, darling," Tonya moved in quickly, slipping her arm possessively through his, "when did you get back?"

Gently freeing his arm, without taking his eyes from the well-stacked blonde, he replied, "About an hour ago." Then he moved closer to Lucy. "I saw the Loadstar when it landed, but I didn't know it brought an angel from Heaven!"

Swaying toward Rusty, more from drink, than because of his charm, Lucy smiled up at him, "You're cute. I like you—'cuz you know what you want!"

Paul Eddy approached. "Don't you think you've had enough to drink, Lucy?"

"Not yet," she giggled. "I'm beginning to like Paygoo. Reminds me of hiding in the tall grass in Alabama—remember, Paul?"

As he turned to beat a hasty retreat, Tonya spoke up. "Don't worry, Mr. Eddy. I'll take Lucy to her quarters and help her get set for the night."

"Is there anything to drink there?" Lucy was not quite ready to give up yet.

As Paul rejoined Stud and Brownfield, Tonya turned to Ole, and in a voice as cold as the ice in the drink she held, ordered, "Ole, please help me get Miss Dodson to her quarters—and bring some gin and tonic along."

"Oh, hell," moaned Ole, "and I thought we were gonna have a party tonight."

"Go on with the party, folks," Rusty cheerfully volunteered, "no need to stop. I'll take Miss Dodson to her quarters. I won't need any help!"

Tonya gave him a look that would have downed a squadron of Jap fighters.

"Bush," August Brownfield shouted. "You are not a squadron commander, nor a member of the staff. Remove yourself immediately."

Everyone turned at this loud interruption. With all eyes focused upon him, Rusty had no alternative but to reply with an exaggerated salute and the "Aye, aye, sir," that made Brownfield livid with rage—as he well knew. Then, with a cocky smile to the group, he sauntered insolently away.

Tonya took one of Lucy Dodson's arms firmly. What with Rusty's early return, she considered it only helpful of her to tuck the secretary in for the night without further delay. An imperious nod from Tonya to Ole Nelson, and he took Lucy's other arm. Between them they guided her more or less steadily out of the clubhouse.

This byplay did not interest the Shark leader tonight. However, getting down to business with Paul Eddy did. Gilbert Withcomb had retired immediately after dinner. Since he had no ear for honest facts, and was not a competitor at heart, it was just as well.

Stud spoke bitterly. "Sure, the Sharks will be backed

one hundred per cent. No more pilots, no staff at all—
what in hell do you expect me to do?"

"Don't worry, Francis," Eddy said, "we're with you in
spirit, even if we aren't in body."

"Paul, twisting the knife won't help any."

"I don't get it. What on earth are you talking about?"

"I've been stabbed in the back before. I know the feeling pretty well, my friend."

"How can I explain?" Eddy said. "The United States
is in a national emergency. We may be attacked any day.
All military personnel are frozen where they stand. There's
nothing anyone can do about it, that's all. But your supplies will keep coming—that I'll guarantee!"

"Hell, why can't they see this is the powder keg of the
world?" Stud argued. "This theater deserves first consideration."

"Maybe so. However, there are those who wonder which
end of the keg the fuse is on."

"While we're waiting for FEAMCO," Brownfield
moaned, "the Japs will wipe us off the map."

Stud was angry now. He was talking loudly. "When I
supplied the names of old friends to recruit for this organization, I didn't have the faintest idea that FEAMCO was
running the show. Here we are fighting for democracy,
and you charge a bonus of $10,000 a head for every bas-
tard we contact in the services. There is only one thing
wrong—your outfit is making too goddamn much profit on
everything that's done."

The distributor of Lend-Lease started to stand up as if he refused to take another insult. "Now look here, Francis, you're getting completely out of hand." Then he sat down.

"What do you suggest telling the Empress?" Stud demanded. "Did you come all this distance to placate us with words?"

"No, not exactly, Francis. That's just part of my mission."

"Well, let's get to the point then. What are you over here for?" The angry man began to hold back his fury, willing to listen, because it was just possible the trip was not for an extra buck.

"Something that I'm not at liberty to discuss. So let's forget it."

"Oh-no-you-don't—li'l Lucy can take off her own pants!" Lucy Dodson staggered and fell backward across the bed. Tonya took advantage of this accident to finish slipping the tight dress from around her ankles, as Lucy continued, "Thatsh what li'l Lucy learned to do in the tall grass in Alabama!"

"Only trying to help, dearie," Tonya said with irritation. "The only dry cleaner in Paygoo is the river at the bottom of the hill!"

"Well, what about him?" Lucy pointed to Ole, standing

57

beside the bed, practically devouring the scantily clad blonde. "How come he gets a front row seat?"

"Ole, shove off please," ordered Tonya.

"Let the lady speak for herself." The squadron leader leaned back against the dresser. "It would be a pity if she chose thee, instead of me!"

"Get out!" Tonya shouted, firing one of Lucy's shoes at him with unerring accuracy. "And stay out!"

Being familiar with Tonya's temper, Ole quickly put the door between them. Something more lethal than a shoe might come next. For a moment, he leaned against the door, trying to think of a way to outwit Tonya and regain entry. Then drunkenly remembering something about "two's company; three's a crowd," he shuddered and staggered off down the path.

"Here's another drink, Lucy." Tonya handed a glass to the nude figure on the bed. "By the way, what are your plans for tomorrow?"

"Gonna go Toyling first . . ." She paused in thought, her lower lip quivering. Then, as the tears started in what was evidently the beginning of a crying jag: "Should say Paul is gonna leave me there—all alone—poor li'l Lucy . . ."

"Oh, he wouldn't. It's obvious he's very fond of you," pacified Tonya, again pulling the sheet over the nude body.

"Ohhh—yes he would, he don' wan' me any more—wan's to get rid of me. Says somebody he can trust has to be at the ol' factory. But I know better. He jus' don' love me——"

58

Her voice rose in a hysterical sob as she added, "But I love him!"

"You must be mistaken. Look how concerned he was you might have too much to drink. He was worried about you!"

"Worried, pig's eye! Jus' afraid I'd talk too much—tell his big ol' secret—stupid ol' Hess message!" Lucy flailed her leg, pulling the sheet down again.

"There now, cover up or you'll catch cold," soothed Tonya, again replacing the sheet. "Don't worry about the old Hess message. Which Hess was he worried about?"

"Oh, you know—Rudolph Hess that landed his plane in Scotland—but li'l Lucy can't tell about it. Big secret. Can't tell."

"Oh, that Hess. Kind of stupid landing his plane in Scotland, wasn't it?" Tonya's interest was definitely alerted. This could be something worth while.

"No, it wasn't. He had to bring big message from Hitler. But it's a big secret. Can't tell you about it—big secret." Lucy pressed the sheet tight around her body, as though admiring the dips and rises.

"Of course. We are all keeping the big secret. Here, have another drink, it'll keep you from taking cold." Tonya handed her another gin and tonic. "We all have to keep the secret, don't we?"

Recollection of the third-ranking Nazi, Rudolph Hess, flying to Scotland was fresh in Tonya's mind. First news releases had mentioned his bringing a message of amity.

TONYA

Hitler had denied this. Hess was now imprisoned in England. Later publicity releases claimed he was insane. That was what the public was supposed to believe.

"Not more'n twenty people know what's in the message—but li'l Lucy knows!" she boasted, hugging the drink close.

"Oh, great!" Tonya realized a drunken stupor was about to overcome her little pigeon. "How'd you find out?"

"Paul let me decode sumpin' he shouldn't of. The President made him come all-l-l the way over here just to find out if it's true." Lucy's words were coming slower and slower, and her eyes were closing.

Tonya seated herself on the side of the bed. "We must all tell the truth, don't you think, Lucy?" she coaxed.

" 'Spose you're right. But if it's true, we're helping the wrong pee-ple—'n you know that—'cuz you're Russian—an' you're takin' all these li'l Chinamen to fight for you." She lifted the glass to her lips, no longer bothering to open her eyes.

"Was that what the message said?" Tonya asked cautiously.

Bit by bit Tonya extracted the complete contents of the message from Lucy.

An immediate peace with France and England was proposed. For this, the Germans agreed to concentrate their undivided forces upon Russia, which they described as a menace to the world. Japan agreed to help by attacking

Russia from the other side. If England and France didn't choose to go along with the proposal, they would rue the day.

It explained, with documentary evidence, just how, when and where Russia was recruiting the greatest source of manpower in the world—China, which was referred to as a sleeping giant, whose numbers needed only education before it would roll over everything.

Part of the message beseeched England to warn her ally, the United States. It explained how the Empress and her bandit-general husband were playing right into Russia's hands by selling Allied arms to Mao Tse-tung. The minute the supplies stopped coming, Mao would run this pair into the ocean.

Contrary to general belief, it stated that the Empress maintained some excellent connections in Japan. The Japanese arms market was limited for obvious reasons, but mainly because the Japs insisted upon trading manufactured goods—and the Empress always insisted on gold.

Lucy was scarcely capable of knowing whether this information was true or false, right or wrong. Presently she was quite incapable of being any further use to Tonya, or anyone else for that matter. Tonya covered her one last time, and departed for the clubhouse, congratulating herself on a good night's work—if it were followed up properly.

"Nice to have a double blade to work with on this

smooth character Eddy," she said to herself. "Now let's see, what can I do to discourage Stud's late hour visit tonight?"

The clubhouse was all but closed for the night. Eddy, Stud and Brownfield were the last dogs to be hung. Judging by the conversation, all three were about ready to fold.

"How's Miss Dodson?" asked Eddy, obviously welcoming a change of subject—and scenery.

"Resting peacefully for the night," Tonya answered. "But just wait till that hangover meets the morning sun. Wow!"

Auggie appeared weary as he rose. "Looks as if this is as far as any of us go tonight, so I'm going to hit the hay." He turned to Tonya. "We'd better say good night, dear. I've got a heavy schedule tomorrow."

Tonya tossed a disdainful glance in the direction of her husband as she proceeded to seat herself between Stud and Eddy. Her reply was cool and final, "Good night, dear."

Flushing in anger, Auggie repeated firmly, "I said, I think we'd better retire, dear. I have a very heavy schedule tomorrow." He shoved his chair into place under the table.

"I know, *dear*," she replied coldly. "Run along and get your rest. I'm going to have a nightcap. Colonel Stud or Mr. Eddy will walk me to my quarters." She smiled directly at Eddy. "Won't you?"

From previous experience Brownfield knew better than to pursue a losing battle. With a "Good night, gentlemen," he turned and departed.

The three at the table waited until they heard the resounding slam of the screen door before continuing conversation.

After waiting for the nightcap to disappear, Stud directed his attention to Tonya, "Well, if you've finished your drink, Toni, I'll walk over with you. I'd like to discuss a few things to be done tomorrow."

"If they're for tomorrow, we can discuss them in the morning. I'll walk over later with Paul." She reached for her glass and turned away.

Sensing that his exec's wife might have plans which did not include him, Stud decided on one more college try. "There are some papers you should look over before our discussion in the morning. I'll drop them by a little later."

"That won't be necessary. I may be out quite late. Paul is leaving tomorrow and I have several things to discuss with him—as official Group Historian, you know. I'll get the papers in the morning."

Stud concluded this was not his night. He picked up his cap.

"Well, good night, Paul. Night, Toni. See you in the morning."

Tonya settled back, drink in hand.

"That was as clever a bit of maneuvering as I've seen

in a long time." Paul grinned. "What'll we talk about?"

"Well, we could talk about how broad your shoulders are. Or how strong you are——" Her eyes caressed him openly.

"This is hardly the place for that," Paul said self-consciously.

"We could go over to my place. For Paygoo it's very nice. I'll buy you a drink, while I get comfortable." Chest forward, she moved her shoulders invitingly.

"Thanks, but Stud might drop by. And I haven't the slightest interest in his papers."

"Neither have I. But I bet there are papers you wouldn't like anyone to read."

"Can't imagine what they could be." He hesitated. "I haven't any papers."

"I know, but some people do. And they even fly them into enemy territory." She peered deep into her glass.

"What on earth are you getting at? You've left me somewhere along the line. I'm not too sharp tonight. Maybe I'm tired."

"I wonder if a certain German pilot was tired—or lost, when he landed in Scotland." She raised her eyes, looking squarely into his.

Paul stiffened. His voice seemed anxious. "Maybe I'll take you up on the drink. Shall we go?"

Walking toward the hostel, he wondered just how much this woman knew. Could Lucy have possibly dropped something, after he had cautioned her so carefully? Their departure for Toyling tomorrow could not take place as scheduled without his knowing. Paul Eddy had to know.

As his hostess pulled drapes across the windows, he eyed the room's contents. The floor and walls were covered with colorful Indian prayer rugs, beautifully woven. From the top of several exquisite pieces of teakwood furniture, sightless eyes stared out of carved wooden heads. Balinese. Male and female.

A large brass key unlocked the doors of a teakwood cabinet, disclosing an ample supply of liquor and glasses. Even an anxious mind could not overlook the beauty of the long slender fingers which expertly poured and handed him the scotch and soda. An occasional sip lowered the tepid-tasting contents of the glass as the guest waited, seated upon the edge of the bed. Johnny Walker Black Label made up somewhat for the absence of ice in the drink.

Behind the adjoining bathroom door, a nude, exact in all dimensions, was preparing for comfort. The reproduction reflected from a full length mirror was pleasant, even to its owner. A favorite French perfume was being dabbed here and there in the proper places.

This pleasant sight emerged, clad only in a filmy robe. The narrow waist was emphasized considerably by a tight sash. The rest of the garment hung loosely, leaving little for the imagination. Contrasting colors accentuated the meeting of the thighs. The nipples of poorly concealed breasts nodded yes with each step.

During the interlude, after removing an uncomfortable tie and coat, the man seated on the bed had unloosened a few of his top shirt buttons. Up until the grand entry, he was still anxious to know how much she knew. But now some doubt began to grow as to just what it was he wanted to know. A form in all its glory was moving lithely toward him, as free as a cloud taking shape. Never before had he seen hips, thighs and belly run into one another in sweeter curves.

Soft sweet sounds came from exquisitely formed lips, shaped ovally, like a ripe plum with a single bite out being offered to another. The remaining shirt buttons were unloosened, one after the other, by long slender fingers.

"I'm rather handy with buttons," murmured Tonya, "but not so good with zippers." Her hand passed lightly over the object.

"I—I—don't know what to say," Paul stammered when words finally came.

"Don't say anything. Let's play some music instead." Tonya whirled gracefully across the room to a phonograph. "I'll put on my favorite record. I think you'll like it."

Any thought of how much, or how little, this woman knew of his business, left Paul Eddy's mind completely as Tonya knelt to crank the record player. The translucent robe tightened across the widened thighs, making loin hol-

lows and vee between cheeks stand out in all their eloquence.

In the few seconds it took Paul to get around to untying
the robe's sash, his neat clothes had been scattered all over
the room. The phonograph played *"J' attendrai"* over and
over again.

Colonel Stud was too hard of hearing to catch the notes
of the music floating through the night. But Chuck Reynolds snored spasmodically a few snorts, then propped
himself up on an elbow to look over at the next bunk.
Rusty Bush was awake, he knew, because his hands were
locked together under the back of his neck.

"Hey, hey, Rusty, can you hear that damn music?"

"Certainly. What about it?" Rusty didn't move a muscle.

"Just wondered, cuz most nights when it wakes me, *you*
ain't in the sack!"

"Oh, shut up and go back to sleep. You need your rest."
Rusty pulled the pillow around so it covered both ears.

Paygoo served two breakfasts, one early, and one late.

Lucy couldn't be dragged to either one. Immaculate as ever, Paul Eddy cordially greeted the late eaters, and pulled up a chair opposite Mrs. Brownfield. A short time later the two were left alone with their coffee. Stud and his staff had professed a busy day. Usually this meant a ride about the area.

Paul leaned toward her across the table. "Toni, I've got to ask a favor of you."

"We've already proved we work well together, Paul." Looking down shyly, she fluttered long eyelashes. "What else can I do?"

"There's been too much rumor already. Let's not have any more. It can bring us a great deal of harm and confusion."

"You amaze me, Paul." She looked hurt. "I thought only men kiss and tell."

"That's not what I mean." He flushed. "I'm referring to that ridiculous story my secretary made up last night. She was drunk. It's nothing but a tall tale. But Heaven forbid the Empress ever gets wind of it. She'd never understand, I'm afraid."

"True, Orientals don't think as we do, do they?" Tonya agreed. "You know you're causing me a lot of extra work, I've already written this in my historical diary. It seems to fit in pretty well with some of my other observations."

"Yes, I suppose." Paul was obviously giving some serious thought to the matter. "However, there are ways I can

68

make it worth your while. I'll talk to Stud before I go, and arrange to have your salary increased."

"You are a darling! Double will do. Five hundred doesn't go far these days, especially on a job like this."

"That's about the only way for the time being. But if you use proper discretion—more or less pattern your remarks after Gil Withcomb's—there'll be plenty of gravy for all of us, I promise." He pushed back his chair and rose.

"I'll try, but this Withcomb I can't take." Tonya shivered. "Anything else I can do?" She left her lips protruding ovally.

After a session like last night, he wanted to change the subject. "Why, yes, help my secretary pull herself together. I'll see Stud about changing your pay status." He departed without further words.

"Am I taking you north today, Mr. Eddy?" inquired Stud's pilot adjutant as Paul entered the bamboo shack called headquarters.

"As soon as possible, Al, after I have a few words with the colonel. You can crank her up anytime."

"Mind giving Plummer a hand, Brownfield?" Stud asked.

"Yes sir, yes sir," obliged Auggie, not realizing he was merely being removed from hearing distance.

69

After a few preliminary remarks, Eddy asked, "How much is Mrs. Brownfield getting a month?"

"Five hundred. Why?"

"Not very much, especially for the responsibility of important historical data. I want the amount doubled—one thousand from now on." He turned away, lighting a cigarette to avoid Francis Stud's eyes.

"Good God, man, that'll put her two hundred fifty over my squadron commanders. What can I do about that?" He slapped the table with the flat of his hand.

"Simple, Francis. Just instruct your paymaster to fill out the necessary papers. I'll sign them." He blew out the match, tossing it at the can, still not looking at the Shark leader.

Prior to boarding the colonel's Beech for Toyling, Paul's eyes met Tonya's momentarily. "Good luck, keep up the good work," he said by way of farewell.

The door of the plane closed, and the dust from it as it taxied down the strip forced the small group to turn their backs.

"Hope they're lucky, and arrive safely," said Auggie as his watery eyes watched the Beech stagger slightly, then continue to climb.

"Some people make their own luck," Stud said sourly, looking at Tonya.

"How's that?" questioned Brownfield.

"Nothing—nothing at all."

70

Brownfield turned and headed down the line to give a few ostentatious orders.

Tonya and Stud walked slowly to the jeep. Tonya was wondering how much Sam Choy would give for her little secret. She turned slowly to Stud. "By the way, Francis, when is Sam Choy due in again?"

He stopped and stared at her. "Good God, woman, don't tell me you want to make the Chinaman too!"

5 · A Nest of Eaglets

"NEVER THOUGHT I'd live to see the day," Chuck Reynolds sighed with relief. "We've got all the equipment on the last god-damn plane. All we gotta do now is keep 'em flyin'— for you silly bastards."

"Hell, what are you so proud of?" Rusty asked. "It's November and you guys been at this for eight stinking months. 'Bout time you got your thumbs outa your butts!"

"Any flyin' this morning?" asked Chuck, reaching for a well-chewed cigar stub laying on the tool box.

"Eight planes—scheduled for dogfights."

"You flyin'?" He bit the end from the stub and spat it at his feet.

"Yeah, Brownfield has me paired off with Dick Plant," Rusty said, "that little hotshot from the Air Corps. Tryin' to show me up, I guess. The guy's about half my weight— one hell of an advantage!"

"Think it'll do 'em good?"

"Hell, yes, when you're pulling twelve G's, a hundred pounds makes a difference of twelve hundred. You gotta turn in bigger circles—or stall out!" Rusty moved both hands in demonstration of the planes' movements.

"I get it," Chuck nodded, "the one who turns the smallest circles gets on the other's tail—right?"

"Right—assuming they're both equal in flying ability."

"How long does a dogfight last?"

"We limit them to ten minutes, or until one chases the other below five thousand. We start at fifteen thousand."

"Then you only need gas to climb up, ten minutes at full throttle, and enough to land." You could almost hear the cogs clicking over in the rough mechanic's brain.

"Go on, brilliant. I'm listening."

"If your plane is short about thirty gallons—which you won't need anyhow—at six pounds to a gallon—that would be one hundred eighty pounds. Would that help any?"

"Christ, yes," exclaimed Rusty. "I'd have the same advantage Brownfield thinks Plant has over me."

"Leave it to dad, m'boy. Mind you, no hard feelin's for Dick, but every chance I get, that son-of-a-bitch, Brownfield, is gonna get the shaft!" Chuck shook a greasy finger at Rusty.

"I'm with you all the way, Dad." Rusty was smiling. "You always been this smart?"

Thrusting out his broad chest, Chuck gave an arrogant grin.

"Did I ever tell you 'bout my three day liberty, Rusty?"

"Nope—what'd you do besides get drunk?" Rusty squatted in the shade of the wing.

"I got all duded up, and strolled into town. These G.I. clothes weren't for Chuck—no sirree—mine was hand tailored."

"Where was this, Chuck?"

"A joint down south, I'd rather forget. As I was saying, ol' Chuck sits himself down on a bar stool, pushes back his pith helmet, and admires the guy in the mirror. I says to myself, 'Charles, you're sure a handsome son-of-a-bitch!' Then I tells the bartender to line 'em up! I polished off that line of drinks like liquor was goin' outa style. Then I noticed a beautiful blonde, seated all alone in one of the booths. 'Parently, she'd been there for some time. It was dark when I came in—guess I hadn't noticed. I nodded. The blonde graciously returned my greetin'. Ol' Chuck moves over and bows polite-like, and says, 'This is not at all formal, ma'am, but can a lonesome Air Corps sergeant buy one for a most charming lady?'

"The lady accepted, and we had the most elevated talk— mostly 'bout world affairs—until the bartender shouted, 'Last call before closin' time!'

"When I was escortin' her home, she fell in my arms. Never in my life had I kissed lips so soft. After invitin' me into her apartment, I felt the softness of those beautiful lips—again—and again." Chuck's eyes closed in esthetic recollection.

"Gee, Chuck," teased Rusty, "who'd ever figure you for such a Romeo! Did you ever make her?"

"Dunno—but I recollect feeling sheer undies, which covered a gorgeous body."

Several others had gathered to attend a conversation of this stature. One spoke up, "For Christ's sake, what *did* happen?"

"Well, I'll tell you now—that shining sun woke me up. I was in bed. When I reached over to put my arm around that gal, I discovered the sheer underclothes were made of flour sacks. That blond hair had turned a dirty, stringy gray.

"At my touch, the charming lady rolled over. I saw why those were the softest lips I'd ever kissed—not a god-damn tooth in her head!"

Roars of laughter poured from the audience. As Chuck sat there, slowly shaking his head from side to side, a sheepish grin creased his rugged features. A great guy. Whenever he drank, trouble and confusion walked arm in arm.

Each Shark deserved Paygoo for a reason.

The pilots and the mechanics, regardless of why they were there, were anxious for the flying to begin. The sooner, the better. Whether any or all would be capable of actual combat flying remained to be seen. Outside of a handful of professed "democracy fighters," the rest were soldiers of fortune in the true sense. Under no flag. Kill for money. There was a $500 bonus for each Japanese plane shot down.

TONYA

Several of Francis Stud's old flying acquaintances, long since retired, had been given special permission in 1941 to recruit pilots secretly from the Navy and Air Corps; that is, up until October of that year. Lavish promises were given. The recruits would be flying superb equipment, manufactured in China, versus antique aircraft piloted by nearsighted Japanese in thick-lensed glasses. Cameras, guns, jewelry and liquor—almost anything one desired—could be had at a fraction of the price they cost at home. A valet-interpreter would be furnished each pilot.

The clincher was United States money deposited in the Chase National Bank, in New York City.

Few persons had any knowledge of these negotiations. Even fewer had any accurate information. The press at large was excluded. The military was ordered to look the other way. The necessary personnel disappeared from the U. S. Services like a person walking alone on one of Casablanca's darkest streets.

As to exactly what was going on, the top figure in China and the United States head man were the two people who came closest to knowing. Complete agreement was impossible. Each neglected to inform the other honestly of his personal reasons.

The mere existence of United States combat pilots in the Far East was sufficient to annoy Japan. Ultimatums were published: "If the pilots, disguised as missionaries on their passports, are not removed, Japan must consider this a war-like act." Et cetera.

American bases and ships of the fleet in the Pacific were kept in ignorance as to what was taking place. They had no knowledge of recent developments with Japan.

The Empress knew a separate peace between China and Japan could be negotiated. This would throw the Japanese at Russia's throat, something the Nips would relish. An old hatred had increased since Japan's last victory over Russia. The Japanese realized the commies were taking over what Japan considered belonged to her. They wanted no quarrel with the United States, even if she did view them with suspicion. Since the time Commodore Perry had sailed into Tokyo Bay and forced trade upon Japan, there had been nothing but admiration for America.

The Empress held the match. A deadline was approaching. A powder keg was at her feet, fused on both ends. Which end to light was the question. It was a tough decision. Power madness could drive her to light both ends, trusting to luck that the right one would go off first. Her judgment could be overpowered by personal greed.

As Tonya and Auggie entered the headquarters shack, they found Francis Stud studying cracks in the bamboo wall, obviously in another world. The couple's noisy entrance did not so much as cause him to flicker an eyelash. The two stopped talking long enough to step closer and peer at the colonel with more than a little concern. On the edge of a deep seam in his leathery face sat a black fly, just as motionless. The insect broke the stillness first. It rubbed its front feet together, probably in awe of the depths of the facial chasms.

Auggie was next to break the silence. "Colonel, would you like a cigarette?"

Without a change of expression, or the lift of an eyelid, Stud accepted the proffered cigarette from the pack. Holding it crosswise between thumb and forefinger, he extended his tongue and proceeded to lick the ready-rolled cigarette from one end to the other.

"Where have you been?" Tonya addressed him. "Anybody I know?"

The colonel glanced down at the wet cigarette which needed no rolling, and crumbled it in his fist. Spasmodically, the hand clenched the remains as if to crush out the last spark of life. A warning to anyone crossing his path.

"Anything else I can do?" Auggie spoke apologetically, as though he were the cause of all Stud's weighty problems. "You know you can count on me, sir."

"Are the planes set for this afternoon's dogfight practice?" Stud inquired.

"Yes, sir. Eight. The first two take off at 1300. The

most interesting one will be Dick Plant versus Bush. My dough is on the ex-Air Corps boy. How about you?" He glanced at his wife. "That wise guy Bush is gonna get chased right out of the sky!"

By way of answer Stud glanced at his wrist watch and commented: "Our third detachment will be arriving at the railroad station in about thirty minutes. Have you made arrangements?"

"Yes, sir, everything's taken care of, Colonel."

"Then you'd better get the lead out—we'll see you at lunch." The palavering exec was swished away without any more to-do than the pesky black fly.

Tonya waited until Auggie left before she probed. "What's the matter? Eddy interfere with your plans?"

"No more than usual," Stud muttered. "No more than usual."

But Tonya knew he wouldn't be so concerned about the usual. Could he, too, know about the Hess message?

"Something's eating you! Don't forget, this is me, Tonya, you're talking to. I know better. What did Eddy say to upset you so? Maybe I can help." She seated herself on the corner of his desk, one bare leg swinging free.

Stud stood fast. The lines in his face deepened as the lips pressed hard together. After a spell, except for the eyes, the grim countenance began to soften somewhat.

"Yes, there is something," he said finally, looking up at her, "and not enough time left to do anything about it. It's finally dawned . . . they're using me . . . that's all.

79

I can hardly blame the Empress, but my own country—
that's the bitter pill to swallow. Somebody has to be sac-
rificed for the good of others, I know, but I'm sick and
tired of being the goat.

"Eddy says the Japs will be jumping the United States
practically any day. And I believe it! It's beginning to
look like we're picking the day, not Japan."

"Do you mean we're only here to help badger the Nips
into a fight?" she asked in disbelief.

"Precisely, my dear. Like slapping them with a glove
and saying, 'Choose your weapons and name the place!'
Otherwise, they wouldn't be closing us out just before the
action starts."

"How long do you think it'll be?" Tonya's question was
based neither on fear nor on a feeling she should be
making conversation. If Stud's presumption was correct,
negotiations had to be made quickly to sell the information
she had obtained from Eddy's secretary to more than one
source.

"A matter of weeks. Probably the first of next year,"
prophesied Stud.

Now Tonya knew she must get to Kunking as soon as
possible, or it would be too late. She thought fast.

"How long is Eddy going to stay in China?" She
alighted from the desk and walked around to Stud.

"Not very long. A few days at most. He's smart enough
to leave before the fireworks start."

"I've got an idea," suggested Tonya. "With the last of

80

the group arriving today, why not pack up and fly to Kunking tomorrow? If we shoot down some planes, they're bound to keep us going."

"I can't help but agree. We're not going to get in any training. Besides, there's no air raid warning system here. As soon as our new arrivals get checked out in a couple of weeks, we'll go."

"Let's you and I fly up first, to get things ready," she wheedled. "You promised you'd take me."

"I know, but——"

"We can be alone—not have to worry about Auggie." She leaned forward invitingly.

Their trip to Kunking was set for the following morning. It had been fairly simple; turning her back and placing one foot on a chair, while she bent over to examine a shoe, was all it took.

The train halted on a narrow-gauge track before the Paygoo station. The tiny steam engine had pulled ten small cars all the way from Rangoon. Most of the passengers were departing in two directions, because the cars were completely open on both sides. The squadron of new recruits, however, remained by the tracks.

Ten minutes later Brownfield arrived, late as usual.

A cloud of brown dust followed a fast-moving jeep that

was heading straight for the station, making no attempt to slow down. A second later, a crash would have been unavoidable, but the brakes held. It reminded the new arrivals of a baseball player sliding into third.

Until now, no one could possibly have guessed a five-ton truck was following the jeep in close formation. With the sudden stop, the truck careened and skidded to one side to avoid a rear-end collision. The driver had been guaranteed a court-martial if he lost his escort.

A bare-headed man in khaki shorts and bush jacket came tearing out of the jeep, wiping his watering eyes with a handkerchief. The truck driver remained seated until he was thoroughly reprimanded for whatever it was that he should, or should not, have done.

These two could have been a comedy team for all the new arrivals knew. But, as the dust settled slightly, the white lettering on the side of the jeep became legible: "Lt.-Col. August Brownfield, Executive Officer, FLYING SHARKS."

"If I was crazy enough to believe this was Paradise," exclaimed one of the recruits in a Texas accent, "then I should've known it'd be run by idiots!"

The man wore a perpetual grin which stood for fear, happiness, sorrow or pain. It never changed. Neither did his unruly black hair, which protruded from his head like spear points. No amount of oil and combing kept it down for long.

"All right, all right! Third Detachment, *fall in!*" commanded a voice in a well over-done Georgia accent. The speaker's graying temples, erect bearing, clear blue eyes and well-tanned skin tended to make him appear taller and handsomer than he actually was, and more mature than his thirty-five years.

The customary dressing down Brownfield held in readiness for newcomers was kept in abeyance for a while. He looked like a bug-eyed fish, brought up from great depths, who needed pressure to live. His mouth opened and closed several times without making a sound. These people were standing at attention. They were in platoon front, in two ranks. This was impossible. Such military etiquette was foreign here.

"Flight Leader Cortland Lee Smith reporting the Third Detachment, all present and accounted for, suh!" chanted the Southern voice. Smith's heels clicked smartly, and he held a snappy salute.

The salute from the confused exec looked more as if he were wiping his forehead than anything else. Finally, he mumbled, "At ease," and the spell was broken.

The Flying Sharks had no actual rank, merely pay classification for their respective positions. Most of them acted accordingly, too. Anyone but Auggie Brownfield would have been able to get along with men who practiced discipline for a change, but all Auggie could think of was that somewhere in this lineup stood one or more capable of seducing Tonya—or vice versa.

"Smith, have your men fall out and climb aboard the

truck," ordered Auggie. "You ride with me. The truck can pick up the baggage after lunch."

"It's certainly splendid of you all to pick us up, Colonel," drawled Smith. "Beautiful country, this inland Burma."

"This afternoon you men are going to see some real seasoned veterans in action. You've got a lot of hard work ahead before you catch up with the early arrivals."

"Gee, that's great," said the Texan. "I'd like to be counting some of those five-hundred-dollar bills soon. Who's got the most planes so far?"

"We'll talk about it later." Auggie reddened at being caught in such a gross exaggeration. "There's no time if we're gonna get chow and make it out to the field."

"Certainly, suh," agreed Smith. Turning to the group, "In due time you'll get the word. Now let's get on the truck."

"Only one other thing," Auggie addressed the group, "if you don't obey orders, we can court-martial you here, too. I just finished five last week. Driver, remember my instructions, or you'll get a court surer 'n hell."

The jeep carrying Smith and Brownfield lurched off to a good head start, gradually raising a curtain of choking dust. The Texan managed to grab the seat beside the driver of the truck.

"I don't give a hootin' damn what he said," stated the lanky Texan, "you'll never live to be court-martialed if you eat that bastard's dust all the way to the camp!"

"Don't worry, pal, I have no intention of it."

"My name's Bob Truelove," the lanky Texan said holding out his hand. "From Fort Worth."

The driver shook it, smiling, and mounted to his seat.

"Say, what about this court-martial crap?" asked Bob. "Was he on the level?"

"Hell, no, he keeps threatening, but all they can do is fire you. We're civilians."

"That's what I thought. Why did he clam up when I asked about shooting down planes?"

"Oh, that blow-hard! Hell, we just finished assembling the last plane. Nobody's been in combat. As far as that goes, there's been damn little flying. Period!"

"Might've known there'd be a catch," sighed Bob with disgust. "How about women? Any good-lookin' natives?"

"All I've found are pretty crummy. Have to get blind drunk to make out with any of 'em." The driver shook his head. "Man, you're in for a surprise. This is a real rathole!"

Finally the truck came to a grinding halt in front of the clubhouse. On a sheltered lanai stood Tonya, chatting with the three squadron commanders. No one else was in sight. The driver turned to his passenger, who had suddenly disengaged himself from further conversation.

"What'cha grinnin' at?"

"Who's grinnin'?" Truelove spoke without taking his eyes from Tonya. "Man, you lied to me, that's a hunk o' lovin' stuff if I ever saw one. What's she doing down here?"

"Oh, that's Tonya Brownfield, Group Historian," the driver informed him with sarcasm. "Dunno' how much history's being written. Should be plenty, the way she's making out 'round here!"

"Any relation of that loud-mouth exec? His sis or daughter?"

"What a dreamer!" laughed the driver. "She's missus— Brownfield's wife!"

"I don't give a damn. Even if she's got V.D., I want it!"

As the new arrivals piled off the truck and filed into the clubhouse, Tonya's conversation with the three squadron leaders gradually ceased. Each newcomer was given the once over—from head to toe—as he passed. Her glance lingered on a few, as Tonya weeded out the most logical for further use.

Everyone left promptly after lunch that day. Sufficient transportation was available to drive the privileged few to the airstrip. Others split up into congenial gatherings, and proceeded to walk the approximate mile and a half. A rather sweet melody entertained them as they walked— a chorus, composed of Allison aircraft engines warming up at varied r.p.m.'s.

On the ready room wall, a flight schedule was written on a blackboard that hung at a considerable tilt. Whoever had driven the supporting nail, had not bothered to center it. The Sharks tilted their heads to read and discuss the schedule, as if the entire Group were suffering from an epidemic of sore necks.

Stud poked his head into the ready room. "It's about 1300. Where's the schedule, Brownfield?"

"On the board, Colonel. Be with you in a minute, sir." The exec was busy giving Dick Plant and Rusty Bush his boring rendition of the art of dogfighting.

"If these pilots fly at the angle their names are posted, God help us," commented Stud as he twisted his neck to one side in order to read, "or we'll ground-loop a few more into spare parts."

"Where's Reynolds?" screamed Auggie, rushing out of the shack. "I ordered him to fix that board a month ago."

Doc Ward was almost knocked off balance as the infuriated man brushed past.

"The Group's going to have its first coronary if he doesn't slow down," the flight surgeon predicted.

"Are a few bets on the dogfights in order?" Tonya smiled as she moved over and touched Rusty's arm.

"Bet my body against yours," whispered the ex-Marine. "When can I pay off?"

"Afraid there isn't time," Tonya answered in a low voice. "Francis and I are flying to Kunking in the morning."

Rusty raised his voice. "My time's available tonight."

"You take a lot for granted," Tonya replied angrily. "Don't think I can't live without you!"

At the sound of her voice, Francis Stud moved in to see what was going on.

"Why don't you get airborne, Bush? If you're good enough, there's a squadron leader's pay classification avail-

TONYA

able for the winner." The old man really meant business.

"You're covered." Rusty's eyes narrowed to mere slits. "Don't forget you said it in front of witnesses!"

"That'll be enough out of you, Bush," the Shark leader warned.

"Don't worry, I'll give you a chance to get it back. Wanna' double your money by taking on any of your pets —Sanderson, Jackson, Nelson?"

"I don't want to repeat . . ."

"Hell, I'd take that trio on one after the other, the same day!" Rusty spoke in defiance.

"Rusty, please go," cautioned Tonya, laying a restraining hand on his arm, "before you say too much. After all, we came out to root for all of you."

"Yeah, I know," Rusty snarled as he pulled away from her. "You ghouls came out hoping we won't—but you don't wanna miss it if we do!"

"Now, Rusty . . ."

"By the way, don't forget our little personal bet." After a knowing glance at Stud, he added, "I'll collect it tonight."

"Bush!" roared Stud, rage mounting in his voice, "You . . ."

"Yes, sir." Rusty saluted sharply. "I understand it's sometimes hard to take competition," he added.

Words of reply failed Stud. By the time he recovered his wits, Rusty was climbing into his plane.

The centrifugal starter in Number Fourteen whirred in

88

a rising crescendo. Engaging the starter produced a few coughs of ugly black smoke, then the engine settled down to a melodious roar. As Rusty tested the P-40 and checked the gauges, a satisfied grin spread over his face. He was short on gas—thirty gallons, to be exact.

Chuck Reynolds stood at the wing tip anxiously waiting an okay signal. Rusty blew the rugged mechanic a kiss. On this occasion, it stood for more than "everything's okay"; it added, "thanks for shorting my gas."

It would have taken a heavy rasp to wipe off the cat-eating grin which creased the mechanic's features. In Reynolds' vocabulary, a message for Garcia meant a shaft for Brownfield.

Picking up his microphone, Rusty called, "Shark 26 from Shark 14, how do you receive me—how do you receive me?"

"Loud and clear. Am I coming through?" Dick Plant answered.

"Roger, coming in loud and clear," verified Rusty. "Your plane okay, too?"

"Okay. Lead off, Hotshot, I'll follow you upstairs," Dick answered.

The two P-40's taxied out and took off, one after the other. As Number 14 climbed in a left-hand turn, Number 26 slowly closed the take-off gap by circling more sharply, until joined up. Few words were spoken on the way up to 15,000 feet.

"Feel in shape?" called Rusty.

"Never felt better in my life," answered his opponent cheerfully. "You take first advantage."

Rusty knew the importance of physical fitness. In order to win he must be able to pull tighter turns than his opponent and not "black out." By being in good physical condition, he could pull a number of G's while "gray," and still be in control of the aircraft.

The P-40's were directly over the field, heading south. Number 26 throttled to cruising, holding course and altitude. Number 14 completed a 180° turn, and headed north, climbing to 16,000 feet. This was a 1,000-foot advantage for the first five minutes. At this point both reversed courses and headed toward the other, maintaining the 1,000-foot differential. Rusty signaled the start by wobbling his wings as he passed directly over Dick.

On the ground below, Stud clicked his stop watch to time the first five minutes. The group around him tilted their heads back to follow the action. Between the blackboard in the ready room, and the planes above, the Sharks were getting their share of neck calisthenics.

The fight was on!

Rusty descended gradually, always keeping his opponent directly below, careful not to lose his altitude advantage. Too clever to dive and over-run. Occasionally a wing dipped for a better view.

Almost as in a groove, Rusty settled, until positioned about two hundred yards directly behind Plant. Dick tightened up a left turn, but the plane behind was turning just above and inside his turn. The first P-40 shuddered and stalled out, losing precious altitude. Plant reversed and tightened up a turn to the right—again stalling out— with Rusty clinging inside the turn. In desperation to shake loose, Dick dove to 5,000 feet, the bottom limit. When he pulled back and climbed with the diving speed, his opponent was still tucked in behind his tail. A few more stalling turns, and the first phase was over. They were below 5,000 feet!

Then the two planes climbed back to 15,000 so that the other could start with the advantage. As they parted to head in opposite directions, Plant knew the best he could salvage was a draw.

One plane settled down over the other, much the same as before. But as they went into a high G-turn, the similar- ity to the first match ceased to exist. Obviously Rusty was turning in smaller circles, thanks to his lighter weight, and not stalling out. In a minute, he would have worked his way around on 26's tail, and Plant's advantage would be gone.

Before this could happen, Dick leveled his wings and pulled away from his opponent. He called over his radio, "Did you have a full load of gas before you took off?"

"Sure I did," Rusty laughed. "Wanna check?"

"You're damn right. As soon as we land!"

Plant headed for the other plane, head on, planning to force his opponent to veer off in a turn first, thinking a collision was imminent. Rusty was wise to this old trick; he had used it himself. Neither altered a collision course. At the last possible second, Rusty decided to duck under the on-coming plane and start his turn. It didn't work!

A jolting, blinding crash stunned him for a few seconds. As he came to his senses, the plane was heading straight down, rolling out of control. Earth was coming up to meet him fast! A glance told him the canopy was smashed in. There was only one wing; the other was gone!

An eternity passed while he tried to free himself from the cockpit. He was oblivious to pain from the slipstream that was cutting and pounding him against the damaged cockpit before he was able to fall clear.

As his chute snapped open, he quickly looked about for his opponent. Rusty saw Dick's plane just before it crashed into the ground. An unopened white chute trailed from the tail.

6 · Three for Tea

THE WEATHER WAS UNUSUAL that November of 1941. The high terrain was piled even higher by blankets of clouds. A twin Beechcraft wandered above. Occasionally it poked an inquisitive nose around the white formations, trying to locate a hole or a familiar landmark. Somewhere, down below, had to be Kunking, China.

Al Plummer not only knew this poorly charted, vast terrain, he respected it as well. He knew that fate allowed these peaks a greater share of airmen than the Japanese were permitted to take. That was why he had become Francis Stud's personal pilot.

"Gonna make it today, Al?" questioned Stud, beside Plummer in the co-pilot's seat.

"I think so," Al replied none too reassuringly. "If only I could locate the mountains on the edge of the lakes."

Stud shifted uncomfortably, peering out the window at the clouds.

Kunking rested in a great basin, located high in the mountains. Near the city were three large lakes, com-

93

pletely surrounded by jagged ranges, suburbs of the Himalayas.

The capital city boasted of no radio station on which an airplane could home in. But if a pilot could definitely recognize a mountain tip, then he could easily let his plane down through the overcast. With any ceiling at all, he would spot one of the lakes. Then, following the lake-shore, he would eventually come to the airstrip located nearby.

"We're okay now." Al pointed to the left. "See that big baby down there? I'd recognize that peak in my sleep. I'll start letting down on a three-hundred-degree heading."

"You're sure it's the one?" Stud asked nervously. Then in a lighter vein: "This isn't a dinner table, you don't get seconds here!"

"I'd stake my life on this." Al banked the plane around.

"That's just dandy," said Stud, "if you can do it without including mine!"

Al throttled back and started down.

A white mist of clouds soon enveloped the Beech. According to the instruments, it was on a 300-degree heading, descending at a rate of 500 feet per minute.

In a few seconds, turbulence began to pitch and roll the plane so badly that control became something of a problem. Instrument indicators vibrated back and forth and up and down. Averaging out the mean reading on several at a time was a mental chore.

"Think it's too bad?" asked Stud. "Maybe we'd better climb out."

"No, sir, it'll be okay. Should smooth out before long."

"Hope you're right!" He noticed beads of perspiration were running down the pilot's temples, while ice was forming on the wing.

"See anything yet?" asked Al, not daring to take his eyes from the instrument panel.

"It's smoother now." Stud was even more relieved as he added, "Yes, we're over water. I can see it every now and then."

"So do I now," Al said as they broke through. "By the way, how's our passenger coming along?"

The colonel didn't have to answer, for Tonya had left her seat and stood behind them. Apparently enjoying every minute, she chided: "Until you shook me to pieces, I was having the nicest nap."

"I'm a bad boy." Al smiled. "Sorry if I disturbed your beauty sleep."

"And I thought being a pilot was an asset." Stud shook his head in a hopeless gesture. "Now I'm beginning to wonder!"

"Why was that supposed to be so terrible?" Tonya pursed her lips poutingly at Stud.

"If I had my career to do over," stated the colonel with a straight face, "all of the pursuit pilots would be women."

"Do you think I'd make a good one, Francis?"

"You have no fear," he said seriously. "Besides, no female would bat an eye at shooting a man she hated, even
if he was coming down in a chute!"

"If that's the way you feel," needled Tonya, "let's go
back to Paygoo. Some of the fellows are flight instructors.
They wouldn't mind teaching me."

"Don't I know!"

Embarrassed by the conversation, Al interrupted.
"Where shall I stay, Colonel?"

After a moment's thought, Stud replied: "Better stay at
the field and watch the plane. These monkeys might steal
an engine if you don't."

"How right you are!" Al didn't want to get involved with
the boss; he had a few nefarious plans of his own.

Anyone having access to trips with any degree of regu-
larity could make a fortune the easy way—that is, if he
didn't care how it was done.

The Americans hanging around Asia who joined Stud's
staff for convenience were interested only in making
money. With the Shark affiliation they became virtually
immune to any laws. For some of the things they got away
with, an ordinary Chinese would be executed.

Although he didn't look the part, Al Plummer was a rich
man. Al made out at both ends of the line. On the return

trip, dope was flown to Rangoon, where it was sold to sailors who smuggled the misery all over the world. With the proceeds in rupees, a handsome profit could be made on the return trip to China, on the rate of exchange. First, the rupees were traded on the black market for Chinese dollars. This money, in turn, was taken to the Bank of China and changed into gold certificates, which remained intact until a way was found to get them back to the United States.

The Shark leader and his companion had no sooner left the field than Al called his Chinese contact, Men Low, a well-educated young man, employed as a cashier at the Bank of China in Kunking, who never bragged about knowing anything, even to advance himself. This would have been useless, as well as dangerous, in his case. Quiet and unassuming, Low was taken for granted like the rest of his countrymen.

Lunch was arranged at Tso Lin's, an exclusive restaurant next to the Plaza near the bank. About the only time Low showed any spark of personality was during these occasional lunches with Al.

"How was the trip, Al?" inquired the Chinese, smiling as he waited for his friend to be seated at the corner table.

"Like to never made it in. I had no idea how important my boss's business was, but nothing was going to stop me."

"You really surprised me. The weather has been very poor." Men Low reached for Al's cup. "Care for some tea?"

"I suppose—long as that's the best you got." Then Al changed the subject. "Got your list of the best places to exchange rupees today?"

"Yes, but they won't be to your advantage for a few days."

"How's that?" asked the American, lifting his eyebrows. "Oh, I get it—our charming Empress's dear little brother Tom Tung has done it again!"

"The rate should be stabilized again in a couple of days," consoled Low. "How long will you be here?"

"All depends on when Francis Stud wants to go back. I don't know how long I can stall him."

Tom Tung, president of the Bank of China, was a financial wizard. At least, he did well in keeping as much wealth as possible in the hands of the Tung family. Without a doubt, Tom was the most loyal man the Empress had under her, but she hated to give credit to any man, even her brother.

The organization in power collected from the masses they kept starved. However, in order to stay in power, they had to pay troops and various other help to run their regime. Fortunately, the help was not in the habit of being paid on a weekly basis. A period of months sometimes passed before a payday was declared for the loyal followers. Then, suddenly, the rate of exchange would fluctuate just after payday. This was a period of just such a fluctuation.

"I sure hope you can stay a few days, Al," said Low. "It's very risky if I have to do it without your being here."

"What's the matter? You afraid?" Al spoke impatiently. "Or don't you like your cut?"

"Please, Al, believe me." Low raised his hands to stop his associate from talking so loudly. "Not only am I risking a good thing, but my life as well!"

"Think anybody's getting suspicious?" Plummer asked. He was not in the least concerned with Low's problems. "I've got over ten thousand rupees with me."

"Don't worry, anything I take, I believe the Empress can well afford," the Chinaman said vengefully. "When I think of all the hard-earned money American-Chinese are sending to relatives over here, and they're only getting part of it!"

"How's that?" The pilot frowned as if there might be something he was missing out on.

"Simple," said Low in a resigned voice. "Every dollar has to clear the Bank of China. And they keep a big cut. That's why!"

On the other side of town Francis Stud was proudly showing Tonya one of his recent acquisitions, a large building which was to be the Sharks' Number One Hostel when they arrived. The ancient, three-story, castle-like construction of stone blocks was located on the side of a hill. For many years this had been an exclusive military academy for the sons of wealthy men. Aside from the lack of facilities and running water, the place appeared completely adequate and very impressive.

"Would you like to pick your room, Toni?" offered the granite-faced leader. "Mine is on the third floor."

"Then I'll take the two rooms across the hall from yours."

"Two rooms!" exclaimed Stud. "They're not connected, you know."

"Knock a hole in the wall and put a door in," said Tonya matter of factly, "if you're contemplating being invited over. It wouldn't be proper without a suite, Francis, now would it?"

"I guess you're right," Stud condescended, although he realized there wasn't too much space available, "but I figured being on the top floor would take care of it. Very little traffic."

"As long as we're here for a few days," said Tonya, as if mentally decorating her suite, "can't the workmen put the door in now?"

"Afraid it'll have to wait till tomorrow, Toni." Stud glanced at his watch. "The Empress invited me to tea in an hour, and it takes that long to get there."

"Will you take me some place nice afterward?" Tonya was thinking of having Stud make a few purchases for her new suite.

"Sure thing! We'll go someplace nice for dinner." He took her arm and guided her through the lower floor to the exit.

"What do you want for dinner, Francis?" As the question brought a lustful eye upon her figure, she laughed and quickly added, "I mean besides that!"

The conversation at the Palace had taken on a more serious note, once the flowery amenities of lunch were over. The Empress had suggested the foursome retire to the Jade Room for further discussion.

"Mr. Eddy," asked the Empress coolly, as they seated themselves about the room, "am I to assume your country is not happy with us?"

"Please, Your Highness," Sam Choy spoke up quickly, trying to avoid a scene, "I don't believe you understand This is merely routine."

"Humph," grunted the General, which meant, "I guess we'll have to claim more battles to keep them happy."

The Empress turned and gave her husband a sharp glance. "Keep out of this, Stoney!"

"Personally, I believe it's just an ugly rumor," Paul Eddy said suavely. "What the President asked for was very little. All I'm doing is making a cursory examination so he can get a couple of die-hard Congressmen out of his hair."

"Sure, that's all," agreed Sam Choy, leaving his seat beside Eddy and trotting across the room to stand beside the Empress, as though his presence verified his statement.

"No matter what was said," the Empress insisted, "the way my people are starving and suffering to help make a better world for democracy is above suspicion. All we ask for is money and supplies with which to carry on. The Chinese are the people getting killed. No amount of money can bring back the lives of the thousands of Chinese who have died for democracy."

As the Empress ran out of breath, Stoney added, "Humph—humph," complaining, "yes, I even went through one of your ceremonies of becoming a Christian. I caught cold from that icy holy water."

"I'm certain the General understands," Sam said as the tenseness of the situation increased. "We'll be able to work everything out satisfactorily." He trotted back across the room to his chair beside Eddy again, as if he were adding reassurance to his statement by his presence.

"About all I need," said Eddy, not wishing to create any further hard feelings, "is your word on the issues in question."

"I believe I can answer most of these quite simply," Sam said. "The majority of the battles have been observed by one of your own generals, George Wellstock."

General Wellstock had been in China for many years, and even prided himself in speaking the language—after a fashion. But West Point had taught him that a general's place was in the command post, working out tactics on a map. This he did expertly, as fast as the information came in. He did not stop to analyze the information or its sources. After all, this was the way they worked out field problems at Fort Benning, Georgia.

Sam spoke conclusively. "Our dealings with Mao Tse-Tung are grossly exaggerated, Paul. We haven't got along too well, but all we've given him is some rice for some starving people. Sure, he'd like to take over, but not because of Russia." He rose and trotted back to stand beside the Empress.

"All this I believe," Eddy agreed. "Now, how about the most insane rumor of all—your relationship to Japan?"

"The most unbelievable lie of all!" stated the Empress emphatically, as she took over from her ambassador. "There's no Japanese I would trust, and they know it! The story probably originated in Japan." It was obvious her patience was at an end.

"Please forgive me for carrying out an unpleasant duty, your Highness," Eddy apologized. "Rest assured I shall put Washington straight in this matter. My humble thanks for your kind and generous hospitality. I must bid you good-day. I am returning to Toyling this afternoon."

After this trying session, the Empress began pacing back and forth, without saying a word. Occasionally she stopped and braced an elbow against her bosom to support her chin in the palm of a hand. The fingers turned white as they curled over and sank long nails into the lower lip. It gave the illusion of a heavy load on the mind, producing physical bulk.

Her dramatics offered the group an opportunity for a quiet exit.

Left alone, the Empress gradually regained composure. She ordered tea for two. The next appointment was due. She anticipated very little trouble from the succeeding visitor. To cope with Francis Stud took no great mental effort.

But Stud arrived with a companion.

The First Lady wasn't too skillful, if she was trying to mask her displeasure. Tonya Brownfield's reputation had spread exceedingly fast, even in a land where communications are poor.

"Your Highness," said Stud awkwardly, "may I present Tonya Brownfield, the Group Historian."

"How do you do. Please be seated," returned the Empress coldly. Then turning to the servant she said, "Wong, change that tea for two—bring tea for three." Returning her attention to Stud's companion she added, "I believe I had the pleasure of meeting Mr. Brownfield while he was representing the Westlake Aircraft Company."

"Yes, August said you were an extremely charming person," Tonya's undertone was obvious, "even though he couldn't sell you any airplanes."

"My dear, he made a great mistake in not taking you with him," bantered the Empress. "It would be difficult to turn you down."

"Happy you see it that way." Tonya's tone caused the Empress to narrow her eyes, making them seem even longer.

Sam Choy suddenly appeared, and Tonya excused herself by saying, "I understand the Palace has some beautiful gardens. Would you mind if Ambassador Choy escorted me through them? No doubt you and Colonel Stud have a few matters you would like to discuss privately."

As Tonya and Sam Choy departed, the Empress turned to Stud. "To what do I owe the honor of this visit, dear Colonel?"

"Mostly routine. Keeping the Empress informed." But his eyes were gazing at an overseas cap which his gnarled fingers were twisting back and forth.

"Oh, come now, Francis, I know you better than that. Has this woman anything to do with it?"

"Who? Tonya? Certainly not!" Stud's eyes met those of the Empress. "I'd like to get my own deal straightened out before it's too late."

"I assumed we had an understanding, Francis," said the Empress, trying to appear shocked. "There's no reason why you shouldn't have all the money you can ever spend."

"It's not that I distrust you," apologized the Shark leader, "but I'd feel happier if it's in writing."

"My dear friend, don't you realize, the ways to the greatest fortunes cannot be put in writing!" Even as a young girl the Empress added her own proverbs to the already lengthy list existing in China, voicing things people like to hear, yet not believing a word of them herself.

"I don't quite understand."

"You make your own fortune—like Brownfield's wife.

If you see an opportunity, take advantage of it. The sky's the limit. When we catch some people, however, we execute them."

"I think I see what you mean," Stud replied slowly, giving his words a great deal of thought.

When Sam Choy told the Empress of the information the Shark Historian agreed to leave out of her book, she was furious.

"That rumor Eddy was talking about came from Rudolph Hess," she stormed. "Sam, get off a cable to the President. Tell him he must agree to send more supplies, and faster."

Sam did not like the look of cold, glittering menace in her eyes. "I think you're acting hastily, Your Highness," he warned. "How long are you giving the President?"

"Two days!"

The Empress was ready to light up the world.

As the car carried them down the bumpy, cobblestone road from the Palace, Stud was silent. But his companion was bubbling over with joy.

"Did the Empress turn you down or something, Francis?"

"Far from it," Stud said in all seriousness. "Did you enjoy the gardens?"

"Not the right time of year for gardens." Tonya was still very pleased. "But I can inform my publisher the first five thousand books are already sold."

For the next two days, Tonya was happy supervising the decoration of the new suite. Stud, however, was at an age where two days brought his enthusiasm to a standstill. He had to insist they return to Paygoo.

Enroute to the airport, they encountered a strange procession headed for the cemetery which bordered the airport. Leading, on horseback, rode a Chinese officer. Directly behind him, four foot soldiers with rifles were herding a young Chinaman along between them. The well-dressed prisoner's hands were wired together behind his back. A bright red feather was fastened to the black hair. A snake-like column of rickshaws and ragged pedestrians followed.

"A thief on his way to the graveyard," commented Stud calmly. "They're going to shoot him."

"Can we go over?" Tonya asked. "I have my camera. I'd like to take a picture."

The procession came to a halt at the edge of the cemetery, which gave the appearance of being covered with tiny hills. In China, the caskets are placed on top of the ground and covered over with mounds of earth.

Tonya, unabashed by the gruesomeness of what was about to take place, alighted from the car and moved close for a picture.

The quiet, unassuming young prisoner was forced to kneel while the officer barked commands to the four soldiers. They waited with cocked rifles for the signal to fire. The victim turned his head toward the camera a moment before the bullets knocked him forward—dead.

As Stud walked Tonya back to the car, he said, "Looked like that guy was saying something to you just before they shot him."

"He did say something," Tonya replied numbly.

"Good thing you can't speak Chinese." Stud laughed.

"He spoke in English!" Tonya had to stop walking in order to get the words out. "He said, 'Lady, tell Al Plummer I won't be able to meet him.'"

7 · Hong Kong Interlude

BECAUSE OF ITS GEOGRAPHICAL position and excellent communications, Hong Kong is the headquarters for numerous newspaper correspondents and radio newsmen. Now, in early December, most of these men felt safe, in spite of the Japanese occupying all the coastal sections except those few controlled by the British.

Among the newsmen loafing around the Hong Kong Hotel was Choy's friend, Gilbert Withcomb. On special leave, he was putting out the same slanted news, but living better. Besides, there was the odd chance of his running into a sideline story, and picking up an extra buck or two.

Withcomb was sitting near the bar with Ross Sparks of the Associated Press.

"That joker looks awful familiar," said Sparks, pointing to a distinguished-looking Japanese. "Do you recognize him, Gil?"

"Prince Satake the Nip Premier." Withcomb turned to get a better view. "He's a little off the beaten track."

Sparks took a healthy gulp from the scotch and soda he held. "You know something, I smell a story."

"I don't think there's anything to get excited about," Withcomb said glumly. "Probably on vacation or something."

"No, no. That guy is waiting for a date, and it's damn important!" He added, as if to himself, "I wonder if it could be a dame."

Withcomb answered indifferently. "Whatever it is, that telephone appears to have solved it. He's leaving in a hurry."

"Come on." Sparks slapped down a bill for the drinks. "Let's tail him and find out!"

In response to the Associated Press man's enthusiasm, Gil Withcomb slumped even further down into the chair. "Go ahead. Two of us would be too obvious."

Apparently the Prince didn't know, or didn't care, that Ross Sparks was riding on the steam tramway with him up the side of Victoria Peak. Ross loitered behind at a safe distance, while Satake walked briskly for the equivalent of three steep blocks. Sparks watched him enter a large house that jutted over the side of the peak. "Tung" he read on the mail box.

For the next few minutes, Sparks stood in thought, catching his breath. No doubt Withcomb either knew, or, with his connections, could easily locate some answers. However, Sparks decided it would be better for him to chance it alone. The airport was a logical check point. If not, then the tramway could be haunted day and night. A pity he wasn't invited inside!

At Kai Tak Airport, the Associated Press took note of Prince Satake's departure. The identification markings on a DC-3 parked on the airstrip looked as if they had been freshly painted over. Further browsing around, and Ross Sparks located an American pilot called "One-Eye" Hoskins, who had acquired this nickname because, by a peculiar quirk, nature had given him only one eyebrow. At a distance, with black hair and dark complexion, Hoskins gave the impression of having one eye missing.

The first day, getting acquainted and questioning One-Eye only brought on an avalanche of double talk. By the second day, he showed signs of becoming more conversational. Judging by nervous actions, One-Eye was in need of a drink. Ross Sparks obliged him. The two left by cab for the nearest bar. Upon arriving, each telephoned and left the same number, in case they were needed elsewhere.

"What'll you have, One-Eye?"

"Make mine a double scotch and soda. I feel like I just came in from the Mongolian Desert."

"Where do you stem from?"

"Raised in California," answered the pilot as if it were a long time ago. "But I've been kicking around the Far East for six years. About every two years, I go back home for a month. Time enough to spend all my money having a good time gettting drunk."

As the afternoon wore into evening, the pilot became more loquacious. But the scotch had thickened his tongue, and Sparks had to ask him to repeat many statements.

"Then the Empress is here," Sparks insisted, as he tried to dwell on the subject, "having some kind of parley with Satake."

"Didn't say who with—or what for," corrected the drunken pilot, " 'cause I don't know. All I said was I brought her here 'n' I'm taking her back to Kunking."

That night Japanese troops began moving across the peninsula to take Hong Kong. The larger guns could be heard in the distance. Terrified, thousands of people, of every nationality ran for every means of transportation available to take them away from the oncoming danger.

Only a small portion of these, women and children, were permitted to board the DC-3 with the Empress. Captain One-Eye Hoskins had miraculously sobered up with the gravity of the situation. He was trying desperately to get the plane door closed.

"Sorry, that's all!" One-Eye realized the plane would never take off with another person aboard. Then he noticed Gil Withcomb frantically pushing people aside, trying to make his way to the door. Fright had bitten into the newsman's face.

"Wait! *Wait for me!*" screamed Withcomb, struggling against the mob in an effort to get closer.

"Sorry, friend," One-Eye shouted, "but we're only taking women and children. We're full up."

"You gotta make room for me! I'm a news correspondent," shrilled the terrified Withcomb. "I've got diplomatic immunity!"

In reply, Hoskins closed the door, leaving Withcomb to struggle in the churning crowd outside the plane.

Ross Sparks stood at a distance, watching One-Eye climb out of Hong Kong and fly out of sight. "I hope I live through this," he said to himself, "so I can find out what that meeting was about. It won't be news, but I'd sure like to know!"

8 · A Black Night

PAYGOO TIME, the fiery ball of the sun hung halfway into the dense jungle to the west—a molten ladle pouring a golden hue over the surrounding plains.

The airstrip was closing for the night. The last mechanic was leaving his ward on the field, with no intention of seeing it for at least twelve hours. Gurkha guards would baby-sit the P-40's until their crews returned in the early morning.

An all-out working schedule had been in effect for the past six weeks, Sundays included. The last of the Third Detachment had finally managed a few familiarization flights in the P-40's with their new military modifications. A few days earlier, a number of Lend-Lease trucks for China had pulled in from Rangoon. These were now being loaded with equipment for the trip north to Kunking, for supplies had to be trucked into China via the perilous Burma Road.

Rusty Bush and Bob Truelove were waiting for the line to secure, and for Chuck Reynolds to remove the outer layer of grease from his arms with 100-octane gas.

114

"C'mon, Chuck, let's go to chow," Rusty urged, "there's a good feed waiting for us."

"How come?" The mechanic did not even look up, continuing to wipe his huge arms.

" 'Cause it's Sunday, man," Truelove drawled. "We always have steak once a week, remember?"

"By golly, you're right. Only day of the week I can keep track of. After breakfast that drunken sky-pilot Frockman blows his bourbon breath in my face and says, 'Those who want to skip an hour's work can do so by attending my Sunday services.' Other than that, I couldn't begin to tell you the day of the month, if my life depended on it!"

After a moment's thought, Rusty laughed. "It's been Sunday, December the seventh, all day long Chuck, and I guess it'll stay that way till midnight!"

"Who gives a damn?" Truelove growled, the perennial grin on his face belying his tone. "It's December seventh. So what? Just another day 'n nothing happening."

"We c'n always hope, can't we?" Rusty was concentrating on a means to get Tonya alone later that night.

"Yeah, hope we hurry and get out of this damn place. Another three weeks and we done spent all of '41 in this hell hole!" Chuck said.

"Speakin' about our padre, Frockman," Truelove said, "did Stud find him out here too?"

"Naw." Chuck threw down the dirty rag he'd been using. "Ol' Frocky was an Air Corps padre, getting in a

115

heap o' trouble drinking back home. Would've been shang-haied out, if he hadn't agreed to resign 'n join the Sharks and straighten hisself up. Now he's working on everybody 'cepting hisself."

"Why? You need a little saving, Bob?" Rusty cocked his head inquisitively at Truelove, suppressing a smile.

"Not me! Not that kind anyhow."

"What other kind is there?"

"Darned if I know, but I overheard the padre telling Toni, 'The best way is down on your knees, woman.' Not knowing what it was all about, I said, 'Count me in too!'"

"I'll bet'cha it was something more fun than praying if he was holding Toni's interest," Chuck laughed.

The ex-Marine's expression changed from a teasing smile to a flush of anger. As men go, his veneer of being a gentleman was thinner than most, but Rusty was there when the blue chips were down. Whatever else Tonya might be, she was a woman, and must be protected.

"Let's knock it off!" he said firmly. "Any female would have a hard time in the spot Toni's in."

"You know," said Chuck, to change the subject, "talking about eating, did I ever tell you about . . ."

"No, but I can believe it," Bob said. Rusty continued to glare at them.

". . . 'bout my first hitch in the army? How I'd spent the whole four years cussin' the chow 'n telling my buddies how good we ate back home . . ."

"What's so good to eat in Arkansas?"

"Well, I'll tell you. After my first four years, I went home. My folks wuz mighty proud. Me 'n my tailored G.I.'s. My Mom greets me at the door and she says, 'Charles, welcome home. I've had your favorite dishes cooking all day.'

"As we went in the kitchen, I says, 'I smell sumpin' sorta funny like.'

" 'You bet you do, son,' she says. 'Sit right down. They must've starved you in the army.'

"I watched her load up a platter of chitlin's, boiled okra, corn bread fried in bacon grease, and some of the mos' beautiful black-eyed peas covered with about a half inch o' hog fat . . ."

"What! No dumplings?" Bob interrupted.

"Now that you mention it, we had them too!"

"I'm glad," Rusty said. "Without dumplings, a meal is hardly complete."

"Ma stood there beaming down at me, waiting fer me to ask fer seconds. But I didn't. After a few bites, I stopped.

" 'What's a matter, son, sumpin' troublin' you?' she says.

" 'Naw, Ma, just thinking, that's all.'

" ' 'Bout what, son?'

" 'About my lying, Ma.'

" 'I thought we reared you better. But even if'n you did, you shouldn't let that take your appetite.'

" 'A guy can enlist and travel all around the world without knowing what he's been doing. I had to come home to find out.'

117

" 'Find out what?'

" 'That I'd been bragging about eating slop all my life and didn't know it!' "

Bob and Rusty laughed together. The three climbed into a jeep and headed for the clubhouse.

No one really had a right to complain about the meals served at Paygoo. Most of the griping about the fare came from boredom, or not enough to talk about. The food, shipped in by rail each day, was prepared by a Rangoon catering service. It was wholesome and tasty. This company employed Indians for the entire mess detail—cooks, waiters and dishwashers. They were well-mannered and capable men, who had migrated to Burma for a pay incentive. They worked three out of four years, a system that allowed them to remain at home with their families every fourth year without having to work.

After the Sunday steak dinner, Colonel Francis Stud permitted himself to be cornered for a few questions. This was not his usual pattern. Stud liked the common folks in platoon front so they couldn't talk back.

"Will the Group be moving no'th shortly, Colonel?" Cortland Lee Smith asked.

"Very shortly, Smith, very shortly." Stud would have liked to pack up immediately. He didn't wish to discuss the matter with Smith.

"I certainly agree with your principles, Colonel, suh," Smith said unctuously in his exaggerated Georgian accent. "Saving China is a cause well wo'th fighting for."

The old Escadrille flyer, Stud's friend who recruited pilots, had placed Smith in charge of the Group prior to their departure from San Francisco. He had held the rank of captain in the Air Corps Reserve before resigning to join the Group. The Sharks needed his stable maturity to balance them out. He was like someone who could be trusted with a dear one who found it necessary to make a trip to Forest Lawn.

"What made you volunteer, Smith? You're quite different from the run of the mill we get. Somewhat older too. When did you go through flight school?"

"Kelly Field, suh, in 1929."

"It's a wonder our paths haven't crossed before. Been flying ever since?"

"No, suh, I took a refresher course in 1940, after the President declared a national emergency. Been assigned to active duty ever since. I left a very profitable jewelry business in Atlanta to come over heah."

The Shark leader's eyes brightened. He enjoyed rubbing elbows with success. Memory of the tough times during his early years was still clear to Francis Stud. If he had anything to do with it, there would never be a repetition of such years for him.

Now, although a bit late in life, Francis Stud had discovered the pleasure that could be offered by the opposite sex. Once forced away from his ungodly large family for economic reasons, he had found that women were attracted to him sexually. This was a source of pride to him.

He sought proof from all the females he encountered, regardless of their affiliations.

"Are you a married man?" inquired Stud.

"Oh, no, suh!" Smith turned his head to Stud in surprise, as if this should be obvious. "The men in my family line always took time to distinguish themselves first in the service before taking on a wife."

Stud remembered that Cortland Lee Smith had previously laid claim to a long line of important military blood. "That makes sense," agreed Stud. "Before this is over, you'll probably have all the requirements you need." He forced what was intended as a smile.

"I come from a stock that believes in fighting for the underdog, Colonel, suh!" Cortland Lee Smith was dramatically fierce. "We throw caution to the winds. Never has a Lee or a Smith fought for money. I'm ready to give my life, if necessary, but not for money!"

"Admirable, very admirable," exclaimed Stud, taken aback by such gallantry. "But I'm curious to know how you became interested in China."

"Colonel, suh, I had the privilege and honor of listening to the Empress when she made an address at the Shrine Auditorium in Atlanta. A magnificent lady—so brilliant, so sincere, so brave, so humble! When her words rang out across the hall about the sacrifice, the hardships and determined war against oppression, I silently vowed to offer my life."

On a nearby table, an olive drab blanket was spread

over the end of a long table in preparation for the nightly poker game. It prevented the cards from sliding, and made them easier to pick up without being shown. Tonya had the unpopular habit of standing behind this horseshoe seating arrangement, kibitzing on one or another of the players' hands. Occasionally fresh faces appeared among the regulars at the table, but not for long. Sooner or later they and their money departed.

"Just who does that son-of-a-bitch think he's kidding?" Truelove drawled as he peeked at the cards cupped in his hands.

"Who's a son-of-a-bitch?" echoed Reynolds, who obviously thought his hand was good.

"That Pocahontas lover, Smith. He's snowing the old man with all this fight for democracy. Man, you don't know how lucky you are! The Third Detachment had to take that crap all the way over."

"Sometimes social standing can make some people feel uncomfortable," taunted Kirk Jackson as he threw in his hand.

"Not if he got it the way you squadron leaders did." Rusty was thinking of how Kirk, Bob Sanderson and Ole Nelson had talked themselves into squadron leader spots merely by being in the first detachment to arrive. Some of the pilots to come later, like Rusty, had at least twice the flying experience.

"Can we help it if we're lucky?" Kirk grinned.

"Do you call luck multiplying your total time by four?

Even then, you'd have been out of luck if Toni hadn't fixed you up with Stud," Rusty said.

"You don't have to make derogatory remarks, Rusty," interceded Sanderson.

"Puh-leese, fellows, watch your language," cautioned Nelson. "The exec's frau is coming back."

"You can bet nobody's said anything the lady hasn't heard before." Truelove pushed a ten-dollar chip into the stack. "Can anyone stand a small raise?"

"Any raise you can muster, I can double." Chuck's attention was focused upon the curvaceous Tonya, in tight-fitting slacks and matching sweater, gliding toward them.

Truelove gave Tonya an approving glance. "Bet she needs a shoehorn to get in that outfit."

Nelson's eyebrows rose. "You're complaining?"

"Wonder what the Padre and Toni have been cooking up," said Rusty.

"Hope they haven't encouraged Smith to sing. That's about all I need," Bob moaned. "I've been holding second best hands all night."

"Second best only counts in horseshoes," Kirk laughed.

"Cards for the losers," called Sanderson.

"I'm out," Ole said.

"Kirk, how many?"

"Sorry, I've folded."

Rusty held up three fingers, and Sanderson dealt the indicated number. "A pair of openers, an honest man."

"Slip me the right one in here," Bob held his four hold cards apart so that the dealer could insert the draw card.

"Two of a kind for me." Chuck threw away two cards.

"A pair of kings and a kicker."

"Everybody folding except Rusty, Bob and Chuck," observed Tonya.

"I'm only staying in to keep them honest," explained Rusty, "and I pass!"

"Check without looking." Bob was waiting for Chuck.

"Not too proud of these, but I'll waste twenty-five bucks, seeing's how I'm ahead."

The game was distracted as Smith raised his voice above the others. "Reverend Frockman has requested my singing 'The Lord's Prayer' to close out this Sunday."

"Oh, no!" Bob groaned loudly. "I'll up that fifty." Eager to recoup from a bad evening, he didn't wait for Rusty's bet.

"Nice of you to save my money. Be my guest." Rusty threw in his cards, and moved over beside Tonya.

"OUR—FATHER—WHO ART IN HEA—VEN——" sang out Smith.

"Doing anything tonight, Toni?" Rusty whispered.

"Please, Rusty, be quiet!"

"HAL-LOW—ED BE THY NAME——"

"But, Toni, I—"

"Shh—Sorry, not tonight, Rusty." She turned her back to him.

"ON EARTH—AS IT IS IN HEA——VEN——"

"You and Stud have work to do, I know." Clenching his
fists, Rusty headed for the bunkhouse, not caring if Smith
ever finished.

"Ole Arkansas Traveler, I've got 'em this time," assured
Bob. "Raise you a hundred."

"FOR THINE IS THE KINGDOM——"

"Tex, I'd hate to win, but I'm forced to call you." Chuck
covered the bet.

"Can you beat it?" Bob proudly laid down his ace high
spade flush, and started to rake in the chips.

"FOREVER——AMEN——"

"Amen," repeated Chuck. "Four little boat hooks win
where I come from."

As the mechanic racked in the winnings with grimy
fingers and started to stack them, Bob sat staring at four
sevens and an ace of hearts. His smoldering eyes con-
trasted with his silly grin.

Dragging Smith by the arm, Frockman staggered up
to the table. "Let's show our appreciation and give our
vocalist a hand."

"Sure, give him a hand." Bob rose from the poker table
and turned around.

Before anyone realized what was happening, least of
all Smith, Truelove's fist had connected squarely on the
Georgian's aristocratic nose, knocking him flat on his back.

The racket was not quelled until August Brownfield

stormed into the clubhouse. No one could give the exec a satisfactory explanation, least of all Smith, holding a bloody handkerchief to his face, tears gushing from his eyes.

"All right—all right—time to hit the sack," Auggie screamed. "I'm turning the lights out!"

During the commotion Stud and Tonya had disappeared in the direction of her quarters.

By 1:00 A.M. practically the entire Shark camp was fast asleep. A moonless night covered Paygoo with a cloak of pitch black darkness. The night was soundless, except for the faint strains of "*J' attendrai*" drifting from Tonya's quarters. This would continue until the Gurkha guards changed.

Music playing in the radio shack disturbed no one. It couldn't. The tones were coming through a set of earphones. Little Blanco White, ex-Navy radioman, had the base's high-powered receiver turned to Hawaiian music. Blanco had been stationed in the Islands. His dream was to retire there someday. Mornings invariably found his short wiry body sprawled across the bed, with his earphones still on.

Blanco's receiving set was almost unique; there were only four like it in the whole world: one in the United States and three others had been shipped to various parts of the British Empire. The set not only reached halfway around the face of the globe, but a split-wave-tube device prevented jamming by the enemy. How the Sharks had gained possession of this priceless equipment from the docks of Rangoon was a dark secret.

The set was manufactured and assembled by its inventor, James McDougall, of Los Angeles, California. England had to be at war before the Defense Department would finally give the little bearded scientist his first chance to prove that his split-wave tube would work. Back when Billy Mitchell proved a bomb could sink a battleship, McDougall had perfected a device to steer the fins on bombs without possible jamming. He called it a "guided missile." Both Mitchell and McDougall had been tossed out.

"The Japanese have attacked Pearl Harbor," repeatedly echoing in his ears, jarred Blanco from his sleep.

"This must be a dream," Blanco thought as he jumped out of bed and turned up the volume. It sounded real. He listened carefully as the broadcast related the disaster. It couldn't be! This announcer had to be joking. Nobody would be stupid enough to attack a fortress as he remembered Pearl Harbor!

Finally Blanco decided this was on the level.

Immediately he picked up the phone and rang for Stud's quarters. Cranking ring after ring without success, he kept mumbling, "Wonder if the old man's turned stone deaf."

There were only four connections on the line: the clubhouse, the flight line, headquarters shack and the colonel's quarters. Blanco tried them all to no avail. Not knowing what else to do, he ran for August Brownfield.

"What in hell's going on?" was Auggie's irritated response to the pounding on the door.

"I don't know, sir, but Pearl Harbor's being bombed by the Japs!"

"Who are you?" Auggie pulled back the mosquito net, reaching for the light switch and his trousers at the same time.

"White, sir, the radioman."

"Blanco, there's been enough trouble for one night," Auggie warned. "I don't need any more practical jokes. Who put you up to this, anyhow?"

"God-damn it," said the excited radioman, when Brownfield finally opened the door and let him in, "if you'd get on your damn pants and come down to the radio shack, you can listen for yourself!"

The exec no longer doubted that something mighty strange was happening. Hurriedly he slipped into his trousers, and the two headed for the jeep and the radio shack.

Auggie listened motionless to the report of the catastrophe that had struck Pearl Harbor. In the dim light his flushed face slowly turned the color of his white hair. Thoughtfully he removed the earphones.

"What'll we do?" asked Blanco.

"I'll call the colonel."

"No use. I've already tried a dozen times. He must be in town."

"Let me try." Auggie grew more excited every time his ring brought no answer. "My God, we'll be blown up like sitting ducks!"

"How will they find us in the dark?" Blanco asked sensibly.

"Never underestimate the Japs. Those little bastards are smart. How do you think they found Pearl Harbor?"

"It's daylight there."

Brownfield tore through the three bunkhouses like a crazy person, flashing on the lights, and screaming, "Man your planes. Pearl Harbor has been attacked. The Japs are hitting all points simultaneously. We're next!"

"How long before they'll be here?" someone asked with calm logic.

"Any minute! Get out to the field!" The terrified exec's voice rose higher and shriller by the second. "Squadrons will take off in numerical order."

"Don't be so nervous, Brownfield, maybe we can understand you," came another voice.

"Who's nervous?" Auggie shrieked. "You son-of-a-bitch, who's nervous?"

In a matter of ten minutes nearly every P-40 coughed and roared defiantly at being awakened in the middle of the night. Slipstreams were blowing in every direction. Why no one walked, or was blown, into a propeller, the Lord only knows. Six trucks, three on each side of the runway, provided runway lights with their almost completely blacked-out lenses.

The exhausts flashing intermittently about the field brought the comment, "Looks like giant fireflies are blitzing this joint tonight."

Brownfield was on the ground radio. "Okay, Sanderson, take off."

"I'm not warmed up yet." Sandy's voice was barely audible in the static.

"To hell with it! *Take off!*" roared the florid-faced exec into the mike.

Robert Sanderson III promptly got under way, and a few seconds later taxied a wing tip through a propeller. He ordered his second in command to take over.

As each of the First Squadron planes roared on take-off, their engines sputtered miserably, for the only warm up was the length of the strip. Only half of them made it into the black night air. The others came to a grinding, sliding stop in a cloud of dust in the uncleared area bordering the field. Landing gears were shorn away. Wing tips tore and bent. Propeller blades folded back to look like umbrella stays.

Doc Ward, standing by viewing the confused operation, muttered, "I knew this vacation of mine was too good to last." He turned his head toward the end of the strip as the sound of metal tearing over rocky surfaces again shattered the night. "Guess I better get set to go to work."

At the first signs of disturbance in camp, Colonel Stud had every intention of leaving Tonya's quarters diplomatically, after he had dressed in the dark. The picture changed rapidly as he heard his precious planes being fired up, and listened to the first clatter through the rocks at the end of the runway.

"Turn on the light, Toni."

"What is it, Francis?"

"Get my bush jacket—quick!"

The Shark leader was oblivious to the sight of Tonya's nude body now. Hurriedly he slipped on his shoes, without socks, not bothering to lace them. His undershorts stayed on the floor, as he slid into his trousers.

"Wait for me," called a very frightened female.

Francis might just as well have waited a second longer. As he started to run through the door into the dark, both arms were halfway into the sleeves of his jacket. The trousers weren't secured and fell around his ankles. He stumbled across the sill, making a beautiful three-point landing on his craggy chin and bony knees.

The light from the open door was sufficient to prove that the colonel did not present a very romantic sight as he climbed to his feet.

9. Only The Young Sleep Sound

STUD DIDN'T BOTHER chopping dragon tails to locate the head of the tempest. He knew better. Like a homing pigeon the jeep bumped through the dark, straight to radio control beside the strip.

"Colonel Stud!" cried the amazed Blanco above the clamor. "We've been looking all over for you."

"Never mind that!" Francis cut the bewildered boy short. "Where's Brownfield?"

"In the tower, sir . . ." Blanco was shoved to one side to make access to the stairway leading to the glassed-in section.

When Stud saw Auggie, an overwhelming desire to become a painter came over him. In the center of a maelstrom, a would-be emperor was in his glory. No doubt Nero would have been proud of his modern-day counterpart. Sometimes history becomes so repetitious it is monotonous, but nearly two thousand years of history are capable of supplying one improvement. Now Francis Stud was getting precisely the same effect, only in animation.

131

"Give me that mike!" Stud ordered, practically tearing the instrument from the exec's hand.

"Glad you finally made it!" panted the breathless Auggie. "I've had my hands full, here all alone. It's lucky I got the news as quick as I did."

"So I see." The Shark leader gritted his teeth in anger. Then he spoke slowly and evenly into the microphone. "Attention all pilots—attention all pilots—cut your engines—remain where you are—I repeat, remain where you are."

Over the receiver, a voice came back, loud and clear. "Sorry, Colonel, I'm fifteen thousand feet over God knows what, and if I cut my engine, I'll be God knows where!"

Aghast, the colonel shouted back, "This pertains to planes on the ground only. I repeat, GROUND ONLY!"

"But—but, Colonel, the Japs are in Pearl Harbor. We'll be next. They'll probably be here any minute."

"Don't know about that, but I'll take a chance on the Japs bombing in the middle of the night rather than lose the whole damn bunch this way!"

Once the master switch was pushed to the off position, the propellers around the field rotated quickly to a stand still, one after the other. The suddenness of it all turned the place into a state of unearthly silence in comparison to a minute before. Even the excited personnel stopped talking, as though waiting for an explosion. The distant drone of the ten airborne P-40's was all that could be heard.

"How many are up?" asked Stud.

"Nine or ten—I th-think," Auggie stammered. "Why, sir?"

"Don't 'why' me! What are their orders?"

"Well—to—uh—to seek out the enemy, and shoot them down." Hearing his own words repeating the orders, the exec flushed at the ridiculousness of them.

"About as easy as finding the man in the moon tonight! Brownfield, don't you realize there isn't so much as a street light within five hundred miles of Paygoo? They'll be lucky to find their way back!"

"If the engines were leaned out, they might last until daylight," Auggie suggested hopefully.

"Perhaps, but they'll probably be over Timbuktu by then."

"What'll we do?"

"Call them down. Tell them to look for a gas fire at the end of the runway in five minutes."

"Yes, sir." Auggie turned to make the call, as Stud headed down the stairway.

Anxious faces reflected the glow from a pile of gasoline-soaked rags. Each time the fire died down, Chuck Reynolds' voice boomed out, "C'mon, you fire bugs, get the lead out, throw some more gas on! Keep the home fires burning!"

While Reynolds was occupied with the bucket brigade, Blanco White appeared. "Colonel Brownfield sent me with a message, Chuck."

"Now what?"

"You should find something besides 100-octane for fire wood. You're wasting too much."

"That stupid son-of-bitch! Not to mention the lives, but the planes—they'll use more gas in an hour than we could all night!"

"Okay, Chuck, I'll tell him what you said."

"I've forgotten already."

"You said he was a stupid son-of-a-bitch," teased Blanco, as he disappeared into the dark.

"I sure hope they spot it soon," Sandy said regretfully, "I feel doubly bad 'cause my plane got banged up and I'm not up there too!"

"We won't have this headache in China," Stud predicted.

"Why, Colonel, offhand I'd think it would be far worse. The terrain and everything . . ."

"True, the country is more rugged. Yet, surprising as it may seem, the Chinese have a very efficient direction-finding system."

"What's that?" asked Sandy.

"A primitive system of common, ordinary telephones throughout the country. Every little village calls in and gives the number of planes, the heading and time overhead. There's a plotting room in Kunking where the calls are taken and marked on a large-scale map. It was developed by tracking Jap planes. Necessity is the mother of invention. These Chinese are great inventors!" Stud smiled.

"Well, I'll be—some warning system!" exclaimed Sandy. "But I don't quite see how it would help tonight."

"I've listened in a couple of times. There's about twenty people talking all at once. Didn't make too much sense to me! But as long as planes are within reach of a ground station, it does. All the pilot has to do is call in and ask what village he's over."

"How can they tell us from the Japs?" Sandy asked, puzzled.

"Doesn't make any difference. We'd know how many we had up that day, and approximately where they were. If they weren't ours, they'd be Japs. In case a pilot's lost, he knows his heading. If not, he can circle over a town and let 'em call in."

"How long they been out?" Chuck's face was so smeared with grease and smoke that only his powerful shoulders and arms identified him.

"It's 2:35," advised the Colonel, turning in the firelight to see his watch. "Sandy, run over to control and see if we're making radio contact."

"Yes, sir!"

"Reynolds, we're going to have to get a guard on the damaged planes off the field."

"Already taken care of, Colonel," said Chuck, wiping still more grease on his face with the back of his hairy arm.

"Who'd you get?" asked Stud.

"The Gurkhas. Who else?"

"When it gets light we'll take a look and see how many we can salvage."

135

"Nearly all eight, I'd say."

"You'll have to pick a detail and get on them right away. They'll have to stay behind until it's done, so pick your men accordingly."

"I take it lucky ol' Charles is staying with 'em till the job's done." The line chief did not seem unhappy at the prospect.

"You guessed right, Reynolds."

"Won't be able to fix 'em any too good, Colonel. Most of the equipment is packed and ready to go north."

"Just enough to get them in the air. If the landing gear is damaged and won't retract, let it go. I'll leave some of the new pilots behind. They can fly them up as they're ready."

"I gotcha. Hammer out the prop blades enough so's they won't fly apart, and let 'em go."

Robert Sanderson III came running across the airstrip toward them. He arrived out of breath. "They're making radio contact all right, Colonel, but they can't see our fire."

"Build up the fire and keep it going," instructed Stud. "I'd better give Brownfield a hand."

"Got any idea where they are?" Chuck asked.

"Unless I miss my guess, they're circling, looking for the fire." The old aviator took off toward the tower.

None of the pilots had flown beyond the Paygoo area in daylight. Experience told the Shark leader that his pilots, in their enthusiasm, had neglected to keep an accurate account of time, headings or airspeed. His rough guess was that they had followed a general easterly course in an interception attempt.

Instructions to head due west without deviating for exactly one hour brought the stray P-40's within sight of the fire. From there on, most managed to set down without mishap. Two planes ground-looped because the trucks provided such poor ground lighting. They were lucky to have only one wing tip damaged.

"Let's secure. Maybe we can get a couple hours' sleep before dawn," Stud said dejectedly.

"Yes, sir, just as soon as we disperse the aircraft," agreed Auggie.

"Let them be. I don't know how in hell they could be any more spread out than they are. I doubt if the Japs could find them even in daylight!"

The greatest liability of age in wartime is the inability to rest when given the opportunity. Ninety per cent of the Group were in their early twenties. In spite of everything that had happened, most of the camp was sound asleep inside of fifteen minutes. Only the top level, the drunk and the frightened remained awake until dawn.

Tonya had not gone near the airstrip during the activity. After her visitor had left in such an unexpected hurry,

Tonya dressed and proceeded to the clubhouse. Having already gone through evacuations of Shanghai and Hanoi, she chose to keep an eye on the possessions she had gathered in the interim. They would be hard to come by again.

As Tonya flicked on the light in the club, she was startled to find a motionless form seated beside the bar. Apparently the Group chaplain had remained to protect something too.

"You startled me," exclaimed Tonya, as she walked over to the bar. "I didn't expect to find anyone here."

"Where else?" said Frockman quite normally, considering how much liquor he had obviously stowed away. He turned slowly, and with some difficulty focused his glassy eyes upon her. "When I first joined the Group, the good commander of this beautiful base assigned me to some additional duties."

"What on earth are you talking about?"

"My earthly employer said I was getting too much money for the few souls that would need saving in this outfit. I would have to pinch-hit with a couple of extra duties. So, I became mess officer and guardian of the whisky. Apparently, the colonel believes humanity can survive on only one virtue—sobriety. Pity he hasn't bothered to look up the meaning of the word."

"You're a real martyr, Frocky, willing to die at your battle station for a principle."

"What's that?" The clergyman was so enthralled by his own eloquence that Tonya's words eluded him.

"Meaning, dead drunk on the floor beside the bar— drinking all the booze yourself to save the Sharks from a fate worse than death!"

"I'm glad you understand," said the chaplain. Then with an exaggerated, and somewhat unsteady, bow: "Would you care to join me?"

"Had it ever occurred to you, even *your* services might be needed more elsewhere?"

"My dear woman, my practices differ somewhat from your Catholicism. I rely upon a distinguished medical officer like Dr. Ward to pronounce them dead first. After this formality is over, they are nailed in the best available casket and resting beside a freshly dug grave before my services are required."

"It's all over then." Tonya was becoming exasperated.

"I beg to differ. Not until I give a parting salutation that will last them from here to eternity, is it over!"

For the remaining hours of the night, the Shark high command stayed glued to all forms of communication: radio, wire and telephone. It was becoming apparent that contacting RAF Headquarters in Rangoon would accomplish nothing until in the morning. Each call from Colonel Stud brought the same sleepy answer from a sergeant with a cockney accent: "As I said before, the Air Marshal is the only one who can answer that, sir, I really can't say."

139

"Has Mingladon Field been alerted?"

"Alerted, you say, for what?"

"Christ, man, haven't you heard about Pearl Harbor, and all the ships sinking?"

"The Pearl Harbor is sinking sir?" said the cockney accent in amazement. "Blimey, governor, for the life of me I couldn't even tell you how many bloody funnels she had!"

"Hell, connect me with the Marshal immediately," demanded the infuriated leader. "He'll understand what I'm talking about!"

"As I said before, sir, it's against regulations. I have to think of me orders, you know."

"To hell with regulations and damn your orders!"

"If you'll call after ten A.M., I'm certain the Air Marshal will . . ."

Stud slammed the receiver down. He sat motionless. Except for the gnarled fingers beating a tattoo on the large crate that served as a table, it would have been impossible to tell if he was nervous. Finally, the fingers stopped and reached for the dead cigarette which had been hanging on his lower lip for the last half hour. He mashed the unlighted butt into small particles on the side of the table.

"Let's try Singapore again," Auggie suggested, thinking anything would be better than the infernal silence.

"All right, go ahead." Stud was staring into space.

140

With this call, co-operation from the other end of the line was a little better. After a series of switchboard operators and orderlies, an English voice answered, "Are you there? Are you there?"

"Hello—hello—Colonel Brownfield speaking. Who am I talking to?"

"Brigadier Howell, Chief of Staff. I say, are you American Army?"

"No, an American volunteer group of flyers, the Flying Sharks, Paygoo, Burma. We're checking to find out if there is any threat of Japanese air power over Singapore."

"Great Heavens, no! This is an impregnable naval base, my good fellow!"

"Is anything happening out of the ordinary?"

"Let me think a moment—oh, I say, we had a corking good party at the Raffles Hotel last Saturday night!"

"Great!"

"I had the pleasure of meeting some of your blokes a short time ago. They stopped three days en route to Rangoon. Jolly good fellows. I say, give them my regards like a good fellow."

"Thanks for everything, Brigadier."

"What's that?"

"Nice talking to you. Good-bye." Brownfield had had enough light chit-chat from the Brigadier. He hadn't the slightest intention of inquiring as to who the Englishman had met in the Third Detachment.

"Nothing happening around Singapore, I take it," commented Stud.

"If there is, then the Chief of Staff isn't the least bit worried."

"We know one thing for sure," reflected the old man, as the fingers renewed their strumming on the table.

"Yes?"

"The last plane has gone out of Hong Kong, and the Japs are pushing down the peninsula."

"Will that take long?"

"No, because the British put all their fortifications in Singapore. There's nothing in Hong Kong."

"Maybe we should relax a bit." The exec sounded somewhat relieved for a change.

"With no alert system and Chieng Mai, Thailand, only three hundred miles away—don't be silly! The Nips have pursuit planes based there. I know. Bombers I haven't heard about. Our information nowadays isn't too trustworthy. These Burmese are turning pro-Jap so fast it'd make your head swim. We'll have to get rolling as soon as it gets daylight."

With dawn, the airstrip maintained a constant two-plane patrol for an alert system. This was relieved every two hours. Sufficient warning was available to drive the trucks out of camp; and time for all flyable aircraft to take to the sky. In the event the Japanese came, they would gather few sitting ducks.

Most of the remaining packing presented no problem.

The heavier equipment had already been stowed on board the trucks. With everyone displaying an eagerness to leave Paygoo, the lighter gear and personal effects were being loaded rapidly. Only the things from Tonya's quarters involved any specialized attention. The quantities of teakwood, both furniture and carvings, had to be packed just so, in order to survive the long journey. Expensive Indian prayer rugs must be protected from weather, dirt, and grease.

Since Tonya fancied herself as a Far Eastern holding corporation of some kind, she took pains to insist upon all this protection from the elements and thieving hands. Very few of these possessions, however, actually belonged to her. Robert Sanderson III had the expensive hobby of collecting beautiful old rugs; and Kirk Jackson had a slightly lesser amount invested in teakwood. Another major stockholder's items weren't so bulky—Ole Nelson's hobby was collecting star sapphires, rubies and other precious stones. Tonya permitted these to ride in a money belt around her tiny waist.

Tonya knew that in the future she would collect for this trust.

The war news, traveling fast, announced the beginning of a long hike for approximately seven per cent of Burma's population. These were Indians, most of whom had lived and worked in Burma for generations, keeping pretty much to themselves. Being more dependable and trustworthy than the Burmese, these migrants were paid higher wages; consequently, they enjoyed a better living. This fact, combined with religious differences, made them not only a select minority group, but an envied one. The growing pro-Japanese attitude of the Burmese did not help quiet their fears either.

Now, with Japan on the march, they knew they had to go.

Many of these Indians were stopping by the airstrip, trying to sell some of their most precious belongings. Money for air fare or boat passage would be needed when they reached the west coast of Burma. They knew the fare would be dear. Akyab was the only jumping-off point for anyone.

The first Indians to pass in the morning had pried most of the Sharks loose from their spare cash. Later passers, after most of the rupees were gone, were pleading to get small amounts, even for extremely valuable gems. At this point, Tonya, who knew her stones, was practically out of her mind.

"Toni, I'm telling you the truth, I haven't an anna to my name," Stud spoke with finality.

"Me either," concurred her husband. "You cleaned me out about an hour ago."

"I don't believe either of you!" Tonya angrily whirled away from the two seated in the clubhouse. Out on the lanai, where the bartering was going on, she stopped and thought desperately, "Doc, Frocky, Sandy, Kirk, Ole,

144

Rusty, I've asked them all. If only Al Plummer had made his trip to Rangoon, he'd have all the money I could use."

Rusty smiled as he watched the lines deepen between her brows.

"Like being in the middle of the ocean without a drop to drink, eh, Toni?" he taunted.

"This is an opportunity of a lifetime. You'll never get a chance like this again." Her voice was all sweetness. "Are you sure you haven't any more? I'll pay you back as soon as we get to Kunking."

"Search me." Rusty turned his pants pockets inside out.

"You could dig some up if you wanted to. You're just mad about last night." She strode off.

Rusty grinned, stuffing in the pulled-out pockets as he watched Tonya walk back into the clubhouse. As he turned, one of the more persistent Indians, who still had hopes there were a few rupees left, displayed several stones he had not shown previously.

"Sahib, look—very good." The Hindu proudly held the deep-cut stone for Rusty to admire. It weighed at least ten carats, and sparkled in the sunlight.

"Nice," commented Rusty. "That's a good-looking topaz, friend."

"No—no—Sahib—veree good," corrected the man, shaking his head. He meant it was not a topaz, but he couldn't think of the right word in English.

"It could be the bottom of a beer bottle for all I know.

145

Probably is too! But it's pretty." Rusty took the glittering pale yellow object and turned it over in the palm of his hand.

"Good buy—fifty rupees," wheedled the old man.

"All I've got is fifteen." Rusty opened his wallet so the man could see. Then he handed back the glittering stone.

"You take, Sahib." He placed the stone in a small black felt bag, and slipped it into Rusty's hand, as if it were a life's savings.

Still believing that fifteen rupees was about twice the amount it was worth, Rusty laughed and guaranteed: "Don't feel so bad. Believe me, if I run into you in India, you can have it back at the same price."

Believing the purchase was next to valueless, Rusty stuck it into his pocket until it could be stored with some equally worthless mementoes. Tonya never saw it. If she had, she would have recognized a most rare and perfect stone—a yellow sapphire!

10 · Gangway For An Officer

PEARL HARBOR DAY STARTED, officially, at 7:55 A.M., December 7, 1941. But a handful of American men, and one Russian wench, will remember Paygoo Day a lot better. It started at 12:55 A.M., December 8, 1941.

Colonel Francis Stud was willing to become a day older without the formality of crossing the International Date Line. Seeing the rising sun in China tomorrow was uppermost in his mind. He was hurriedly giving last minute orders: some would travel by convoy; others would fly; a few must remain.

"Brownfield, start the convoy rolling!"

When the colonel waved his arm forward, the exec went into action. Brownfield's jeep skidded to a halt beside each truck as Auggie jammed on the brakes. Every driver received the same blast of verbal orders, judging by their expression from a distance.

"Know what he reminds me of?" Chuck asked Rusty.

"No, I'll bite."

"An old mother hen chewing out her young 'uns for

147

doing sump'in they ain't old enough to know about."

Rusty laughed, and continued cramming his personal belongings into the small baggage compartment of the P-40. The available space would barely accommodate his case of scotch and carton of soda, let alone anything else. Finally, the weight of a shoulder held the baggage door closed until the lock could be snapped. He stepped back cautiously and waited, hoping the door would fly open now, instead of in the air.

"Let's hope," Rusty spoke quietly, as if fearing the sound of his voice might spring the lock.

"Yeah, let's hope they don't leave Brownfield here!" Chuck moaned. "I don't mind being without women, don't even care if the Japs bomb . . . but staying with that son-of-a-bitch is worse than death."

"Don't worry, I'm afraid the old man is stuck with Auggie."

"Dunno about that. Have to wait till the Beech takes off 'fore I'll breathe again."

"Who's in Kunking to take care of the planes? This convoy won't be there for a week."

"At least forty mechs are already there," Chuck said.

"I remember now. They left before I came over in the second detachment."

"Looks like they're boarding the Beech." Chuck pointed toward the plane. "Take care of yourself, Rusty."

"Guess it's about that time. So long, Chuck." Rusty

climbed into the cockpit, and sat waiting for Sandy to give a radio check. Sanderson had been assigned as a fighter group commander for the trip. Forty-nine of the P-40's were flyable. Twenty planes in the Third Group, twenty in the Second, and nine from the First—after last night's activity.

There was a definite reason for the anxiety in getting the Beech underway. Word was coming from Singapore by radio. Apparently, things were not quite so peaceful as Brigadier Howell had predicted they would be. Also, Rangoon's Air Marshal was on the telephone, demanding to talk with the Sharks' commanding officer.

"What's happening?" questioned a very nervous Tonya, terminating a more pleasant mercenary conversation with the colonel's pilot.

The lines in Stud's forehead deepened. "Blanco says the Japs are bombing Singapore. Most of the planes were caught on the ground. But the tough news is a Jap Zero can outmaneuver a Spitfire."

"You mean a Zero can shoot down a Spitfire?" Al Plummer's mouth dropped open.

"Not can, but did!" confirmed Stud.

"Are you going to answer the phone, Colonel?" Blanco reminded Stud. "The Air Marshal sounded pretty hot, and he's still waiting."

"Sure I will!" Stud said with a smirk. "Tell the Marshal to call after ten A.M."

149

"Tell him to call back in an hour?" asked the radioman in all sincerity, noting that his watch said nine.

"I mean tomorrow, in Kunking!"

"Yes, sir. I'll tell him you've left, sir."

"You do that, Blanco."

"Maybe it's important, Francis." Tonya seemed doubtful. "Don't you think you'd better talk to him?"

"I know what he wants. We'd better get out of here."

"How do you know?"

"In the first place, these planes belong to the British, and in the second place, it's a lot safer in China."

"Oh, I see. Now they want us in Rangoon to help defend it."

"They haven't been attacked yet, but they will be," predicted Stud. "Let's go!"

The Reverend Frockman was already fast asleep, chair seat back in a comfortable position. When the left engine started, he mumbled something in his sleep. Round little Doc Ward smiled; he fully enjoyed lending a hand to assist Tonya. His hand shoved on the seat of a well-rounded, tight-fitting pair of slacks as he boosted her up.

"Permit me," he said helpfully. "It's not often I have the pleasure."

"What?" Tonya seemed unaware of Doc's thrill.

"That money belt around your middle reminds me of a boa constrictor after dinner."

The right engine of the Beech coughed and started. Turning his back, Stud muttered and brushed uselessly at a few dark oil spots the slipstream had spattered on his immaculate khaki trousers. He would have been inside, but he was waiting for the exec's jeep, which was now heading straight for him at great speed.

Auggie scrambled out, reached back for a well-stuffed canvas traveling bag, and ran puffing up to the colonel.

"All ready—let's go!" he shouted breathlessly above the noise of the idling propellers.

"Want us to take your bag?" asked Stud, motioning to the heavy case.

"No thanks, I'll put it aboard."

"Got everything you need?"

"Right here." Auggie patted the canvas covering in his arms.

"You'd better keep it with you then, because you're staying!"

"Staying?" Auggie's jaw dropped.

"Somebody has to remain in charge. You're second in command."

"I suppose so." The exec's head and shoulders dropped in dejection, like the Indian's in the "End of the Trail."

"My hands are full. Rank has its problems, you know," Stud added consolingly.

"Yes, and I should know something else by now," Auggie said bitterly.

"What?"

"That rank has its privileges too!"

Very few words were spoken by the group standing on

151

the strip as the P-40's took off, one after the other, following the Twin Beech northward. Hands shaded the eyes of
the remaining Sharks as they watched the last plane until
it was out of sight. There would either be plenty of time
to work on the aircraft later, or there would be no time.

The dust from the ground convoy was visible for some
time, as they plodded along the great plains road leading
to the Burma Road connection. Provided the enemy didn't
attack, the going would be easy for the first leg of the 700-
mile trip. Later, in northern Burma and southern China,
the Burma Road began its hairpin turns over steep ranges.
Some places the trucks would be laboring at 9,000 feet.
The members of the convoy would be viewing some of the
most rugged terrain in the world, overlooking fever-ridden
valleys. Once in the mountainous sections, even the Japs
would find difficulty in bombing or strafing. Faulty equipment and deep gorges would be their enemy.

A capable, but unpopular, gentleman had been placed
in command of the long trip. He looked more like an owl
than anything else. With two beautifully colored black
eyes, and his beak encased in white adhesive tape, Cortland Lee Smith would remain under cover until the effects
wore away. Brownfield had placed Smith in command,
and had promised to take care of the person who committed the dastardly act. Truelove was promised a court-
martial—at a later date!

"S'pose they'll gas up at Lashio," commented Chuck as
he headed for the line shack to get the crew working on

the disabled P-40's. "That's the only good-sized town on the way."

"I doubt it," disagreed Bob Truelove, one of the recent arrivals left behind to ferry the planes if Chuck's crew succeeded in their repair work.

"How come?" questioned Chuck.

"The old man's too anxious to get to China. They'll stop at Toyling. I understand that American hostel of FEAMCO's is really something," explained Bob with a yearning note in his voice.

"'Spose you're right," agreed Chuck. Then after a moment he added, "Sure, that's the joint where that scrumptious blonde shacks up."

"Who in hell are you talking about?"

"Paul Eddy's private stuff."

"But you've never been in China," insisted Bob. "How come you know so much?"

"Oh, I forgot. Lucy Dodson came through here before you guys got here. Never got too close to her myself, because the brass had her roped off in officers' country. Guess they were scared some greasy mech might soil her with his grimy lunch hooks, or sumpin'."

"You mean, she stays there?"

"Toni says the gal told her Eddy was leavin' her in Toyling."

"I'll be damned!" grinned Bob lecherously. "Arkansas traveler, you're gonna have to fix a plane, so a Texan can go traveling."

153

"Thought you only came for five-hundred-dollar bills, Tex," laughed Chuck.

"Don't be silly. I like what you spend 'em on a lot better."

"Yeah, while your plane's gettin' gas and you're eatin' dinner, you can do a lot!"

"Man, you don't know it, but I've had trouble starting a plane for three days!"

With the departure of the planes and convoy, the camp seemed deserted. The few remaining Sharks were spread over a wide area, faced with the colossal task of repairing eleven very sick P-40's. In a way it was a blessing, because with so little time, fewer thoughts could be given to the prospect of a Jap air raid.

The capable and trusty Gurkhas' duties were multiplied twofold. Previously, guard details were necessary only during the hours of darkness. Now, these excellent soldiers had something to occupy their days as well. Judging by their smiles, an extra load was not only exciting, but appreciated. These Gurkhas had not seen action for a long time, and they obviously craved a good fight.

"All ho-kay, Cap-tan!"

The Gurkha sergeant-major had come from nowhere, it seemed, to report to Line Chief Reynolds. Chuck and the brown, muscular soldier understood each other remarkably well. Pidgin English, combined with a few Burmese words, were all that were necessary for a deep friendship and a mutual admiration.

"Hi there, Champ," Chuck returned affectionately. "What's okay?"

"Air raid—ho-kay." The Gurkha smiled, pointing east and up to the sky.

"Can you testo, Champ?"

"Ho-kay—ho-kay," nodded the man proudly, and trotted off in the direction of his headquarters.

In a couple of minutes, Chuck heard a series of sharp blasts from a bugle. A second later, a bugler answered at some distance to the east, followed by still another call further away.

The native soldier returned, trotting quickly as before. When he stopped before Chuck, the exercise was unnoticeable in his breathing.

"Champ, you sure are in great shape." Chuck smiled in admiration.

"Ho-kay?"

"Ho-kay. How far away is the last bugle, Champ?"

The Gurkha hesitated a moment, then held up five fingers.

"You mean five miles?" The man nodded. As an afterthought, Chuck mumbled to himself: "No, he means five kilometers—about enough time to run off the field and make a swan dive into a slit trench."

Not fully understanding, the Gurkha again questioned, "Ho-kay, Cap-tan?"

"Ho-kay, thanks."

Outside of a few interruptions from the frustrated exec,

the remainder of Pearl Harbor Day found all hands busy until sunset. The Gurkhas had completed slit trenches in every direction a man might choose to run to safety. Six of the eleven planes had been raised by block and tackle from their prone positions, and each now stood balanced upon three steel supports.

As the day ended, Chuck spotted a jeep bumping cross-country toward him. His dark scowl changed to one of pleasant surprise at seeing Truelove behind the wheel.

"Come out to pick you up, Chuck."

"Gee, for a minute I thought you was ol' happy puss," Chuck sighed with relief, "coming out for a final chew on me old arse."

"You too! Didn't figure he had time for anyone but me."

"Been on you too?" Chuck continued his futile effort at wiping grease from his hands with an equally greasy rag.

"Yeah, he'd have court-martialed me today, he said, if he'd had four people who knew enough about a court to even sit in on one." Bob grinned. "You'd have thought I killed Smith."

"Maybe there'd be less paperwork if you had." Chuck threw down the greasy rag in despair.

"Guess there's no defense against a self-righteous, psalm-singing hypocrite in this league," Bob said with resignation.

"A thought comes to mind." Chuck scratched his chin with greasy fingers.

"Yeah?"

"That old white-haired bastard is so nervous he's about ready to shed his skin any minute. And with night coming on . . ." A devilish light came into the mechanic's eyes.

Truelove leaned forward in interest. "Keep traveling, boy. I'm follin' you . . ."

"Start needling him tonight, and I'll lay you ten to one there'll be a jeep a-catching up with that there convoy tomorrow!"

"Man, you and I travel the same road! Let's roll."

They climbed into the jeep and bounced over the rough, roadless section of the base.

Chuck shook his head solemnly. "Come to think of it, it's a crying shame that nice white-haired old man having to stay here, while his beautiful young wife goes to cold, cold China with nobody to protect her."

"You know what, man, it's our sacred duty to help him out." Bob's voice was equally serious. "Why, down in Texas, we wouldn't think of leaving one of our heifers unpertected!"

"Even if the Japs don't bomb her, the wolves might eat his poor li'l wife." A grin flicked at the corners of the mechanic's mouth.

"Yeah, if there's any left after the head of the wolf pack gets through."

As the jeep rolled to a jolting stop in front of the club-house, Truelove, glancing upward, said in a loud voice, "Man, don't that look like a bomber way up there?"

Noting Auggie standing on the steps, Chuck concen-

157

trated his eyes upon the blank sky and replied, "Sure does look like a bomber just went behind that cloud!"

The two stood in concentrated silence, heads back, eyes skyward, until they sensed the strain of their observer. Neither let on they knew the exec was walking toward them.

Auggie was unable to control his curiosity. "Did you fellows see something?"

Bob and Chuck dropped their heads, obviously avoiding his eyes.

"No, nothing. Nothing at all," Chuck said with exaggerated nonchalance.

"Certainly ought to be able to hear them," Auggie insisted anxiously, "unless they've throttled back and are gliding in to bomb."

"Who cares?" said Bob. "Let's have a drink before dinner."

Chuck and Bob proceeded into the clubhouse, leaving Auggie beside the jeep, straining his eyes and ears for the sight or sound of enemy aircraft.

The two had barely seated themselves at the bar when Auggie hurried up. "Are you sure you didn't see something?"

Bob spoke precisely. "Well, you see—I can't rightly say— it's kinda hard to see this time o' day—dusk comes so fast. That's why they pick this hour to bomb."

Auggie paled at this information.

"I just don't see how they can jeopardize a person with

your knowledge of this country," Chuck said seriously.

"Yeah," added Bob, "and all for a few stinkin' airplanes!"

" 'Specially now that we're at war, we need all the intelligent and experienced staff officers we can get." As a morale booster for Auggie, Chuck's statement was a failure.

"How 'bout a drink, sir," offered Truelove.

"Scotch and soda," Auggie accepted.

"Double scotch and soda—heavy on the scotch." Bob winked at the bartender.

"And the idea of sending your wife off without consulting you—why, I know women in China that were . . ." Chuck said. "Oh, well, it couldn't happen to Tonya."

"They sent her off with those wolves, with no protection." Truelove added.

"Wolves in that city think they can buy a woman with a few beautiful pieces of jewelry, but 'course Tonya wouldn't be interested . . ." Chuck's voice trailed off into the obvious.

Auggie squirmed.

"Better have another drink, Colonel," Truelove offered sympathetically.

Auggie accepted the drink of practically straight scotch and guzzled it as if it were the last he would ever have.

"One bomb tonight, or in the morning, and Toni would be a widow surer'n hell!" Chuck's rough voice was emphatic.

Auggie's face was one shade whiter than mom's freshly

bleached sheets. He pushed his glass back for a refill.

Bob rested a reassuring arm across the exec's shoulder. "No need for you to hang around when you're needed so badly elsewhere. We can take care of things here."

"Sure," Chuck agreed, "we got everything under control. No one would ever know the difference if you left."

This, together with the double scotches, decided the course of action for Auggie. He didn't drink often, but he was a quick lush when he did.

Puffing out his chest, Auggie pounded the bar with a fist and cut loose. "Gentlemen, you are absolutely right. My country needs me more than a few stinkin' planes. More planes can be manufactured tomorrow, but it takes twenty years to get the training I possess. Gentlemen, do you realize I graduated from West Point in the Class of '26? It will take someone with my experience to outguess those little yellow bastards! Besides, leaving Tonya alone in China, unprotected, could lead to serious repercussions!"

"For the Chinese, no doubt!" Truelove mumbled.

"What?" asked Auggie, completely unaware of more than the fact Truelove had spoken.

"I said, you're so right."

"I shall depart immediately," Auggie said with authority.

"Right, sir." Chuck was all smiles. "I'll have the jeep gassed and ready to roll first thing in the morning."

Without further words Auggie hurried somewhat unsteadily out of the clubhouse.

The group around the bar cut loose with a roar of laughter. Then, suddenly, they heard the jeep engine rev up, and the wheels churning dust as the clutch took hold. They rushed to the door just as the jeep slackened speed long enough for Auggie to yell: "Truelove, take charge!"

They watched the jeep gathering speed, weaving from one side of the road to the other. Obviously, the exec was on his way. The night breeze carried back a shout which sounded vaguely like, "China, here I come!"

Re-entering the clubhouse, Bob kept shaking his head, as tears of laughter poured down his cheeks. "The silly son-of-a-bitch has been itching to court-martial me all day. Tonight he puts me in charge! All I can say is, gangway for an officer! Christ knows, we can't all be saved."

11 · No Place Like Home

THE COUNTRYSIDE WAS DRAB. So were its people. In the distance stood high mountain ranges, steep and bleak, surrounding the lakes and the city. The Sharks had finally reached the home base Colonel Francis Stud had raved so much about.

Midwinter did not show the ancient city to its best advantage, especially as there was no snow. The buildings were hundreds of years old, with plumbing to match. Most of the construction was of stone block, and of no particular era that any of the Sharks were familiar with. An almost complete lack of symmetry existed between one building and the next. It was hard to believe this construction could have taken place before there was such a thing as architecture.

The city proper, located in the foothills of the mountains, did not appear large enough to house close to half a million inhabitants. Approaching Kunking from the lower levels of the lake, or the airfield, was like standing so close to a painting as not to observe how the artist converged his lines to give a street the necessary depth perception. However, it was no optical illusion here—the streets did become steeper and narrower as you approached the center of the city.

The more recent arrivals to the Group did not rate space in the three-story stone school at the far side of town, called Hostel Number One. They were quartered in rectangular adobe buildings within a mile of the field. This odd assortment of one-story huts was soon designated as Hostel Number Two. Stud had the foresight to place Rusty in charge of this adobe town so as to keep him as far away from Tonya as possible.

In a flat wooden building adjoining the strip Francis Stud was proudly explaining the oriental intricacies of the military operations room to Tonya, Sandy, Kirk and Ole. This was where the continuous telephone calls were sifted, and the information marked on a large-scale map.

"Some of these things are awkward, but Major Chung speaks English and will be happy to give you all the help you need," Stud said.

The major in charge of this small group of Chinese office workers was a scholarly individual in horn-rimmed glasses. His uniform was made of the same cotton khaki as the others, and just as patched.

"This is pretty neat!" Sandy approved heartily. "When you were talking about it in Paygoo, I had my doubts."

The colonel beamed with this show of approval, obviously proud of his affiliations with the Chinese. No doubt this was the first station in the man's life where scrimping and saving were not all-important. He felt as though a goal had been achieved. Somehow the impression stuck that Stud didn't care about ever returning to the United States. Like the American Indians, China had a blood brother.

"We have a cable connection to the States via India in the next room," Stud continued, motioning for the group to follow. "All of the battle reports originate, or are received, here." He pointed to a telephone. "This is a direct line to the Empress. We're having one connected to Hostel One in a couple of days."

"What about Adobe Town, Colonel?" Kirk asked, smiling.

"Rusty and his new wards won't be concerned. Which reminds me, Sandy, you are the only pilot allowed in operations." Then nodding to the other two squadron commanders, he added, "Of course, Kirk or Ole will be here in your absence."

Nelson and Tonya were standing before a bulletin board, comparing two sets of messages fastened to it by thumbtacks. The top sheet of one Ole read aloud:

Singapore, December 8, 1941.—63 killed and 133 injured in Jap air raids on Singapore, but Japanese units were being "mopped up" in an attempted land invasion of Malaya from the north, a British communiqué declared.

Japanese warcraft which had landed troops at two places in northern Malaya near the Thailand border were heavily machine-gunned, the British announced.

A later communiqué tonight said that there also had been two Jap landings in southern Thailand and "mopping up" continued near Kota Bahru on the Gulf of Siam just inside northern Malaya from the Thailand border.

"Whew, plenty happened that first day. I wonder what's happened since," commented Ole.

"That's not up to date," Stud said. "The ninth and tenth are in the basket."

Ole picked the sheets from their container and proceeded to thumb through the stack backward.

"My God! Two English super-dreadnoughts, the *Prince of Wales* and the *Repulse*, were sunk today outside of Singapore!"

"How?" asked Kirk. Being ex-Navy, this seemed impossible to him.

"By ten Jap bombers."

"Unbelievable!"

Ole grinned for Stud's benefit, saying, "Good thing we only have one ex-Navy squadron commander, or the Sharks would be sunk too!"

This brought a short laugh from Stud. Being old-school Army, he wasn't any too fond of the Navy. He didn't care to have it known that over half his pilots were ex-Navy. In addition to Tonya's intercession, Kirk's appointment as squadron commander had been mainly to appease these Navy pilots.

Nelson continued: "Estimates some 200,000 specially

trained Nips, jungle fighters, have been unloaded on the Malay Peninsula in the last couple of days. Be in Burma to cut off the road before long. Looks like all the American Islands are taking a steady pounding too."

"Which ones?" asked Tonya.

"Midway, Guam and Wake Island."

"Wake Island is the one Rusty would've been on if he hadn't joined the Sharks," Tonya said.

Stud's comment, "Too bad Bush did. The Japs will blow Wake Island off the map," brought a chuckle from the three squadron commanders. Tonya permitted the remark to go unnoticed.

"Looks like the Philippine Islands are in for a shellacking." Sandy was reading over Nelson's shoulder.

"Yes," concurred Stud, "the Japs have established several large beachheads and are on the move for Manila. Both Clark and Nichols Fields were caught with their pants down, like the boys in Singapore. General MacArthur has been called back from retirement to command the troops."

"Who's General MacArthur, Francis?" Tonya moved over close to Stud.

"A World War I General, a great man. Knew him well in the service. The General retired in the early thirties and has been in the islands ever since."

"Think he can do any good?"

"If he can't, nobody can."

"Say, they're using P-40's, aren't they?" inquired Kirk, none too pleasantly.

"Yes," Stud said, "but no plane's got a chance sitting on the ground. Remember that!"

"Yes, sir!" Kirk said seriously. The other two men nodded somberly. They understood.

"The Chinese seem to be the only ones doing any good," Tonya commented, as she flipped through the outgoing file of messages. "They've either fought the Japs to a standstill, or are pushing them back in every case."

Stud, beaming, accepted this as a compliment.

"Then how come China's lost the entire coast and all the industrial cities?" she asked.

Stud glanced at the operations clock on the wall and reset his watch, quickly changing the subject.

"You look like you're expecting someone, Francis."

"I am."

The pilots had been enjoying the change of scenery, if nothing more. They had scoured Kunking for two nights since the Group's arrival, for any excitement the city might have to offer. They found little. Outside of the usual shops with colorful embroidered silk and jade carvings, there were few restaurants an American would care to sit down in. Most of the populace bought food from a large open

167

bazaar in the city center. The rows of roasting fowl looked and smelled good enough; however, the putrid side odors of a city with no sewage disposal system killed any appetite for the newcomers.

A couple of pilots were amusing themselves as they worked by bouncing a Ford station wagon about the rough dry strip. The clay soil of the large dirt field had molded itself into permanent impressions since the rains several months previously. The boys were making a "planes available" list from the aircraft dispersed throughout the entire field.

"How many in commission?" asked Jeff Nichols, a blue-eyed blond from Minnesota. Jeff, twenty-two, had arrived with the last detachment.

"Stop the bumps so I can add," complained Ross Dickey, a youthful contrast to Jeff. His Italian ancestry had blessed him with a full head of black curly hair and lustrous dark eyes to match his fine swarthy features.

"How's this then?" Jeff took the vehicle out of gear and braked it slowly to a standstill.

"Thirty-nine, forty, forty-one," Ross counted aloud.

"Pretty good, out of fifty. Let's go post them on the blackboard."

Returning to the pilots' alert shack, the station wagon passed a row of wooden hangars alongside the field, facing the city. None was painted. The few antiquated Curtiss Hawk fighters and dual-seated trainers the Chinese had left were hidden in places less obvious to bombers.

Jeff indicated a group of better-dressed Chinese civilians seated on their haunches beside one of the hangars. "Wonder what they're waiting for. Must've been there all night. I'd swear I saw some of the same ones yesterday."

"I can't read that chicken track writing on the wall," Ross answered, "but they're waiting for a seat on a CNAC plane."

"I guess that's the ticket office."

"Yup, and it costs a bundle to ride over the 'Hump' into India, I hear tell."

"Poor bastards, I don't 'spose they really know where to go—except away." Jeff shook his head sorrowfully.

The station wagon proceeded slowly along the buildings, heading for the alert shack near operations. They passed a straight-backed elderly Chinese, dressed in a combination of occidental and oriental clothes, gazing out over the field. The high collar of an oriental silk shirt with the dark suit and black felt soft hat made him look like a missionary. Neither of the boys paid him any particular attention.

But a few hundred feet ahead was a sight that perked up the two pilots considerably—a rear view of a well-proportioned Chinese woman in native black silk, with high collar and slit skirt. She was strolling in the direction they were heading.

"Hey, slow down a bit," Ross said.

"Why?"

"Let's get a look at her face!"

169

"Wow! I see whatcha mean!"

Neither of the fellows could give even a rough guess as to the woman's age, behind the flawless creamy skin and naturally rosy cheeks. It could have been anywhere from twenty-five to forty. But it was completely unimportant to them after she returned their smiles of introduction.

"Back up, Jeff."

"Okay. Give me time to get in gear." Jeff fumbled hurriedly trying to get the car in reverse. "Bet she can't speak a word of English!"

"Who cares!"

The dust created by the wagon's sudden stop and abrupt backing up caused the woman to shield part of her face in a white lace handkerchief. In their enthusiasm, the boys paid no attention to the elderly Chinese watching as they piled out of the wagon from both sides. Nor did they notice that he had started toward them.

"Hi there, beautiful!" Ross spoke first. "Where you goin' all alone?"

Looking into the laughing eyes blinking above the handkerchief, Jeff moved in close. "I told you she couldn't speak English. Here, let me try."

"Go ahead. The only word I remember to ask for is water, and that ain't what I wanna ask for!"

"Hobuhow," greeted Jeff. Then grinning from ear to ear he pointed to the station wagon and said, "Likee ridee, velly glood car?"

The woman nodded. Ross held the door open, placing her between the two of them. They noticed the elderly man had approached to within a few yards of the car, but Ross slammed the door shut.

"Whatcha waitin' on?" asked Ross.

Jeff hesitated. "Looks like he wants a ride too," he said innocently.

"Probably her father. Let's get rolling, we don't need him."

Jeff put the car in motion so fast that the old man was left holding his arms over his face in a feeble attempt to ward off the cloud of dust. For a few minutes the speed and rough ground jostled their passenger so badly she couldn't have talked if she had wanted to.

"Slow down, Jeff, so's we can show the gal our airplanes." Ross wanted no more bumps, now that the old man was safely behind.

Jeff pointed to several parked P-40's and grinned widely. "We brought America's latest fighters just to keep the Jap bombers off you, baby."

"We sure did," chimed in Ross. "You haven't another worry in the world. We're here just to look after the likes of you!"

The next few words dropped the boys' mouths wide open. The pretty little passenger spoke in flawless English. "It's a great honor and privilege to be associating with handsome American heroes."

171

After a pause, Jeff regained his composure. "Gee, Ross, she speaks English perfectly!" His tone of surprise was exceeded only by the look on his face.

"Damned if she doesn't!" Ross turned in the seat to face her.

"My name's Jeff Nichols. This is Ross Dickey. What's yours?"

"Susie Tung," came the somewhat shy reply.

Now that the formalities of a proper introduction were over, the trio laughingly settled down to enjoy themselves. They drove about the area for better than an hour, before finally driving up and parking in front of operations.

Whether or not their actions were visible from within the building, the two pilots could not have cared less. They hadn't the faintest idea of how the personnel functioned inside; nor did they know that only squadron commanders had permission to enter. The two had volunteered to show their guest how things were run in operations, and they were going to do just that. Even if they had to play it by ear.

As they left the car, and headed for the entrance, both fellows put an arm around Susie with exaggerated friendliness. Ross laughed and said, "Think we ought to introduce the old man to what we found?"

Before Jeff could answer, the door to operations opened, and Stud stepped out. The old man stopped dead in his tracks, as though shot, at the sight of the two pilots holding on to Susie Tung. All but the deep lines in his face blanched.

Jeff released a hold on Susie and jumped forward, taking Stud's arm. "Colonel, what's wrong, are you sick—do you feel all right?"

The colonel jerked his arm free and stiffened. "It's all right, Nichols, I'm okay!"

Stud was in the process of raising his hand to salute when Jeff cut it short. "Colonel, like you to meet our friend, Susie Tung."

The woman spoke softly as her eyes twinkled. "Thank you, Jeff, but the colonel and I have already had the pleasure."

"Your Highness," Stud mumbled humbly, from under bowed head. He was standing at rigid attention with his fingertips touching the seams of his trousers.

"Your Highness!" exclaimed Ross in complete astonishment.

Jeff blushed to the roots of his blond hair. "You—you mean," he stuttered, "y-you m-mean this is the Em-Empress of China!"

The Shark leader stood aghast, unable to speak, wondering what on earth the pilots might have said or done previously, and afraid to give way to thought of what might have taken place.

Finally Her Highness broke the ice. Smiling, she said, "We had a wonderful time, didn't we, boys?"

"Your Highness, are you sure everything is all right?" Stud's question was a mixture of doubt and hope!

"Don't worry, Francis, the boys only had one complaint."

Stud almost closed his eyes in anticipation of the worst. "What was that?"

"There has been no catsup in the dining room, and I promised to send for some."

The expression that swept over Stud's face was like that of a man being reborn.

"How is the General?" he inquired.

With this, the two pilots reddened simultaneously, remembering a man in a black felt hat left behind in a cloud of dust. With an understanding look at each other, the boys started toward the station wagon in double time.

"Where do you think you're going?" demanded Stud sternly.

"Well, sir, we know where the General is," Jeff said, "just thought we'd better go pick him up and bring him back."

The way Stud shrugged his shoulders, he apparently believed the whole world was crazy, except himself.

Jeff and Ross were unable to locate the Empress' husband. During their absence, CNAC had arrived, gassed and departed on a return flight to India. Stoney had been waiting at the airport for it to bring Major General George Wellstock, U. S. Army, who had been attached as an observer to China for the past five years. Wellstock had shoved off for Calcutta unexpectedly a few days pre-

174

viously, and the Empress was most anxious to learn what he had accomplished there. The unimaginative observer had been easy to handle thus far, and she wanted to keep it that way.

Later that afternoon, a meeting was held in one of the vacant airfield buildings Stud had chosen for headquarters. The four, seated around a homemade wooden table, had all the expressions of good poker players. But in this game the players concealed all the cards in their sleeves.

"You say help is on the way. What help? And how soon?" The Empress was no longer sweet Susie Tung, she was the guiding force.

As he spoke, George Wellstock didn't sound any too optimistic. "More than likely spring."

"My dear General, that's going to be a little too late I'm afraid," insisted the Empress. "The spring rains will bring beautiful wild flowers—and the Japanese troops will be marching up the Burma Road to pick them!"

"Harumph," sighed her husband, meaning: "Mao Tse-tung always said I'd see things his way some day. If things get bad enough, we can always take our gold and fly to the United States until the war is over."

"No, we won't, Stoney," the Empress was firm. "There's another way."

The eyes of the wiry little observer shone large and encouragingly from behind thick glasses. "Certainly, there has to be." Thoughts that anyone had approached Japan with a separate peace had never entered his gray head.

175

"I still say aircraft is the only answer," Stud insisted, "but it will take squadrons of cargo planes to fly supplies."

"From which direction?" queried Wellstock, interrupting the Shark leader's dream.

"Over the Hump from India."

"Don't you think that's a little far-fetched, Francis? Keeping the Burma Road open is our only hope. I'm willing to fly a few of my Chinese staff to Rangoon, and give Sir Archibald Wavell a hand."

"Even if the Road is open, it won't do any good," Stud said stubbornly.

"Why not?"

"The Jap navy has control of the sea, that's why. No ships will be coming into Rangoon in the future."

With the conclusion of the meeting, George Wellstock advised he would use the cover of early morning darkness to fly to Rangoon, landing shortly after sunrise. Begrudgingly Stud relinquished his Beechcraft and pilot to be used for the trip. China would send troops to support the British Colonial forces only if George deemed this an absolute necessity.

Adobe Town was beginning to appear halfway livable after nearly three days of elbow grease, and a bit of paint. Even a bar had been fashioned from one of the smaller buildings. Some of the more artistic members had painted murals on the adobe walls. Inside, two vivacious Mexican dancing girls with low-cut blouses were displaying their pretty legs. A toreador was taunting a fiery black bull with a red cape. Outside, over the door hung a sign: WEL-COME TO EL GORDO.

At first Rusty had been downright belligerent upon being assigned the responsibility of making Hostel Two out of Adobe Town. He knew the boss was deliberately separating him from Tonya. But now, a feeling of relief came over him, a satisfaction that it had happened this way.

After sunset, the ex-marine showered in the new wash room his boys had just completed. During this absence, a Chinese orderly had placed a large brazier full of glowing red charcoal on a low stand at the foot of his cot. The room was quiet, warm and comfortable.

Sprawled on his back, without a stitch on, Rusty stared at the ceiling and wondered if coming over to China had been the smart thing to do.

The none too familiar sound of high heels, clicking down a board walk, interrupted Rusty's meditation. Undoubtedly, someone with cowboy boots, he thought. But the steps were too fast and close together to be a man's. The clicking stopped in front of his door.

"Yoo—hoo—Rus-tee," came a familiar voice together with a light tapping on the door.

"Just a minute." Rusty jumped off the bed and threw on a brightly colored silk robe.

177

"Are you decent, Rusty?"

"Yeah, c'mon in, Toni."

As Tonya entered the quarters with grace and freshness, Rusty tried to conceal his surprise.

"Whatcha doin' out here, slumming or something?" he asked.

Tonya stepped close. He could feel the cool night air from her body. "Thought you might like some company for dinner," she murmured.

"Good idea. I'll get dressed and we can go over to the mess hall. Let me see—what time is it?—maybe we can stop by El Gordo and have a couple of drinks first."

"El Gordo means the fat one! What on earth are you talking about, Rusty?"

"That's Adobe Town's new bar," grinned Rusty, his eyes twinkling in the lamp light.

"Ohh—Rus-tee—I haven't seen you in so-o-o long." Her slender arms crept slowly up his chest until the hands locked behind his neck. Her body pressed close to the thin silk robe. "Let's eat in here—it's so much cozier!"

"Not supposed to be allowed." He rubbed his nose softly along her cheek.

"Since when?"

"Old man's orders."

Pressing close against him, Tonya insisted Rusty call for the orderly.

In answer to the call, a young Chinese entered quietly

from the darkness and stood silently just inside the door-way.

"Do you speak English, boy?" asked Tonya.

"Chin acts as an interpreter."

At the mention of interpreter, the Chinese beamed proudly. His knowledge of English, however, was any-thing but fluent. Lines of amusement played about Rusty's mouth as Chin tried to explain his duties, and Tonya's insistence developed into anger.

"Boy," she screamed in exasperation, "two whisky soda, two Chinese dinners, chop-chop—savvy?"

After Chin left, Rusty complimented, "You sure know how to get your way, baby."

"I should. I've handled boys in the Orient before."

Chin understood a great deal more than he had pre-viously, mainly, never to argue with Tonya.

"Have you heard from your ever-lovin'?"

"Not a word—" Tonya raked the coals in the burner with the small poker—"but I'm sure nothing's happened or I would have heard."

"No news is good news." Rusty paused a moment. "It's hard to imagine you two being married. Does Auggie ever make love to you any more?"

"I won't let him."

"Never?"

Tonya seemed amused as she thought back. "Once in a while, after a terrible brawl."

"Yes—?"

"The last time he tried to beat me up—he was in his pajama pants—I grabbed a pair of scissors and jabbed him in the belly!"

"Gee whiz! Sounds like rough play!"

"It only stung him," she laughed. "He tore off all my clothes and had me on the floor."

"I've heard of people getting their sex out of beating someone with a whip, but never cutting each other up. No wonder I've been left out in the cold lately. I'm outclassed!"

"You're not. I'm here, aren't I?"

"Yeah—but——" Jap fighters—O.K.—he knew how to deal with, but scissor-wielding women—?

"But you don't love me?"

"I s'pose you're psychic."

"I don't have to be."

"Well—?"

"If you were in love, you'd have grabbed me in your arms when I first came in. We could have been in bed and completely relaxed by now—instead of standing here dressed and waiting for dinner to be served."

A gentle knock turned their attention to the door.

"Come in, Chin," Rusty called.

The Chinese entered without the dinner or drinks, and stood motionless, not knowing how to start.

"Where are the drinks and dinner, boy?" Tonya was annoyed at this interruption.

180

"No time flo dinner," he finally spoke.

"What are you talking about?" demanded Rusty.

"Man call," came the flat reply.

"Man call? From where? What'd he forget, the chickens or the eggs?"

"No chickee, no egg." He turned to Tonya. "Master call—Hostel One—you go chop-chop, savvy?"

"Who in the hell is he talking about?" Tonya turned to Rusty.

"Damned if I know."

"Mista' Bloonfleel, velly mad man, say heem kill someblody."

"He must mean Auggie." Her tone was one of utter disbelief.

"He's not due for another week." Rusty turned to Chin. "Lady's master here?"

Grinning in relief and pleasure at finally being understood, the Chinese nodded his head violently in the affirmative.

Brushing her hand lightly against the front of Rusty's robe, Tonya gave him a quick kiss and departed. "Au revoir, chéri, keep the dinner warm!"

181

12 · Eaglets Become Eagles

JUST ONE WEEK had passed since Auggie's untimely arrival and George Wellstock's departure for Rangoon. The whole world had focused its attention upon the Far East. During this brief period, the steam roller Japan had set in motion looked as though it couldn't be halted. Fear mounted everywhere—as far down under as Australia—that the Japs were invincible.

Seated alone at breakfast, the Shark leader was unmistakably worried, but not over the possibility of the invaders getting this far into the interior. They already had practically all of China that could be of any value to Japan. Come what may, Stud firmly believed America would eventually get in gear, and the war would be won. This would take time. His dilemma was how could he protect his hard-come-by status in life in the meanwhile?

Since Stud's arrival RAF Headquarters in Rangoon had been continuously burning up the wires with messages. They had insisted that all P-40's and pilots be returned to Burma. Now they were threatening. An international incident would undoubtedly arise if the British weren't pacified.

Good old George Wellstock was giving Stud a sizable headache too. George and the four sickly-looking Chinese officers Stoney had assigned as his staff were out near the Thailand border, observing a practically unimpeded march of Japanese toward Rangoon. They were using field glasses for this work, but this and their tired legs were sufficient for them to tell that the enemy was swarming across the southern country at about ten miles a day. It was evident the British commanded natives, had no heart for their job. Now George had joined the Rangoon authorities in demanding Stud fly his little air force to Burma.

A mess attendant poured a third cup of coffee as the Brownfields arrived in time for Auggie to light Stud's fourth after-breakfast cigarette.

"You're both up bright and early," commented Stud facetiously, "trust you rested well."

"Thanks, Francis," returned Tonya cheerfully. "Wish I could say the same for you."

"The colonel does look a bit haggard." Auggie waved out the lighted match.

"Don't doubt it, I lost enough sleep for all of us last night."

"Sour stomach?" suggested Auggie.

"No, receiving all the damn messages from Rangoon. Not only is the Air Marshal pestering me to send planes, but Wellstock's in the act now!"

"George can't order you around," Tonya insisted. "You're not in the Army any more."

"True, but——"

"Then how can he?"

"By getting hold of the Empress. We had a yak fest last night that lasted four hours." Stud motioned the mess boy to bring more coffee.

"And she wants to play all ends against the middle. I know." Tonya shook her head.

"I don't understand." Both Auggie's voice and expression were perplexed.

"You never do!" Tonya glared at him, causing him to flush in embarrassment.

"They have planes of their own," said Tonya, "but couldn't you just send part of ours down and keep everybody happy?"

"I guess I could send down one squadron, then rotate it with the other two later . . ."

Tonya smiled. "All our eggs won't be in one basket that way."

"We wouldn't lose everything, either, if the RAF pulls another Singapore, leaving all the planes on the ground."

"How soon will this be?" Auggie asked.

"Might just as well send them today." Stud's mind was made up.

"It's nine now." Auggie was perking up at the thought of dispersing at least a part of Tonya's male friends. "If we don't hurry up it will be noon before they can take off."

"One or one-thirty is soon enough."

"Why so late?" Auggie seemed anxious.

"The planes should land just as close to sunset as possible. There's little likelihood of any Jap aircraft being airborne at that hour." Stud's statement was one of thought as much as explanation.

"I thought the idea is to run into some Jap planes in order to make some money!"

Stud's reply to this was a look of disdain at Auggie. Then shaking his head hopelessly, he replied, "Not when you're about out of gas!" His tone as much as said "Stupid!"

"Yeah, guess you're right," Auggie said slowly, then asked, "Which squadron shall I alert?"

"Let me see." Stud paused and looked at Tonya. "I don't give a hoot, but be sure Bush goes along with the one you pick."

"Yes, sir, right away, Colonel." Auggie wore a decided smirk as he gave his wife a parting, "Take care of yourself, dear."

Tonya waited a moment, then glanced over her shoulder to be sure her husband was gone. "Why not let him go down and take care of the boys?"

Stud shrugged his shoulders as the mess boy refilled the coffee cups.

"I'd like to get away from his constant jealous bickering," she continued as the boy departed.

"Your dear husband bounces back like a rubber ball."

185

"Meaning?"

"From the danger I mean," said Stud. "He left Paygoo a day after the convoy and beat everybody here by three days!"

Tonya settled a little deeper in her chair, and pouted. "I was just thinking how pleasant it could be, that's all."

The Shark leader smiled as he reached over and patted her hand reassuringly. "Don't worry, Toni, there's a strip or two without roads in these mountains that should be safe enough to suit all three of us. I'll think of some important job from time to time—and have Auggie flown in to take charge!"

Toni straightened up and leaned forward, offering a generous view of her low-cut bodice. "And pick him up when we're damn good and ready?" She smiled in anticipation.

"When we're tired!" he said with an expression of equal anticipation.

Out on the field an unveiling of sorts was about to get under way. One of the pilots had picked up a magazine with a picture of a shark's head painted on the nose of a P-40, somewhere in North Africa. This horrifying caricature had been duplicated upon one of their own aircraft. The P-40 presented a natural silhouette for this head. The spinner formed a nose, protruding beyond the aperture of the air scoop, which became a wide open mouth once it had two rows of jagged teeth.

This part was all right. The entire Group, plus the Empress, who dearly loved sharkfin soup, heartily approved of the insignia. It was immediately adopted. But five little rectangular sketches had been painted on the side in addition to the name of the pilot to be honored by the unveiling.

"On your feet, the exec's approaching our threshold," came a warning voice, which the other pilots ignored. Several were snoozing on cots, with newspapers covering their heads to keep the persistent flies off their faces. A couple of the boys were playing acey-ducey on a table, on which someone had sketched in the playing board with a pencil. The poker game going on at the center table never stopped; however, it occasionally changed a player.

Suddenly the door flew wide open and remained that way, permitting more flies to enter and a few to leave.

"I want the attention of all the First Pursuit Squadron," boomed Auggie.

"No rest for the wicked. I hoped I was dreaming when you said the exec was coming." A sleepy pilot sat up and let his newspapers slide to the floor.

"Where's the CO of the First Pursuit?" demanded Auggie, looking about impatiently.

"Robert Sanderson the Third is presently at operations," Rusty said with exaggerated politeness. "You're just in

187

time for a little presentation that's about to take place!"

"Presentation of what? I have some real important news. The First Pursuit will be leaving for Rangoon at 1300. Go get Sanderson and we'll decide who are the lucky fellows that are gonna go."

Sandy returned by jeep, and entered with the two breathless pilots who had run to notify him.

"Hear we're going to Rangoon," he exclaimed excitedly.

"Pick twenty low-time planes," said Auggie, "and have your gear packed and be ready to take off right after lunch. The old man will have a few words to say before you go, I imagine."

"Boys, this may be the beginning of the five-hundred-dollar bills floating down from heaven." Rusty rubbed his hands together. "With three out sick, no one is going to have to fight for a position!"

It was almost impossible to talk now, with everyone jabbering at one time.

"Mr. Brownfield," shouted Sandy above the din, "we'll need ground crew and some equipment."

"You'll have to count on the Limeys until we can truck some down." It cost Auggie little effort to make himself heard above the noise; he was always shouting or bellowing whatever he had to say.

"That'll take ten days!" Sandy seemed doubtful.

"When I ferried out of Paygoo a couple of days ago," Bob Truelove put in, "Reynolds and his crew were working on the last two wrecks."

"Good idea, I'll phone Reynolds right away. They could make Rangoon early tomorrow." Suddenly Auggie scowled with the realization he had paid Truelove a compliment.

Members of the other two squadrons, highly envious of the pilots making the trip, felt left out. There hadn't been a Jap plane over Kunking for a month, and they doubted if there would be, now that they were here. If the Chinese had intelligence working in enemy territory, then it was logical the Japanese had the same. Besides, Rangoon offered night life, with beautiful Anglo-Indian and Anglo-Burmese girls.

Everyone, from the Empress on down, showed up for the farewell after lunch. The twenty P-40's had been placed in a single line, wingtip to wingtip, the first about a hundred feet from the ready room. Several eloquent words were spoken by the illustrious first lady of the land. Her husband stood silently through it all, like the rock of ages. Francis Stud must have strapped a board on his back, to stand so erect and maneuver through his complete military repertoire.

"Left face, right face, about face, at ease—right-hand salute." The craggy-faced old man commanded loudly and crisply, executing each order himself with exacting precision. Somehow, the line of twenty pilots gave the impression of a row of falling dominoes as they answered his command of right-hand salute.

As the formation broke, Tonya rushed forward and

kissed several goodbye, leaving the most obvious, Rusty, with a platonic hand shake. Apparently, the Far Eastern Holding Corporation was still in business, because several of the fellows were handing Tonya items for safekeeping. Prior to embracing Sandy, she carefully wrapped and knotted one of her white silk scarves around his neck.

Tonya's voice was soft and low as her long fingers tucked the loose ends inside Sandy's flying jacket. "It's especially monogrammed," she murmured.

Stud was excitedly shaking hands, and giving last minute words and advice.

"You're in good hands. Sanderson is the only squadron leader from West Point. You're lucky to be with him."

Auggie, heeling after the Colonel like a puppy, elaborated. "The discipline of those four years, plus the two in the Infantry before flight training will tell—yes sir—I oughtta know, I'm from the Class of '26, and that's meant everything to me!"

The wince of pain that passed over the colonel's face caused Auggie to realize that no more personal experiences were necessary to bolster the reputation of the old trade school.

"Say, Sandy, what's the horse blanket for?" Auggie jovially changed the subject. "To keep the plane warm?"

For the first time Sandy noticed the blanket covering the cowling, from the spinner back to the windshield. In surprise, he answered, "Be hanged if I know!"

"During all the big hullaballoo," Rusty came to their assistance, "we plumb forgot about our own little presentation!"

"Gosh sakes, fellows, let's get on with it," said Sandy impatiently. "Surely you don't expect someone to fly all the way to Rangoon under a blanket!"

"Just a minute," Rusty said. "I'll get the artist himself to unveil his work."

After a shove from Rusty, the embarrassed pilot, not expecting an audience of such proportions to view his art work, walked up the wing stub. He started to speak, but the noise of the crowd drowned him out.

"Quiet, everybody," called Rusty, waving his arms to the crowd for attention.

The hollow-cheeked young pilot started again, once the talking had subsided. "I would like to unveil this in two sections," he said. "The first is a suggestion for a group insignia."

Turning his back, the pilot pulled back the first half of the covering, disclosing a man-eating shark's mouth in brilliant colors.

"That's enough to scare anybody," was the general consensus.

"We wouldn't need any guns if'n we meet the Japs head on with that!" came a voice from the group of pilots.

"Naw," answered Truelove, "we'd scare 'em right out of the sky!"

As the bashful artist hesitated for lack of words, some-one yelled, "That's great, let's see the rest of it!"

"First, let me explain." Raising one hand to quiet the audience the pilot continued, "A custom started in World War One, of painting victories on planes, one national flag for each aircraft put out of action. The rules say five, or a combination of five, make a flyer an ace. We regret being so late, because the man to be honored got his latest victory on December 8, 1941."

The artist jumped off the wing, pulling the blanket with him. The name and rank printed was: Robert Sanderson III, Squadron Leader. Directly below were five tiny rectangular flags. Sandy turned crimson.

"December 8," drawled Truelove. "We were in Pay-goo—that's the night we first——" A grin spread over his features. "Yeah, he got it right on the field there! That's the fifth one he cracked up!"

Standing with the Empress and the colonel, Auggie frowned in bewilderment. "How can he have five flags when no Japs have been shot down yet?"

"You'd better start wearing your glasses," Tonya said. "Those aren't Rising Suns, they're American flags."

"All right, that's enough horseplay," reprimanded Stud, "let's get on our way. I'll deal with the instigator of this later." With the final statement he looked directly at Rusty, who gave him a sheepish grin in return.

The gathering watched the planes take off, one after

the other, with varied emotions. Some were yearning to follow them. Others breathed a sigh of relief that they were permitted to remain. A few, for different reasons, hoped several of the pilots would never return. The majority wished them good hunting, and the best of luck.

"They look mighty pretty," commented Stud, as the planes joined in five flights of four, heading over the field to the southwest.

"If only my eyes didn't bother me so much," bemoaned Auggie, wiping them with a handkerchief, "I'd be right up there with them."

"Yes, dear, I know!" Tonya said. "The Japs don't know how lucky they are!"

Deliberately, Stud walked ahead. Fear that Brownfield might question his own anxiety to fly against the Japs flashed through his mind. He forced a few hacking coughs into the dry atmosphere, to remind them his timely asthma was acting up again.

"Francis, that doesn't sound good." Tonya ran ahead to Stud's assistance. "Come on, I'll drive you to the hostel and put you to bed."

"Sure, I can take over until dark," Auggie said importantly.

After watching his wife help the Shark leader into the car and drive away, Auggie parked his jeep in front of group headquarters. He sat silently. With Truelove and Bush gone, he would have to find a new victim. Recollection of how happy Chuck Reynolds sounded when ordered to Rangoon, instead of Kunking, bothered him. Maybe he'd done him a favor!

Finally Auggie entered Stud's vacant office, walked over to the telephone, hesitated, then plunked himself in the old man's swivel chair. Soon his legs were crossed, and his heavy half-boots rested comfortably on the edge of the large desk. His head finally dropped back. Audible snores were the only evidence that everything in headquarters was under complete control.

Almost the only apparent activity on the field was in operations. The tempo of the many voices, jabbering on the rural telephone network, had been at high ebb for an hour or so after take-off. This, too, died down when the P-40's passed over the border into Burma.

Now the calls were commencing to come in again. With the increased activity, alarm and excitement spread among the personnel in operations. Particles of saliva shot from between the spreading buck teeth of Major Wong as he talked loudly to the members of his staff. Then the Major grabbed the telephone and rang Shark headquarters.

The sharp ring startled the sleeping exec so much he jumped, rolling over backward in the swivel chair. He picked himself up, brushed dust from his uniform with one hand, and reached for the receiver with the other.

"What do you want?"

"Major Wong, operations."

"Yes, Major, what can I do for you?"

"Wish replort gingbow,* Colonel."

"How many planes?" questioned Auggie without undue alarm.

"Twelve, Colonel."

Auggie glanced at his watch. He was thinking the Shark aircraft were undoubtedly the cause of the alarm. Perhaps the boys had spread out, so only twelve were spotted. It was even possible they ran into weather below and were returning to base.

"Those are our own planes," he reassured the Major. "Which way are they heading?"

"Ah—two five zero."

"That's about the right heading for Lashio."

"Blut these, two engine plane, Colonel, over Nantan!"

"What!" screamed Auggie in the Major's ear. "Those are Japs and they're heading straight for us!"

"Good bly, Colonel."

What a moment! Auggie couldn't find his cap anywhere. He knew it had been on the back of his head before he fell asleep, so he dropped on all fours, crawling half under the desk before he finally retrieved it. Then he telephoned Hostel One for Stud.

It took time to relay the message to the colonel. Auggie waited. Every few seconds he leaned over nervously, trying to get a better view of the sky through the window. Then Tonya delivered Stud's reply:

"For Christ's sake, get the planes in the air. And get on

* The Chinese word for "air raid."

195

the radio in operations and vector them to the target!"

Within five minutes spinning propellers indicated twelve P-40's warming, prior to take-off. The other planes were held in reserve. Soon the prestone-cooled Allison engines let out a throaty howl, and started the long run of a high level take-off, four abreast. Kirk Jackson circled his planes around the field once, gaining altitude, then headed due east.

Ground radio told the Shark patrol the twin bombers were approximately one hundred miles northeast of the city. The course of the patrol was altered accordingly, as they continued, climbing to 20,000. Operations radio next reported: "Bombers ahead, fifty miles, hold your course!"

Kirk held his plane so that the magnetic compass remained on a 315-degree heading. There was no worry as to whether to add or subtract the magnetic variation, for on his map a wavy line ran all the way from Rangoon through Kunking, indicating the magnetic variation as zero. With the gross errors existing in the maps of the rugged interior of China, this single item alone was a blessing to inexperienced navigators. On this heading, no correction was needed for wind drift either. The prevailing dry monsoons came from the northwest.

Kirk glanced at his watch. If the Chinese were interpreting the calls and plotting them correctly, contact should come in approximately six minutes. He thought: "Halfway around the earth, nearly a year since I left home, and now I'm only a few minutes away from what I came over for."

The jerky motion of the second hand on the instrument panel clock, as it wound around the dial, made Kirk uneasy. This uneasiness gradually turned to fear. The delightful flamboyancy that caused Kirk to stand out above the run of the mill was gone. He had developed this kind of personality as a ruse, to cover a bad inferiority complex. In earlier days, he had forced himself deliberately to crash a half dozen speeding automobiles, in an attempt to overcome his feelings. Except for the eyes, his face now appeared frozen.

Five of the longest minutes in his life were over, and no enemy in sight. Kirk relaxed. His spirits bounced back rapidly, and he became his own flippant self once again.

Picking up the mike he called, "Just passed the interception point. Must have been ghost riders in the sky. We'll make a 180 and come home for coffee."

No sooner had Kirk hung up his microphone than he was right back where he started.

Ground called: "Negative, do NOT, I repeat, do NOT return base. Change course to 150 degrees. Enemy is heading back for Indo-China."

No Japanese planes were in sight. Either they were tuned in on the Kunking operations frequency, or, more than likely, several of their own ground stations were stashed in the interior relaying messages. Anyway, Kirk's morale was helped somewhat to know the Japs were barreling for home instead of attacking.

For twenty minutes the formation held the new course at 20,000, but saw nothing ahead. Then one of the wingmen pulled alongside the leader, pointing below. There were twelve beautiful silver birds, in perfect formation.

Due to inexperience, the pilots had not realized that bombers would nose down, losing altitude in order to gain speed. They would have been even lower but for the mountain range which lay ahead.

In their enthusiasm, and Jackson's hesitancy, most of the pilots broke formation and dived down individually on the twelve silver-covered medium bombers. As the distance closed, the bright red ball markings, symbolic of the rising sun, stood out plainly on the wingtips.

Kirk saw smoking tracers flying up from the Jap formation, as well as the fighters' fiery balls heading downward. True to their name, they resembled a school of sharks attacking a bunch of hooked tuna aft of a commercial fishing boat.

One bomber turned right, out of the formation, with a smoking engine shooting flames. A second later, the wing disintegrated, flipping the bomber on its side. Slowly it nosed over, picking up speed as it rotated downward. A moment later it exploded, sending up a huge column of smoke from a mountain side.

Two P-40's, abreast, hung on the tail of another bomber, not two hundred yards behind. Pieces of the fuselage were breaking off, due to the combined effect of the .50-calibers and the slipstream. A second later an explosion sprayed the two pursuers with debris. Three larger sections of the bomber appeared to be floating as they fell.

As Kirk looked on, two more bombers burst into flames, plunging earthward with ever increasing speed like the nozzles of two blowtorches.

No longer a tight formation, the bombers skimmed over the last range into French Indo-China separately. Each bomber could hear and feel the death rattle of the .50-calibers from one to two P-40's in hot pursuit.

The squadron leader had kept a fairly accurate check of the course, even to placing circles where four Jap planes had gone down. Soon he noted the French Indo-China border. At this point he circled, and radioed for the pilots to stop the attack and rendezvous over the border town of Mengtz. Most of them were out of sight. Kirk had to circle for forty-five minutes, waiting and calling, before the last one joined up to return to Kunking.

An elated group of American flyers piled out of their planes on the home strip that afternoon. Not only were they all back in one piece, but they were the first to experience combat. Apparently Stud had recuperated quickly from his attack of asthma, for he had both arms around Jackson's slender body, whirling the squadron leader so fast his feet couldn't touch ground.

"If you want anything done, call on the Second Pursuit, Colonel."

"Great work, Kirk," complimented Stud. "Let's get into operations and write up this encounter before you forget part of it."

"A thousand years couldn't make me forget today."

Brownfield drove the colonel and Kirk to operations, leaving the new combat fighters to enthrall those who couldn't make the trip with a recounting of the action. The comments were varied.

"I was so close, I could see the tail gunner slumped over dead."

"When my bomber hit, I was so close the explosion almost got me! What a jar!"

"Any of 'em get away?" questioned an excited greeter.

"Naw, but we chased the last one damn near to Hanoi before we nailed him."

"Look at the holes in this plane," was one observation. "These weren't made by moths!"

"There are only two planes that didn't get hit."

"Whose were those?"

"Kirk, and his wingman, Rocky."

"Don't blame me," said Rocky, "I had to follow Kirk."

"Yeah, I know, but the way Kirk was accepting the big hero act, Stud would never believe he had to be practically forced into his plane with a .45 in his back!"

The victory was celebrated until the wee hours of the following morning. Never before had the Sharks boasted of such a large number of drunks at any one time. Even Brownfield lucked out. He got to sleep in the living room of Tonya's suite—to keep loud staggering celebrators from entering.

No one could say that the Empress didn't take care of her boys. There was another ceremony the following day. The twelve pilots of the great victory were all dressed up, and stood at attention in a line on the edge of the field.

Again Stud practiced his short order drill. Then he added a few words: "Before the medals are presented, I'm happy to report four of yesterday's victories are positively confirmed. The Chinese have spotted the crashes." His next statement raised a moan from the heroes. "If there were any others brought down in enemy territory, we have no way of proving it. Therefore, each of you will receive credit for one third of an aircraft, and $166.67. Don't worry, there's going to be enough for everybody before we're through."

With this, Stud executed a smart about face, and saluted the Empress. Then Her Highness stepped forward, followed by Stoney, Stud and a retinue of high-ranking Chinese military.

As Stud supplied the name of each pilot, the Empress moved in front of the one to be decorated. The flowery words varied, but the endings were pretty much the same: "And for our brave and beloved wingman, I present the Order of the White Cloud."

The pilot acknowledged the ribbon pinned on his blouse, by saluting and thanking Her Highness.

"And for our brave and beloved squadron commander,

Kirk Jackson, I present the Order of the Purple Dragon in addition to the Order of the White Cloud."

No one knew whether Kirk was blushing from embarrassment or conscience.

"Mr. Brownfield," Ross Dicky asked, "what gives with all this Purple Dragon and White Cloud business?"

"Why—er—ah—well—those are ancient and royal orders dating back since—well, since——" For once Auggie was at a loss for words.

"Sounded more like it was sumpin' she made up last night on the spur of the moment!" Ross Dicky turned to his buddy, Jeff Nichols, and added, "C'mon, let's get the hell outa here!"

13. Greetings From The Sharks

NICK, THE GREEK OWNER of the Silver Grill, was the happiest man in Rangoon. His cash register bulged. Business had picked up considerably during the last week, and last night's take was the highest ever. He stayed up counting cash till four o'clock Christmas morning.

With the exception of Robert Sanderson III, the entire First Pursuit had squandered Christmas Eve in this hovel, called a nightclub. The boys were generous. Even the Anglo-native prostitutes fared well for a change, even after giving Nick his cut.

Rusty Bush had been the last to leave. He had promised Chuck Reynolds he would pick him up on the way back to Mingladon Field. Three of them had driven to town together. En route Chuck asked to be dropped at a sailor's hangout near the docks. He claimed the Silver Grill was too fancy for his blood. However, during the course of the evening, Truelove, in a drunken stupor, had become belligerent, and shoved off by himself in the jeep.

Rangoon, the capital, with a population of over 400,000,

was by far the largest and most modern city in Burma. In this metropolis, a fellow should have been able to locate a cab in the early morning hours. Rusty couldn't. The search for the missing Reynolds was conducted through the dark dock area by gharry, a light horse-drawn affair popular in India and Burma.

When finally located, Chuck was seated opposite a tough Irish seaman, bare arms resting on the only table left in one piece, in an effort to prop up a heavy head. Both men's clothing was a mess. Their faces were dirty and smeared with blood. The place was a shambles, with broken glass, chairs and tables strewn about. Among these were a few prone drunks. Whether they had been knocked out by the effects of booze or fists was debatable.

Chuck raised his head slowly as Rusty entered the dive. Despite his puffed features and skinned knuckles, the big grin indicated "Ol' Charles" had been having himself quite a time.

"Hi, Rusty, c'mon in 'n have a drink," Chuck's voice cheerfully boomed across the room, as he lifted an arm in an unsteady, beckoning motion.

Stepping carefully, Rusty made his way to the table. He stood, shaking his head in disbelief.

"What in hell are you taking up now, interior decorating?"

Chuck's bull-necked companion raised his head, displaying a flat nose and receding hairline. In a thick brogue he explained: "A bunch of these Limey scum picked a fight with the Yank here. Thought it a bit uneven, I did, so I lent 'em a hand. Besides, I don't like the bloody bastards, anyhow!"

"The way Chuck can pick allies," said Rusty in grinning admiration, "he should be President of the United States."

Before Rusty could shake Chuck's newly acquired buddy loose at his flop house, it was nearly daylight. Of all the great loves down through the ages, he reflected, the greatest without a doubt is the love of one drunk for another.

Daybreak found the two clickity-clacking down the scenic boulevard which winds along beautiful estates on the way to Mingladon. The field was a good thirty miles from Rangoon.

"Man, are we gonna' be late!" stated Rusty, settling back. "It'll be ten-thirty or eleven before we get there."

"Who cares?" mumbled Chuck, trying to shade his eyes and curl his bulk into a comfortable sleeping position.

As the gharry rounded the next turn, Rusty suddenly shouted, "Stop! Driver, stop!"

The Indian driver pulled over to the left side of the highway. There was a jeep a couple hundred feet from the road. Apparently, it had jumped the curb and flipped over. Rusty climbed out, leaving the driver and the sleeping Reynolds in the gharry.

"Hey, Chuck," he yelled back, "give me a hand, it's our jeep!"

Chuck moaned, as he painfully unfolded, shaking his

head in an effort to come from his stupor. "I'm coming. That son-of-a-bitch would park it way out there!"

Rusty walked toward Chuck with concern. "I'm afraid he's dead."

"Who's dead?"

"Truelove, stupid, he's been crushed underneath all night."

Chuck proceeded to the jeep. Kneeling down, he touched one of the ankles that barely protruded from beneath.

"Gosh, I'm sorry I cussed him now." Tears started to well in the mechanic's bruised eyes. "Ol' Tex was the salt of the earth. Sure gonna' miss him at the poker table."

Rusty rested a comforting hand on the mechanic's shoulder. "C'mon, Chuck, let's roll the damn jeep off his body."

As Chuck added his brawn to Rusty's, the jeep rolled slowly over on its side.

"Careful now," cautioned Chuck, "let's not disfigure him any more than he already is."

"Undertakers do some wonderful things nowadays," consoled Rusty. "Never forget my uncle's funeral, looked the best I'd seen him in twenty years."

The jeep rolled on over and bounced on its springs from the impact, revealing the prone body of the Texan.

"No blood," observed Chuck, "couldn't have bled to death."

"Must've broke his neck instantly. What a blessing!"

Suddenly the corpse raised an arm, pulling the visor of

his cap forward to ward off the sudden sunlight. "Quiet! What do you bastards mean by waking me up with all the god-damn light?"

Chuck rubbed a pair of wet and swollen eyes, shaking his head slowly, "My daddy always said, 'Charles, you're gonna see some terrible things if you don't stop drinking.' "

The only noticeable damage was the jeep's broken windshield. Truelove had lucked out without so much as a scratch. After a brief hassle as to who had enough to pay off the gharry driver, the three drove on to Mingladon Field.

Shortly after 9:00 A.M., they pulled up in front of the two-story wood-frame barracks used for operations. Several of the pilots, sitting on the railing of the porch, had a good laugh out of these late arrivals. But Sanderson couldn't see the joke.

"What's the idea coming in at this hour?" he demanded unpleasantly.

"With your sense of humor, you wouldn't believe it if we told you," Rusty answered with a hopeless gesture as he alighted from the jeep.

"All three of you know a Shark's working day begins at sunrise," reprimanded Sandy. "Being AWOL is gonna' cost you three days' pay apiece."

The dapper little squadron leader would have said more, but he was interrupted by Cortland Smith calling out from inside operations: "R.A.F. radar control thinks they've spotted something on their scope!"

207

"Well, did they or didn't they?" Sandy seemed mad with the world. He turned and walked briskly inside. His intentions were to telephone Vice Air Marshal Dillingsworth personally. However, the squadron leader found that the marshal would not be available until ten o'clock.

"Dunno what's eatin' Sandy," complained Truelove. "The Japs won't bother lousing up a Christmas that's already ruined." He ground out his cigarette as he mounted the steps to the porch.

"All the bugs haven't been ironed out of RAF radar. Hardly had a chance to use it since it's been installed, but this could be it," warned Rusty. "Think I'll drive over and check with the Brewster pilots. C'mon, Chuck, pile out, you can sleep elsewhere."

"Man, that's just what I'm gonna' do." The line chief staggered slightly as he turned toward the barracks.

It was 9:40 when he returned to the squadron area, to find the situation hadn't changed. RAF control was still getting twin blips on their radar scope. Only closer.

"I've got an idea," offered Rusty as he entered the office.

"What?" Sandy stopped wearing a path in the wooden floor, long enough to turn to Rusty. Sandy couldn't conceal his obvious dislike for the ex-Marine, but he was ready to listen to anything.

"Those two satellite fields just north of us, why not disperse half the P-40's between the two fields, and let the rest patrol."

Old and unused for several years, these satellite strips had almost gone back to nature. Recognition of them from the air would be next to impossible. The greenish brown camouflage of a P-40 would blend in perfectly.

Sandy started to object, then remembered Stud's words, "The best plane in the world is useless if it's caught on the ground." Anything the RAF Command might have to yell about would be minor in comparison to the rumpus Stud would raise if his precious planes were caught in a repetition of Singapore, Manila or Pearl Harbor.

During the next ten minutes the RAF command was, to put it mildly, nonplussed. Without instructions, or so much as a by your leave, the P-40's were taking to the air. Stunned as they were, RAF radio immediately tried to contact the Shark C.O. to find out what was taking place. When control was informed why the Sharks had scrambled, the P-40's were ordered to pancake immediately.

In answer to the order, a drawling accent cut into the radio conversation with a statement that perplexed the control operator even further. It informed him he could go to hell and do something that was impossible.

Ten of the P-40's did not even bother to retract their gear. They landed without mishap on the two satellite fields. Sandy was leading the other ten planes upstairs for an 18,000-foot patrol. He had reached an agreement with control whereby the patrol would remain above the field so as not to confuse the blips on the radar scope. As they

209

continued to climb, the vision of the Sharks was directed above and to the east, likely places for the enemy to appear.

Sandy glanced at his watch: 10:10 A.M. He checked his altimeter at 17,500. Nothing but a few scattered clouds to the east, floating at about 16,000. After leveling off at 18,000, he raised a wing for the first time to be certain Mingladon was directly below.

At first glance, Sandy thought the group had drifted away from the field; they hadn't moved laterally, and neither had Mingladon. Instead, there were eight columns of black smoke commencing to rise from the field. The entire formation jumped as the squadron leader's stick shot forward, radios blaring almost simultaneously!

"Jap fighters are strafing!" came from control.

Some fifty Japanese I-97 fighters had flown in from the south at sufficiently low altitude to avoid detection by radar. Like a nest of angry bees the little low-wing planes were making pass after pass over Mingladon. Incendiary bullets had set ablaze practically every aircraft left on the field. Even the hangars and gasoline trucks were going up in fire and smoke. Personnel ran frantically in all directions. There were no slit trenches. With no opposition from air or ground, the little planes with the fixed landing gear literally chased the horrified people fleeing across the open areas. One Shark mechanic threw a wrench in a futile attempt to ward off his low-flying Nip pursuer.

Leaving Mingladon a holocaust, the I-97's hugged the

treetops and expended their remaining ammunition on the city and docks of Rangoon, which lay to the east, as they headed for home.

Sandy's P-40's, upstairs, took too long losing altitude; and Rusty's boys on the satellite fields climbed too high before turning, after taking off to the north. Before either group reached the immediate vicinity of Mingladon, the Japs were on their way.

Planes hugging the terrain are tough to spot from high altitude. For the next half hour, the Sharks milled around the sky above Mingladon. As they were beginning to relax, convinced the day's show was over, RAF control suddenly blasted out that formations of several different types of bombers were twenty miles east of Rangoon. Eighty estimated.

By this time the P-40's were spread over a twenty-five-mile radius from the home base, their altitudes varying from 10,000 to 20,000 feet. Allison engines were not super-charged, and carried a load far above design. Except for this, a few would have been even higher.

At the time Rusty radioed, "twenty-seven twin engine bombers, altitude 16,000 over Rangoon in big Vee formation," they were already releasing destruction upon the helpless city.

Two of Rusty's mates were closing in on the formation from above and behind. As he climbed to a position in front of the bombers, Rusty screamed an unheeded warning over his radio to the two pilots of the P-40's. The two

Sharks caught the maximum fire power the formation possessed on this type of approach.

Rusty had a sudden sick feeling in the pit of his stomach, as he saw the two P-40's, one after the other, drop away from the formation throwing smoke and oil. They headed down in a steep spiral, out of control. The boys had got it from both sides, where there was no armor plate or engine for protection.

Rusty squeezed his trigger briefly to test his six guns. All worked. Then he made a head-on run from slightly below the bombers. Tracers sailed in and around the lead bomber until the last instant, when the fuselage completely filled his gun sight. By reflex, Rusty ducked his head and shot his stick forward to avoid a crash.

Pulling up and around in a Chandelle after the pass, he headed back for another head-on run. But the first one had done the trick! The lead plane was plummeting earthward in a screaming ball of flames. Half the bombers turned left, and the others right, heading for home. No longer was there a tight formation with deadly crossfire.

Three other Sharks appeared on the scene. A mad chase followed as the remaining twenty-six bombers nosed over and headed for Bangkok, each his own separate way. The four Sharks would sit on an enemy tail, chopping away with their machine guns until the bomber either crashed, burned or blew apart. Before the boys ran out of ammunition, at least twelve bombers would never bother Rangoon or any other place again.

On the return trip to base, being out of ammo was damned uncomfortable. Rusty wondered if the strip would be safe for landing, even though the Nips were gone. It was a certainty, the attackers had added insult to injury by bombing after their strafing party.

Three I-97 fighters, coming out of the sun above Rusty, decided his next move. With his throttle wide open, head and shoulders tucked forward, he headed his P-40 straight down. The heavy, streamlined plane picked up over 500 knots before he noticed his airspeed. A cautious glance over the tail told him his pursuers had given up the chase. Another glance, forward, reminded him to pull out, or it would be too late!

Rusty leveled off after almost blacking out from pulling so many G's. The rice paddies skimmed by his blurred vision. Soon, delayed reaction to his close call set in. His legs seemed to jerk the rudder bars. He could hear his heart pounding over the noise and vibration of his plane, pumping blood back into his head so fast that his neck throbbed and ached.

Rusty tried to think, but the only logical conclusion he could come to was to land on one of the satellite fields. He need have little concern about revealing the hiding place now. A swerving landing resulted, mainly caused by muscle spasms in his legs. After rolling to a stop, he quickly taxied the plane into some brush that would hide it from view. A few moments passed before he even bothered to climb out of the cockpit.

The satellite strip looked as though it was deserted, but the action was still going strong in the distance. From overhead, the occasional chatter of machine guns floated down. Rusty could easily distinguish the sound of the Japanese guns from the Sharks. The heavier .50-calibers echoed across the sky much more loudly.

Standing on the wing of his plane, Rusty watched two more flaming wrecks diving down to the southeast. Brush obstructed his view as they crashed into the ground. But an earth-shaking explosion came almost simultaneously with the sight of black smoke rising above the top of the brush.

Rusty soon discovered that he was not the only inhabitant of the satellite field. As he turned to jump off the wing, Reynolds and two of his men approached from the rear of the parked plane.

"Hi, neighbor," Chuck greeted him with a smile.

"Last time I saw you, you were gonna' take a nap. What'cha doin' way over here?"

One of the mechanics laughed. "The way he lit out, none of us expected to see Chuck till we hit China."

"How many Japs did'ya git?" came the obvious question from the little group.

"Four bombers." Rusty took a hitch at his loose belt. "Did anybody bring anything to eat?"

Chuck mentally calculated the bonus money. "Two thousand dollars! That'll more than make up for getting docked three days' pay this morning."

"Yeah, and the day ain't over yet," came a comment.

"It is for me," Rusty said, "unless you guys got some ammo and petrol for this beat-up crate."

"You could use a few patches over those bullet holes too," advised one of Chuck's helpers.

"Hell, it would take three hours or more to cover all those," Rusty said. "The Japs could be back and blast us off the map before then."

"Cool down, boy, cool down. Ol' Charles has just what the doctor ordered."

Rusty looked at him skeptically. "I don't need any doctor. All I need is for Santa Claus to bring me a new plane." He looked at his plane dejectedly.

"Ho-ho-ho and a bottle of rum," sang the line chief, patting his stomach with both hands. Then he added with a wide grin, "Just call me Santa Claus!"

"This is a helluva time to be joking!"

"I ain't kiddin'. Follow me." Chuck stalked off through the brush.

Rusty glanced questionably at the other two mechanics, then proceeded to follow Reynolds. The tall growth somewhat hampered his keeping Chuck in sight. Every few minutes, Rusty would stop to listen, to determine which direction the line chief had taken. At length he reached a clearing. Chuck stood waiting. He turned and pointed. Following the direction indicated, Rusty spotted the tail of a P-40 protruding from the brush on the opposite side of the clearing.

215

"Who'n hell beat me down?"

"No one. It's been here all the time."

"You're crazy. All ten planes took off."

"We got here less than half hour after you guys scrambled. It was here then."

As they approached the plane for a closer inspection, Chuck informed, "I done checked her—full of gas and ammo, and not a bullet hole in her!"

"Engine hot?"

Chuck ran a hairy hand along the exhaust stacks. "Nope, barely warm."

"Well, I'll be a monkey's uncle!" Rusty exclaimed as he noted the number on the plane.

"You're a natural, man, but do you know whose plane this is?" Chuck was more interested in the latter question than he was in Rusty's choice of ancestry or relatives.

"Not to mention any names, but a most distinguished gentleman did take off in this plane with us."

"Who, man, who?" Chuck pushed back his cap and scratched his head. "C'mon, give with the info."

"But to have got here before you arrived, he sure must've beat a hasty retreat when it started getting hot upstairs. You know, I'd of thought he'd got used to the heat where he was raised."

"What in hell are you talking about?"

"This brave gentleman hails from the capital of a southern state, where Peachtree Street runs into Peachtree Avenue, where it crosses Peachtree Boulevard." Rusty turned to Chuck with an exaggerated air of dignity. "We wouldn't want to mention any names, would we?"

As the realization of the implication dawned upon Chuck, he burst forth, "Why, that four-flushing hunk of white trash——"

Rusty placed a placating arm across Chuck's shoulders. "Easy, boy, easy."

"And this was the guy who was gonna die for democracy!" continued Chuck. "The scum we've got out here running this joint makes me sick. First we get an exec that doesn't know his ass from a hot rock, then he brings along a broad that's layin' every pair of pants that comes along for information or money . . ."

"Don't get so riled . . ." Rusty's attempt to halt Chuck's rising anger was useless.

"If that ain't bad enough, a Chinese broad ain't satisfied running her own country on the rocks, she's trying to take ours along with it! And our old man ain't fooling me with all that fight-for-democracy crap. You noticed he was the first to get out of Burma. You ain't seeing him leading any squadrons in battle like he was supposed to. I'll lay you odds, you'll never see the old bastard in any place where there's any shooting either!" Chuck's face was red with anger and he was puffing from the fury of his outburst.

The line chief, shooting off at the mouth, finally got on Rusty's nerves, even though he agreed with him one hundred per cent.

The next thing Chuck knew, Rusty had climbed into

the cockpit of the P-40, and was preparing to go aloft. "What'cha gonna do?" asked Chuck.

"Get away from all your bitching."

"Sorry, but what I said still goes," said Chuck stubbornly, as he knelt on the wing peering into the cockpit.

"You know, Chuck, someone once told me I was free to bitch all I wanted to as long as I confined it to military channels!"

"Back home, maybe so, but out here we're bottlenecked. Starting with three squadron commanders, right on up to ol' craggy puss—where all trails end." Chuck's eyes blazed.

Rusty held his hand on the electric starter. "If Cortland Smith ever shows up, ask him to do me a favor."

"What could Smith do for you?"

"Seeing as how he's got no love for flying, maybe he can taxi my plane back to Mingladon after dark. It's only twenty miles."

Rusty engaged the engine. The roar and slipstream ended further conversation. Chuck beat a hasty retreat off the wing of the plane.

The three ground crew members, with backs turned, held their hats, as they tried to avoid the sticks and stones flying behind the turning plane. Rolling rapidly through the clearing, it disappeared briefly. A few seconds later, the crew heard the throttle open wide. The plane was visible over the brush, climbing to the east.

At 4,000 feet, twenty miles east of Rangoon, a lone P-40

was futilely trying to dogfight with three I-97's. The highly maneuverable little fighters were out-turning the Shark pilot and unmercifully machine-gunning his plane, regardless of where he turned. Whoever he was, he had no excess altitude in which to dive away from his tormentors.

Intent upon a sure kill, the three enemy fighters failed to notice Rusty coming to the rescue. A burst from Rusty's guns, a moment too soon, warned his prospective target in time for him to half snap-roll and head down out of range. Seeing this, his two mates broke off their attack also, nosing down to the east and heading for home. Undoubtedly short on fuel by now, the Japs were uninterested in pursuing anything, but a sure thing.

Out of the corner of his eye, Rusty caught sight of the P-40 heading for Mingladon. He didn't blame the pilot. He knew he wasn't deserting, because if the plane was not nearly out of fuel, then it must look like a sieve.

Rusty soon discovered a P-40 traveled faster than the I-97. His plane closed the distance between himself and one of the home-bound Japs. There would be no firing out of range this time. Obviously the Jap was unaware that he was being followed. His two mates had already disappeared.

Directly behind the I-97, at less than 150 yards, Rusty centered the Jap's vertical fin on his vertical gun sight line. The wings were parallel and slightly below the horizontal marker on the sight. The dot rested between the little man's shoulder blades.

As Rusty squeezed the trigger, setting six machine guns chattering, he screamed: "And a Merry Christmas to you too, you son of a bitch!"

14 · One Man's Misery — Another Man's Meat

WAR IS A TIME FOR GENERALS, for in peace time they are entitled to only a little more pay than the rank below them, and the privilege of standing first in line. Few men of this rank, or those who were striking for this elevated position in the Far East, had anything to write home about—unless they were Japanese.

Now, things were different. From a tree which was supposed to be dead within three weeks, a beautiful plum was growing. As it began to ripen, several hunks of brass who formerly held a pessimistic viewpoint were angling for a big bite.

The Sharks' first week in combat was all it took. By January, 1942, everything else had been shot down, sunk, bowled over, turned to ashes or captured. With Stud's flyers, things were different. The score was 56 to 2 in their favor.

The press ground out the news of a handful of Americans, fighting under a capable leader, destroying heretofore invincible Japanese at every turn of a propeller. And always, the news carried only one man's name: "Francis Stud's Sharks."

By mid-January, a few American generals and staff officers had arrived in India, with only enough privates to carry their luggage. They were itching to get supplies, matériel and personnel rolling, but this took time. In the meantime there was nothing to do but to get as comfortable as possible.

Major General Boliker S. Sittel had arrived from the United States on his first tour of duty overseas just two weeks before to command all American Air Corps in the Far Eastern theater of war. Sittel, who insisted his name be pronounced with a long "i," was in his fifties. Double bags under each eye were mute evidence of easy living and hard drinking during his thirty years of service.

A light khaki blouse, with three stars on each shoulder, was draped over the back of a faded red upholstered, antique chair opposite the general as he sat at breakfast. The overseas cap resting on the seat below, was always deliberately placed to show three smaller stars in preference to the insignia.

He looked up from his newspaper and smiled, when a deep melodious voice asked, "General, could I freshen your coffee?"

"Yes, please, Marva."

Marva was a comely lass from Miami, Florida, with a few brain cells to match her beauty. An attractive red brick house in Calcutta, at 17 Cryer Street, one of the better residential districts, had been purchased in her name four years previously. Paul Eddy had originally advanced the money when he started the FEAMCO plant in Calcutta. This loan had long since been paid in full. The twenty-seven-year-old charmer claimed: "I have enough to retire on now, but these war years are just too good to miss."

Men who work and travel halfway around the globe, often find the extra pay benefits also carry a premium of loneliness. A hundred dollars was a small token for the affection, comfort and consolation the raven-haired resident of Cryer Street could supply.

Boliker had graduated from West Point as one of the most popular men in his class. However, in order to climb ahead during his lengthy military career, he had lost practically every vestige of this early popularity. The brief association with Marva was compensating somewhat for all those years. Recently, the general had acquired the habit of passing on affectionate salutations, not only to his own service, but to the Navy, the Merchant Marine, the FEAMCO employees and the numerous outfits serving the crown. For he had kissed them all by proxy.

"It's hard to believe," muttered Boliker, as he stared intently at the newspaper.

"What's hard to believe?"

"This outfit of Francis Stud's."

223

"The Flying Sharks, you mean?" As Marva rested her foot upon a nearby chair, the loose robe parted, revealing a long slender bare leg and thigh.

"Don't know how they do it!" He shook his head as he turned toward her, letting the paper fall to his lap. "The Japs aren't jeopardizing their bombers, they're only using a few for night raids. Fighters, they send out in daylight. Stud's men have shot down ninety-eight Japs and lost only four of their pilots. What a record! Some outfit to have under your command!"

"Soldiers of fortune, I understand." Marva's second foot joined the first upon the chair, crossing over a pair of slim ankles, and revealing a pair of well-proportioned underpinnings.

"I wonder if that still applies . . ." The general's voice faded. After last night he was content to stare at the electric percolator. One elbow rested on the table, supporting his head with a hand which was clasped over his chin and lips. The fingers of his other hand beat rhythmically on the hard table top.

Raising his head, and turning back to Marva, he took his hand from his chin.

"Now that war is declared, those planes should rightfully come under my command. I'd better check into this immediately."

"I understand these pilots have government contracts with FEAMCO. If you'd brought this up sooner, I could have helped you. FEAMCO's president, Paul Eddy, is a personal friend of mine. He's been here for two weeks trying to locate some missing spare parts for their P-40's. A Pan-American Clipper left their last shipment on Wake Island December seventh." She reached for the cigarettes and extracted one, placing it between her lips.

The general fumbled through his pockets for his lighter. "Where can I locate this Eddy person?"

"You can't. He left two days ago. Probably in the states by now."

"Really doesn't matter too much." He produced the elusive cigarette lighter and held it forward to her.

"Why?" Marva placed her hand on his and guided the ignited lighter to the tip of her cigarette, then settled back as the general proceeded to talk.

"Stud is retired from the service. I can wire Washington and have him called back to active duty. The pilots can be inducted, quite simply, into the Air Corps. Then I would be in a position to direct their activities properly."

Marva was beginning to understand just why the general was so eager to supplant Air Corps upon the rank and file of the Sharks. With a knowing glance at her overnight visitor she suggested: "Then maybe the news releases would read, 'One hundred more Jap planes destroyed was reported by General B. S. Sittel from his Headquarters in India.'"

Boliker's face flushed. In spite of her profession,

Marva was inherently honest. She believed in giving the underdog an even run for his money. Never a month passed without her mailing Paul Eddy ten per cent of her gross—for his original investment. This beat giving a madam back home fifty per cent, and another twenty for police protection. And never being sure!

"As long as the Sharks are doing such an excellent job, why not leave them alone?" she said in a definite mind-your-own-business tone of voice.

"My dear, as commanding general, I have to place the morale of the men under me ahead of my own personal feelings. Having my men fight side by side with people making all that money would only be asking for dissension. It's not right!" He rose and stalked to the window.

"Pardon me, General."

"What is it, my dear?"

"Since I'm a woman, you might consider this a bit stupid—but where are all these flyers whose morale you're so concerned about? I don't even see any airplanes!" This acute observation from Marva was anything but comforting to Boliker.

"I'll see you in a few days." The general was threading his field scarf under his shirt collar, getting ready to tie a neat knot.

"Oh?" Marva raised her eyebrows.

"I'm taking CNAC to Kunking this afternoon."

He slipped his arms into the light khaki jacket and reached for the overseas cap.

"Say hello to 'One-Eye' for me, will you, General?" She rose from the chair, pulling the robe tightly about her slim form.

"Sounds like a Chinese bandit."

"One-Eye Hoskins is an American who flies for CNAC." Marva closed the door behind the general.

Obtaining a seat on CNAC wasn't the easiest thing in the world to accomplish at this time. Passengers bribed ticket agents to replace others fleeing from China. But the return trip, without a waiting list, was equally as difficult. In this case, one was vying with valuable black market goods with a 500 per cent inflation, fare included.

Marva hadn't planned on being so helpful, when she casually mentioned one of her more regular clientele. Now, the name flashed through Boliker's mind, after threats and curses failed to make the Chinese personnel in the CNAC office understand his importance. Not offering a bribe was one of his mistakes, but his expecting to travel for free was completely beyond their comprehension.

Information, however, was volunteered as to the whereabouts of Captain Hoskins. One-Eye could be located at the same hotel in which Sittel and his staff had established headquarters. The general ordered his adjutant to locate Captain Hoskins and bring him immediately.

Presently an expected knock rattled the outside door of the general's suite.

The general hesitated a moment. His extended lips resembled a funnel as his head shot back and a last healthy

227

TONYA

slug of straight scotch poured into them from a water glass. Quickly rinsing the glass, he placed it on the bathroom sink. By his own orders, the command was strictly forbidden to imbibe during working hours. So, a smaller gulp of mouthwash followed the scotch.

Grabbing a stack of papers and a pair of reading glasses, he hurriedly plunked himself into a chair, and quickly spread the papers out upon the coffee table in front of him. He looked impressive. From a cursory examination, any visitor would assume the old boy had been wrapped up in important military affairs since an early hour. However, a more observant visitor might wonder why a man in such an important position read upside down.

After an appreciable pause, the knock was repeated.

"Come in," called Boliker, not looking up. He deliberately lowered the quality of his voice to sound important. This always caused people who knew him well to turn their eyes in his direction. It was so unnatural, compared to his normal high pitch, that they knew something was about to take place.

Glancing up from the paper work, in due time, after he heard the door open and close, the general did a double take. The adjutant stood alone, shifting from one foot to the other in an embarrassed manner.

"Well—" the normal unpleasant high-pitched tone was back again—"I thought I told you to bring Hoskins."

"Begging your pardon, sir," the adjutant hesitated

shyly, "Captain Hoskins acted rather strange. In fact, he seemed a trifle angry."

"Angry, you say?" Boliker grabbed the arms of the chair and bolted to his feet.

"Yes, sir." The adjutant looked at the floor under his feet, as though wishing it would open and let him drop through before further questioning.

"Doesn't he know who I am?" shouted the general as a well-aimed foot connected with the edge of the little table. It went careening across the room against the far wall, strewing the floor with papers.

"Yes, sir," repeated the adjutant.

En route to the bathroom and another drink, the general turned suddenly. "What d'ya mean—yes, sir—yes, sir? Are you just agreeing with me, or does the captain know me?"

"He sure does, sir!" The adjutant stiffened to attention. A hand flew to his mouth as though to halt the impulsive statement he knew had enlightened his superior to the fact that he was withholding some of the facts.

"Well, go on—out with it!" commanded the general in shrill anger.

"If—if—if you insist, sir."

"Certainly I insist!" declared the general emphatically. "I'll be with you in a minute." He proceeded into the bathroom, closing the door behind him.

Boliker held the glass at eye level while he measured a reasonable portion by tilting the bottle at brief intervals to gurgle out the proper amount. However, after the glass was lowered, and prior to consuming the drink, he continued to pour until the glass was close to overflowing. On this occasion, the mouthwash chaser was forgotten. It was just as well. No amount could have covered the telltale odor of a slug like that.

"Now then," he smacked his loose lips audibly as he re-entered the sitting room, "where were we?"

"You were insisting, sir . . ." The adjutant was still standing at attention, as he supplied the line of thought.

"Oh yes, continue." The general had somewhat regained his composure, as he lighted a cigarette. "Why didn't Hoskins show up?"

"He said, 'Sure I know who the general is,' sir, and he called you by name, sir . . ."

"What name?"

"Sittel, sir," trying to infer Hoskins had pronounced the surname correctly.

"You sure that's all?" The threatening tone and inference of a lack of intelligence or honesty in the lieutenant, forced the truth from him.

"He said," continued the young officer, " 'sure I know— I know—' "

"Know who?" demanded the angry man.

"Bullshit Sittel!" the lieutenant advised in a loud, clear voice, his face turning crimson as he finally gave the information.

"Go on," Boliker broke the silence in a subdued voice.

This statement did not shake him nearly so much as did the officer's reluctance. He had overheard the nickname previously, when he was not supposed to be within earshot.

The rest sounded anticlimactic.

"He said to tell you that he wasn't in the service, hadn't been for eight years, and had no plans for ever joining up again. If you want to see him, then you could walk down to the bar where he is or take a flying jump into the ocean. He didn't care which—sir!" The adjutant let out a deep sigh like a balloon deflating.

If the ensuing pause pointed to an emotional outburst, it did not come. Quietly donning cap and blouse, the general picked up his fancy leather swagger stick from the telephone stand, and walked over to open the outer door. He pushed his cap at a jaunty angle with the aid of the swagger stick, and turned to the thoroughly confused young lieutenant.

"If that's the way he wants it—okay!"

In the bar, on the first floor, Al Plummer and One-Eye Hoskins were seated at a corner table discussing urgent business problems. Japanese progress in the Burma area was forcing them to change their theater of operations. The Kunking black market money houses had lost a desire for the Burmese rupee.

TONYA

Rangoon docks along the river were piled high with the accumulated commerce of months. Native coolies refused to unload ships or load truck convoys and railroad cars for shipment north to China. The bulk of the great port's commerce lay stacked on the docks or stuffed in the holds of freighters in the harbor. No more freighters rounded Elephant Point bound for Rangoon. No more freighters left. The harbor had been mined, and old ships had been sunk in the river to block the channel for Japanese naval vessels.

However, neither Al nor One-Eye had the slightest interest in the thousands of tons of equipment and supplies piled up in Rangoon. These were too heavy and bulky for them to handle. Their only interest lay in something light and valuable, which could be concealed under a jacket, or in a map kit. This more or less confined their personal cargo to money and heroin.

Now that CNAC was no longer flying into Burma, new connections were being established in Calcutta. Al Plummer had chosen a somewhat roundabout course of flying the Beechcraft home from Rangoon in order to take care of his personal business in Calcutta. Fares collected from a full plane load of wealthy merchants enroute to India wiped away any doubts he had as to whether he should take this out-of-the-way route back to Kunking.

Once inside the hotel bar, the general had no difficulty in locating Hoskins. It wasn't that the blue CNAC uniform was so familiar, but a dark-haired man with one eyebrow

232

missing gave the appearance of having only one eye. Boliker walked over and stood beside the table, looking down at the two men seated there.

"Pull up a chair, General, I'll buy you a drink." Hoskins indicated the chair next to him.

"You're Captain Hoskins, I take it," Boliker said as he sat down, depositing his cap and stick on an adjoining chair.

"That's right," One-Eye replied. Then he turned to Al, adding, "Like you to meet Al Plummer, one of the Flying Sharks."

"My pleasure." Boliker seemed impressed. "My compliments on the splendid work you men are doing."

"Thanks, General, but I'm not one of the combat flyers. I'm the group adjutant," advised Al.

Turning on the charm when necessary was one of Boliker's strong points. He realized the futility of ordering Hoskins around. So, the men took turns buying scotch and enjoying each other's fabricated conversation.

"Francis Stud's an old friend of mine—knew him well in the service," Boliker bragged.

"Yeah, he speaks of you too, General."

On several occasions Stud had voiced a bitterness toward certain Air Corps officers and the part they played in his separation from the Corps. Hoskins recalled that this placed B. S. Sittel fairly high on Stud's you-know-what list. But this was really no concern of Hoskins'. The general appeared to be an affable gent who could hold his liquor, and that, in his opinion, was all anyone could ask for.

Boliker leaned forward in pretended concern. "I understand the Group is desperate for planes and spare parts."

"Yeah," said Al, "there are twice as many pilots as there are planes in operating order, and it's getting worse. We scoured the Rangoon docks. Parts for everything but a P-40. If replacements don't come from the east coast soon, I'm afraid it'll be too late."

"This will be alleviated shortly. I've cabled Washington to allocate pilots and P-40 parts immediately," lied Boliker, pretending to be the man-of-the-hour.

The only cable sent by Boliker was to Air Corps Headquarters, recommending that a certain first lieutenant be recalled to active duty in the Air Corps. The message also advised that the only logical solution for the disposal of the pilots was to absorb them into the Air Corps—by induction.

Plummer leaned forward in sudden interest. "Does Stud know this?"

"Well—er—no," Boliker faltered, "but I think the sooner I can get to Kunking and tell him, the better."

"I'll be happy to fly you to Kunking with the good news," One-Eye volunteered.

"Me too," offered Al, "but I won't be leaving for a few days."

"I can take you up this afternoon." One-Eye reached out to give the general a companionable pat on the shoulder. The movement of the somewhat inebriated pilot tipped over his glass. The general was alert enough to shoot back his chair to avoid the mixture of scotch and soda dripping over the edge of the table.

"You've got yourself a passenger," accepted Boliker, stooping over to brush at a few wet spots on his trousers.

One-Eye laughed boisterously. "Pardon me," he apologized between outbursts, "but if anyone had ever told me in flight school I'd live to fly over the Himalayas with a three star general as a co-pilot, I'd have said they was drunk!"

"Sorta looks like your dream's come true," commented Al, "only you're the one who's drunk!"

15 · White Scarves

STUD HAD SENT Doc Ward from Kunking to Mingladon to keep the pilots patched up. The good Reverend Frockman went along to bury Robert Sanderson III. Al Plummer had deposited both Doc and Frocky in Rangoon. The Sharks there had sent very little back on the Beechcraft, other than outgoing mail. Most of the letters were to relatives back home.

Tonya, however, had at least a dozen letters from members of the Group. The only package was hers too—a small lumpy bundle. It contained a wallet, a crushed gold wrist watch, a class ring, a battered diary, a few odd coins, and personal papers marked R. Sanderson III. These were knotted inside a dirty silk cloth. On careful inspection one could tell the silk had once been white. It was now covered with ugly brown blood stains. A monogram was visible on a part: "Forever, Tonya."

British colonials, residing in the nearby estates on the road to Mingladon, had been oblivious of the Americans,

236

until preparations for their holiday dinners were so rudely interrupted by the Japanese bombing on Christmas day. Until then, no one appeared to care how, when, where or if, the Sharks ate. Hospitality changed—almost overnight. Now servants were instructed to prepare and transport meals for the visitors three times a day.

The reason was obvious. As at Singapore, only two of the Britishers' fat little Lend-Lease Buffaloes had managed to escape the initial raid on Christmas day. Hence, the city was dependent upon the Sharks for sky protection. Because of them the Japs had been unable to get a bomber over Rangoon during daylight hours. Bombers came after dark, but these flew singly, and the damage was negligible. Watching the enemy being picked off at a safe distance from the town boosted the citizens' morale considerably. These good people had every intention of extending a welcoming hand until the long talked about Spitfires and Hurricanes might arrive from home.

A door from one of the bombed-out RAF barracks rested outdoors none too steadily upon a pair of saw horses. It was covered with a fresh sheet. The contents of various containers placed on this crude table permeated the air with their savor. Strong aromas of coffee, tea, ham, bacon and eggs predominated. A closer look showed the buffet to be loaded with a variety of fresh fruit, jam, jelly and cheeses.

By mid-January, Jap aerial strategy upon Rangoon had almost developed into a routine. Most of the attacks were from fighters only. About once a week they would try to sneak in a formation of bombers. If the Japanese had only made this a daily routine, they could have killed the Sharks with monotony. The fact that occasionally they didn't show up was the only thing that prevented this.

If control didn't report a bogey by 10:30 A.M., the ground crew knew they would have an uninterrupted day to work on the planes. Most of the time RAF Radar would pick up something around 10:00 A.M. and the fighting would start about 11:00 A.M.

Pilots took turns standing by, alternating days. Since the action started, the ground crew had been able to keep only half the P-40's in commission at any one time.

Kirk Jackson had arrived at dusk the previous night with twenty fresh pilots and planes of the Second Pursuit, sent by Colonel Stud to relieve Cortland Smith, who had command after Sanderson was killed. Kirk looked as immaculate as ever, with a snow-white silk scarf knotted neatly at his throat. But for some reason he appeared anything but debonair.

"Smith must be giving Kirk an awful line of crap," Chuck said, his mouth full of food.

"Yeah, Kirk looks pale as a ghost." Rusty rose unsteadily from the bench and headed toward the table.

"Take it easy," Chuck cautioned. "You better sit down." He knew that when Rusty had imbibed a few drinks, his temper was easily aroused.

"Why?" Rusty asked over his shoulder.

" 'Cause you smell like a brewery." The mechanic rose,

leaving his plate on the bench, in an effort to intercept Rusty. It was no use. Rusty brushed his arm aside and proceeded toward Kirk.

"Say, that's a pretty neat scarf you're wearing." Rusty's keen eyes had instantly recognized the trademark.

"Thanks."

In the instant Kirk hesitated, Rusty rubbed an admiring hand across the silk. It was too late for Kirk to do anything but blush when Rusty pulled one end from inside the leather jacket. He read the monogram aloud: "Forever, Tonya."

A titter escaped the bystanders. Kirk jerked the scarf from Rusty's hand and tucked it back inside his jacket.

"The mate to that didn't bring much luck to the guy wearing it." Rusty spoke as though the scarf might be an evil omen, wiping his hands down the side of his trousers as though to rid himself of the contamination of having touched it.

"When I need your advice, I'll ask for it!" Kirk turned and stalked away.

Later that afternoon most of the pilots at Mingladon gathered in front of operations, waiting for the 4:00 P.M. meeting Kirk had called to fill them in on the latest directives from Kunking.

Doc Ward was ribbing Rusty, who had been sleeping most of the day, since his morning's altercation with Kirk. "You're a pretty nice-looking fellow when you get shaved and ain't in a fighting mood."

Rusty gave a sheepish smile. "How're things in Kunking, Doc?"

"Same as ever. Oh, I forgot to tell you—Toni won't be there when you get back."

"Where'd she go?" Rusty visualized another fight with Auggie, and her usual departure for a few days.

Doc eyed Rusty closely. "Hadn't gone anywhere before we left, but I understand she's going to be General Sittel's house guest for a week."

"Meaning what?"

"Oh, he's the high muckey-muck in charge of the Air Corps. His headquarters are in Calcutta. He flew into Kunking about a week ago to have a chat with Stud."

"Going to Calcutta, huh? I hope she doesn't forget to pay The Black Hole of Calcutta a visit!"

General B. S. Sittel's recent visit to China had caused Stud to throw caution to the winds; that is, as far as the individuals who had to fly in his small air force were concerned. Stud knew he had but a few precious months to carve a name for himself in aviation history, and to secure his own personal future.

But Sittel was blocked. Actually, his untimely visit worked to the Shark leader's advantage, in that the warning gave Stud a chance to get a second wind. During Sittel's stay in China, certain P-40 parts Stud's group needed so desperately had finally arrived in Calcutta—

tires, batteries, propellers, solenoids, instruments, oxygen, and ammunition for the .50-caliber machine guns.

Tonya had obliged her boss by delaying the round little general for nearly a week. Thus One-Eye Hoskins had ample time to make enough flights in a CNAC DC-3 to bring in all the parts. It had not been at all hard for her to ingratiate herself with Boliker S. Sittel.

Stud realized this would be his one and only shipment, but it was all he needed to keep himself in an excellent bargaining position. If the general had remained in Calcutta, there was no doubt that the shipment would have been confiscated by his authority. Or, he would have placed a hold on the parts, and would have had Francis Stud and his boys executing close order drill in Air Corps uniforms, under his command, in less than a month.

"All right," promised Stud at the end of their conference, "I'm agreeable to having the Group inducted, just as soon as the Air Corps can supply us completely with aircraft, personnel, post exchanges—the works."

"We'll be able to complete this transition by May, Francis." Sittel beamed at his success in getting such ready co-operation from Stud.

"Let's allow a little leeway and make a definite date, say, the first of July." Stud wanted as much time as possible. Furthermore, the rainy weather would have arrived by July.

As they reached the door of the plane, the two men shook hands on their agreement.

"Have a nice trip." Stud gave a salute in farewell. Then

turning to Tonya, he added, "Hope you can find a few
clothes to buy in Calcutta, Toni."

"I hope so too, I'm nearly threadbare," she complained,
looking up at Sittel in a provocative manner.

"Take care of yourself, dear." Auggie moved toward his
wife.

"I'll only be gone a week," she said, turning her cheek
as he leaned forward to kiss her.

"The hotels in Calcutta are jammed. Were you able to
get a reservation?" Auggie was more curious than concerned.

"That's all taken care of," Sittel interposed. "Toni will
be staying in a beautiful home in the residential section."
Noting Brownfield's expression, he quickly added, "With
an American woman who lives by herself."

"Mind giving me the address, so I can write?" Auggie
was determined to at least know where she was; he would
only be able to guess what she would be doing.

Tonya looked to the general for an answer to this question.

"17 Cryer Street," said General Boliker S. Sittel.

Inside the barracks used as operations, the four o'clock
meeting was under way. Kirk was standing in front of a
large-scale map tacked on the wall opposite the windows.
Jagged pieces of glass pointed from the frames of the windows at odd and sharp angles. Bullet holes in the walls,

floor and ceiling bore mute evidence of the beating the building had taken during the Christmas Day raid, and there was a large circular opening in the ceiling like an incompleted chimney. Another hole of approximately the same diameter in the floor indicated that only a bomb could have made both. One which, fortunately, had failed to explode.

"Is everybody here?" asked Kirk, flexing a yardstick as he held the extreme ends.

"As the group's physician," Doc wisecracked, "I'm certain all bodies are present, but where their minds are I can only guess."

"I don't follow you, Doc," said Kirk.

"Take Rusty here, his mind is probably in The Black Hole of Calcutta."

"Aw, sex is all Doc can think about." Truelove tipped his chair back until it balanced on two legs.

Rusty gave the medic a playful shove with his elbow. "If the quack don't take time to clean his glasses, he's going to fall through that hole in the deck."

"Let's get on with our meeting." Kirk tapped the yardstick on the edge of the table. "Colonel Stud has informed me that the Group is ready to carry on an all-out offensive. We are through waiting for the Japs. From now on, we'll be flying into enemy territory and destroying them before they take off."

"Just how in hell are we going to do this without bombs?" Truelove continued rocking back and forth on the two back legs of his chair.

243

"By strafing. The old man says the Japs' direction-finding equipment is next to useless."

"Oh, great!" moaned Rusty. "If you have a forced landing, don't bother to walk home, stay and have some fish heads and rice!"

"We'll also be on call to help the Colonial troops," continued Kirk, ignoring Rusty's interruption. "Wellstock reports the British command turned down his offer of a supporting division of Chinese. All they need are aircraft to strafe."

Truelove brought the chair down on all fours. "Which brings up a mighty important question."

"What's that?"

"Our contracts state we'll only be called upon to shoot down planes, and that we'll only get paid for the ones the Chinese confirm."

"Yeah, what about that, Kirk?" came a voice from the rear.

Smith stepped to the front. "Maybe I can answer this. Things are different now our country's at war. We're going to have to make sacrifices which weren't originally in the plan."

"Look who's talking." Rusty turned in his seat as if to put his back toward Smith. "Who's going to take us on these clam bakes, you—or Stud?"

"I'm going to lead tomorrow," Kirk said. At the sound of his own voice volunteering this his already pale cheeks paled even more.

At the mention of tomorrow, a member of the First Pursuit sounded off: "Thought you came down here to relieve us. Ain't we supposed to be leaving soon?"

"Day after tomorrow," Smith said.

"Why the wait?"

"Two reasons." Smith again turned to the group. "It'll be a couple of days before I can completely brief Kirk on our operations routine. Some of us will be high cover for the strafing mission tomorrow. Proceed with the briefing, Kirk."

Take-off time was set for 10:30 A.M. the following morning. This hour was chosen in case the enemy might select the same day for a raid of their own. The objective was the airport near the outskirts of Bangkok, Thailand, four hundred miles away. Twelve, noon, was the estimated time of arrival over the target area.

The day ended much the same as any other. The Sharks who didn't have to park aircraft headed for the RAF officers' mess, a rambling one-story wood-frame affair, located near the center of the field. The runways crossed in front of the veranda, facing to the northeast. As the sun was getting ready to plunge out of sight, they sat with a scotch in one hand and a cigarette in the other. Planes took off leisurely. The sound of the Allison engines was more of a purr, unlike the angry roar of a scramble, content to be bedded down for the night.

"I like this time of day," drawled Truelove, holding his scotch and soda up and peering through the contents of the glass with one eye closed, observing the fiery ball of the dying sun.

"Me too," Rusty squinted his deep set eyes as he turned his head to the west. "Wonder why it's so pleasant."

"Don't have to worry about getting shot at until the following day."

The two turned to observe Doc Ward trying to hold the screen door open and steer Frockman out into the fresh air at the same time. Frocky was none too steady.

"Could the Padre get this way in one hour?" Truelove said incredulously. "This place doesn't serve from one to four."

"Probably stacked up enough during lunch to last all afternoon!"

Once outside, the clergyman indignantly brushed his benefactor to one side. Using the porch railing for a supporting guide, he approached Bob and Rusty.

"What's troubling you, Padre? Not enough attendance at the Sunday services?" Bob laughed.

Rusty continued sipping his drink. "He couldn't see them if they did."

"Naw," Doc said. "Frocky's mad about the strafing mission tomorrow."

"For Christ's sake, he ain't going," said Truelove.

"Yeah, what's he got to worry about?"

Frocky braced himself with both arms around a porch post and started talking. "I'm deeply concerned about the pilots who might go down in enemy territory. My learned colleague, Dr. Ward, will be unable to pronounce them dead. Undoubtedly there will be no clergyman of the Christian faith to preside at their funeral."

"That shouldn't be such a problem," Rusty said. "They've been having funerals for guys lost at sea for years. Kinda like an absentee ballot."

"But I won't know whether they are dead or captured." He released one arm from around the post long enough to wave a pointed finger at Rusty. "The prayers I give for the deceased are quite different from the prayers for the living, you know."

"Maybe we can help you, Padre," Rusty offered.

"How?"

"Well, we can usually tell by how hard they're hit, or whether they hit the silk or not."

Doc placed one of the weary man's arms across his shoulders. "C'mon, Frocky, let's hit the sack."

"God bless you," said Frocky, momentarily turning his head back to Rusty and Bob, as the Doc half carried, half led, him away.

At 10:00 A.M. the following morning, Kirk and Smith dropped by RAF Headquarters on a purely routine call. They were surprised to find General Wellstock there. Stoney's wiry gray-haired observer smiled pleasantly as the two squadron leaders entered.

"Good morning, gentlemen," greeted George affably. "I take it you've already met the Vice Air Marshall."

"Good morning, General, Air Marshall," said the two

Sharks in turn, nodding, and saluting as each stepped forward.

Wellstock and the Britisher were standing beside a long table. They had been poring over a map, sketched out in front of them.

"Just checking in, sir," said Smith. "If the Japs don't come over in the next half hour, we'll be on our way to Bangkok."

"Yes, I know." Wellstock nodded approval. "Come over here and take a look at this map."

The four men leaned over the map while the general marked enemy strength and positions in southeast Burma. These were troop concentrations, as of four days ago, when Wellstock last saw the front.

"There should be a large movement of heavy equipment as far over as this by now." His pencil traced a line along a road, a few inches in advance of the front line, as he spoke.

"Looks like they're moving right along," commented Kirk.

"Unfortunately, yes." Wellstock continued tracing his pencil along the map. "See this road just north of the other one?"

"Yes, sir," Kirk and Smith nodded in unison.

"You should find tanks and armored car movement here too." The general tapped his pencil against the map.

"I thought we were supposed to strafe Bangkok!" Kirk sensed something here didn't tally.

"True, but I want you to hit these targets en route home."
Wellstock spoke without lifting his eyes from the map.

The straining silence that followed this order was finally
broken when the Vice Air Marshall cleared his throat
loudly and, with a bit of hawing about, cautioned, "And I
say, old man, don't hit any of our blokes by mistake!"

"Where'll they be?" Kirk sounded dubious.

"Why, along this same road—" the British officer pointed
to the marked section—"but the convoy lorries will be
marked with a white banner of cloth on top."

On the way back to the flight line, Kirk appeared to be
entranced. None of his companion's morale-building chatter caused the slightest change of outward aspect. He was
like a man on his way to execution.

"We're here," said Smith, a moment or so after swinging
from the jeep, noting that the leader of the mission remained motionless in his seat.

"Well, are we going, or aren't we?" Rusty walked over
and stared down at the immobile face in the jeep.

Rusty's voice broke the spell.

"Get ready to go in five minutes." Kirk pushed through
the crowd on the way to the latrine. Due to nervousness,
he had made three times the usual number of trips in that
direction this morning.

"Any changes in the strike?" Rusty directed this to
Smith.

"Nothing important. Wellstock wants the Japs strafed
along the roads on your return from Bangkok."

"What roads?"

The map sketched by Wellstock was produced and unfolded upon the hood of the jeep. Pilots looked over each other's shoulders while Smith pointed a finger, indicating the proper roads. Kirk had returned and was heading for his P-40, before Smith got around to mentioning there might be any possibility of British movement on the roads. Or how such equipment would be recognized.

Radios checked with RAF control for the last time prior to take-off. From then on, radio silence would be in effect. The pilots hoped their arrival over the target area would come as a surprise. At least they could hope.

"The last plane is in the air at 10:35," Smith said to Chuck Reynolds as he walked up from the flight line after ascertaining that all planes had checked out satisfactorily.

"Sure hope it works out." Chuck was watching Smith check his watch.

"If your engines keep running, it will." Smith noticed the cloudiness in Chuck's eyes as the P-40's winged out of sight. "Wish you were going along?"

"No thanks."

Chuck continued to gaze at the horizon even after the planes had disappeared.

"You look like you're thinking about something."

"I am," said Chuck still gazing skyward.

"What?"

"When I left the States, I had hopes of learning to fly after I got here. I was just itching to get my fool head blowed off. Instead I got my rear chewed out for complaining about no action. Now I guess I'm lucky it's my rear and not my head that gets the action." Chuck shook his head and slowly turned away.

On the way to the mission the boys had the sky to themselves. Visibility was almost too clear for comfort. They could see a submarine surfaced about twenty miles south of the point where the flight crossed the Gulf of Martaban. No doubt it was Japanese, and heading for Gyaw, a small occupied Burmese port on the peninsula; but they had no extra fuel to warrant an investigation. This choice target would have to wait.

Long before Bangkok or its airdrome was visible, the blue of the Gulf of Siam glistened peacefully off to the right. Several pilots had turned their radios in on some American music coming out of Saigon. Occasionally the announcer threw in a few words for propaganda purposes, but most of the records went uninterrupted.

The announcer broke in with "Our next selection, 'J' attendrai,' will be for . . ." Static blotted out the name of the party to be honored.

Rusty felt a twinge of jealousy. "I wonder if the announcer knows Tonya too," he thought. "In any event, I hope I get back from this mission, so I can fly to Kunking tomorrow."

Rusty redialed the base frequency. He knew there would be plenty to occupy his mind in a few minutes. The others knew this too, for now Bangkok was in sight. Sunlight sparkled from a gold-plated pagoda in the distance. Below, the P-40's were getting squared away for the attack, and nosing over. All gun switches were checked to determine their readiness. The mixture controls were placed in full rich position. Prayers, unused in recent years, miraculously sifted back through the minds in clear detail. Though most of the flyers were fatalists by their own admission, there were occasions like this one when they silently asked God to prolong that day for another day.

The Sharks weren't invited for lunch, but the Japanese had everything but a band out to greet them. Rapid flares emitted from the barrels of ground guns like so many blinking lights. Terrified personnel ran madly about the field, in and out of planes, as though a giant ant hill had been kicked over. Incendiary bullets quickly set many of the parked aircraft into blazing torches. Some of the other aircraft, which did not burn, sagged as armor-piercing rounds shattered landing gear and structural parts.

For this mission the guns' belts had been loaded alternately with incendiary and armor-piercing bullets. Both were serving their purpose equally well.

Black puffs from anti-aircraft guns were beginning to dirty the clear air. Kirk's planes were so low and were moving over the ground so fast that the heavy guns could not train on them. These guns were firing away at Rusty and the high cover.

Rusty divided his attention between the P-40's below,

and the bursts in the air. Whenever he figured the next volley would have him measured for size he varied his course and altitude slightly.

Camouflage on the P-40's below made them almost impossible to keep in sight. Only during the brief intervals when they streaked across the field with guns wide open were the high cover able to pick them up.

"I'd swear those guys are making more than two passes," Rusty thought as the few minutes dragged on like an eternity. "They are sure pushing their luck sumpin' awful!"

Even as he looked down at the field, a P-40 dug a wing tip into the ground, literally tearing itself to bits as it cart-wheeled along. Propeller, wings, tail section and engine left the rotating craft in a spray of grinding wheel-sparks as each had its turn on the concrete. The center section, housing the pilot, rolled to rest on the lawn in front of one of the larger buildings.

A hard lump swelled in Rusty's throat. He reached for his microphone, planning to call, "Let's go before we wear out our welcome."

Before he could speak, his instrument panel was a mass of flying glass and torn metal. The increased roar of the slipstream on his right caused him to turn in that direction. Two smoking barrels from a Jap fighter were staring him in the eye. Never before had Jap guns sounded quite so loud above the roar of his own propeller.

Automatically he pointed the nose of the P-40 earth-ward. The throttle was pushed wide open. Down he went.

Since there was little diving space left, he started to pull out, keeping full throttle. An occasional tinkle told him that an enemy bullet was expending itself as it ricocheted about inside his fuselage and wings.

Rusty led two pursuing I-97's southward—out over the Gulf of Siam. He soon discovered a P-40 could outrun an I-97 on the flat.

As he saw the two I-97's turn toward Bangkok, Rusty circled back. Now the shoe was on the other foot. Neither Jap looked back. They were too interested in finding new prey over their city. Rusty eased behind each in turn, sending it down in flames.

Rusty spotted several enemy fighters north of the field, but no P-40's. A glance at his watch told him to lean out and head for home. The shot-up gas gauge could tell him nothing. With a great sigh of relief he headed toward Mingladon.

The strafing pilots stayed low on the way home, following the roads in search of enemy equipment. With news of the raid, most of the Japanese had been ordered off the beaten track. Miles were covered without a sign of life. Then, suddenly, a long line of lorries came into view.

Each pilot gave the column the full benefit of six machine guns as he ripped it from one end to the other. Then they continued on.

"Funny thing 'bout those trucks," one pilot radioed his mates.

"Whatcha mean funny?" came back to him.

"All of them had a white marking down the center!"

"Yeah," came the reply, "almost as if they wanted us to recognize them."

The pilots couldn't hear the operators of the convoy of trucks screaming, as they shook their fists toward the planes, "Stop! You bloody bastards, we're British!"

It was a good thing the Sharks were short on gas!

In front of the administration building below, a Japanese major was supervising a grisly detail. Freeing the tangled body from the twisted cockpit of the center section of the crashed plane was proving quite a chore. Search of the wreckage and the body had provided little more than a wallet and a white silk scarf knotted about the dead man's neck.

The major ordered the men to drag what remained of the P-40 and its contents away and burn it. He stooped and released the silk scarf as he noticed some lettering on it.

"Ha-so, 'Forever Tonya-ka!'" His brows furrowed in thought as he stood holding the piece of stained white silk. Like most educated Japanese, the major could read and write English.

One of the soldiers had opened the wallet, and was displaying the picture of a woman he found in it.

"Kirie no ojo-san!" he exclaimed with a toothy grin, meaning, "pretty girl."

Promptly the major called the enlisted man to attention, and slapped him in the face for tampering with information Japanese intelligence might deem valuable.

As the major stared at the photograph, then the scarf, he remembered clearly what had been but a vague recollection a moment before. The face—the name—the place—in Hanoi—in Saigon—information bought—for a high price—paid to this woman—TONYA!

16 · A Maharaja Makes A Loan

THE INDIAN MAID opened and closed the door silently. The occupant of the bedroom was sleeping face down, one knee arched above her waist, the other extended straight. The covering of a single sheet made the smooth-flowing curves underneath more inviting.

It was nearly noon. The owner of the long auburn hair, which spread softly over the pillow, should be in need of tea soon. But the quiet maid had learned better than to jump the gun with this house guest. Bare feet padded noiselessly into the dining room, where the mistress sat, engrossed in manicuring her nails.

"Still sleeping, Sita?" inquired Marva, without taking her eyes from the tiny brush with which she was applying red lacquer to her fingernails.

"Yes, Mem-sahib."

"Go ahead and run her bath." Then, as an afterthought, more or less to herself, Marva added, "I'd better get sleeping beauty on the ball, so we'll be ready when the general's car arrives."

General Sittel wasn't exactly appealing to the mistress of 17 Cryer Street, especially in the hot Calcutta climate. However, he could be extremely useful. He was top brass. In the event the Japs threatened, he was the one to decide who would be evacuated in U. S. aircraft. Many introductions to the proper kind of clientele had already evolved from this association.

Having a house guest of equal caliber to herself had made it a week of festivity for Marva. Tonya, equally if not more beautiful, was every bit as experienced and clever at handling the opposite sex. As a result, the house had been overflowing with flowers, guests and invitations throughout the week. Marva somewhat regretted the end of the visit drawing near. Two beautiful foreign girls in Calcutta could practically write their own ticket.

A pink-cheeked soldier of about eighteen drove up in a green Buick sedan, with "U. S. A. Air Corps" lettered on the side. He wore corporal's chevrons on his khaki shirt. The blond fuzz on his chin made him appear even younger. The ladies, he announced, were to be driven to the general's Grand Hotel suite for the customary three o'clock tea—or cocktail.

"Good afternoon, ladies," General Sittel greeted them warmly. "Glad you came early. It's been a hectic day. Just completed my work a few minutes ago."

"Will that be all, sir?" asked the young corporal.

"Yes, but hang around in the lobby in case I need you."

Tonya seated herself on the large comfortable divan, to await the usual offered drink.

"We're the only ones here." Marva sounded disappointed as she walked about the suite.

"I'm expecting others later." Sittel turned back to Tonya, "Now, what is your pleasure?"

Leaning back, Tonya stretched her long legs out in front of her, crossing her ankles. "Make mine a tall scotch with plenty of ice."

As though tearing his eyes away from the lithe form on the end of the couch, the general turned reluctantly to Marva.

"And you, Marva? The usual?"

"I'll wait awhile." She ground out her cigarette and walked toward the window.

"You seem restless, my dear." He frowned somewhat quizically as he watched her turn back from the window. "Anything wrong?"

"No. Just bored, I guess." Marva reached for another cigarette.

"By the way, I promised the Maharaja I'd pick him up at the Oxford Club at four." The general reached into his pocket and pulled out a wad of bills, clamped together with a gold money clip. Extracting two hundred-rupee notes, he passed them to Marva. "Do me a favor, dear. Take my car and pick him up for me at four? Perhaps you could kill a little time with this until then."

"You don't mind?" Marva directed the inquiry to Tonya.

"Not at all." Tonya could not care less.

"'Bye then. See you later." Marva seemed relieved to be on her way.

After her departure the general poured himself a stiff drink and stood under the large ceiling fan. Between sips from the glass he held in one hand, and puffs on the cigar he held in the other, he spoke.

"Stud's boys are still going to town. The Japs retaliated for the Bangkok attack yesterday. Sent over sixty pursuit and thirty medium bombers."

"What happened?"

"Didn't get close to Rangoon. Nearly half of them were shot down."

"That should make the Sharks' total close to one hundred fifty planes by now." Tonya lifted one foot and pointed the toe of her shoe as though admiring the arch of her foot. "Did we lose any pilots?"

"Three."

"Know who they were?" She lowered her foot and lifted her gaze expectantly to him.

"All the communiqué said was that three of Francis Stud's flyers were lost."

An appreciable pause followed. Each tinkled the ice

against the side of the glasses, as though waiting for the other to speak.

"Something is on your mind, Boliker," Tonya broke the silence.

"I've been doing a little more than thinking about our conversation on the plane."

He turned away from her to refill his glass and prepare a fresh one for her.

"You'll have to clue me in."

"About making money on the rate of exchange in China."

Currently, the Bank of China valued the Chinese dollar at twenty to one American dollar. However, Chinese businessmen preferred the Indian rupee. Anyone with access to air transportation could get from 100 to 150 Chinese dollars, depending upon the locale, for one American dollar. This, traded back into gold certificates through the China Bank, would make a profit of from 400 to 600 per cent.

The general thought of his wife and her money that had financed his military career throughout the years. Now the money was gone. They were in debt. Retirement after the war was inevitable for him.

"I can dispose of the money for you in China," offered Tonya, "but you have to have several thousand dollars to make a trip worth while."

"Yes, I know," said Sittel, doing some mental arithmetic.

He was thinking of using a part of the $50,000 in the headquarters safe. This amount was usually kept on hand to run his small military missions. A few thousand would never be missed—if it were returned within a few days. After all, he would only be borrowing the use of it.

Tonya knew he needed her—or someone—and now that she knew his plan he would have to use and trust her.

"You could give me twenty per cent for my work," she said.

"Certainly. I wouldn't want you to do it for nothing."

"I don't know if you realize that this can be dangerous," Tonya warned, remembering Al Plummer's friend.

"Don't worry, I fully realize that in my position I could be court-martialed." He turned and walked back to the window, then, as he turned back to Tonya, he continued, "Somehow, I can't help but feel justified in taking advantage of this situation personally. The Empress takes the United States for a bunch of jerks. She has insisted that all money our forces spend in China has to go through the Bank at twenty to one. This amounts to our paying for the privilege of fighting in China!"

"That may be true, but it's beyond me," she said. "My only concern is looking after Tonya!"

Ignoring this statement, Boliker continued pacing between the window and the couch. "I'll bet Francis Stud and George Wellstock have been getting fatter than hogs on this setup."

"No, I'm certain neither have," corrected Tonya. "Such a thought would never enter Wellstock's mind. He's so gullible, the Empress is only using him for a patsy! Francis knows most of his staff have been involved at one time or another, but so far he personally has been content just to make a name for himself—it varies in different circles—and to keep in solid with the Empress."

"Being the first Allied Commander to win distinction has really made Francis feel his oats! He even had the gall to send the President a message saying, 'If you give me one hundred fighters, thirty medium, and twelve heavy bombers, I can accomplish the downfall of Japan.'"

"Can't argue with success, General," she smiled.

"So true! So, let's have another drink—to our success!" He was getting awfully thirsty trying to be polite in waiting for his guest to finish her tall drink before replenishing his own.

"I still have some." She held up her glass for him to see.

"I'll just sweeten it then."

As the host was busy with the ice, Tonya continued on the original subject.

"I can't help thinking Stud has some special deal with the Empress. Either that, or he's working himself into a high enough position whereby he can take what he wants! But Francis can't fool me. Every day he shows less and less consideration for those who helped him. As far as the pilots go, he is becoming absolutely ruthless! He doesn't care what happens to them as long as they make a name for him risking their necks—and not his!"

"You'd never convince anyone back home of that. Not now. He's America's Number One hero. I get so tired of reading his messages I hope he never gets around to writing a book!" Sittel handed her the fresh drink, then turned back to the table and took a fresh cigar.

"Why?" asked Tonya with suddenly revived interest, wondering if Stud had decided to take over her book.

"It would probably read like *Mein Kampf!*" Boliker smiled at her over the lighted match he held close to his cigar.

"It might at that!" Tonya laughed.

He seated himself beside her. "You're returning to Kunking in a couple of days?"

"Day after tomorrow. Why?"

"I want to give you five thousand dollars before you go," he said, looking directly at her as though he expected some reaction.

"Don't forget to change it into rupees."

"I won't." He gave her a knowing smile. "And don't you forget to change them into gold certificates for *me!* I'll be there two or three days after you leave. I'll give you your per cent then."

Smiling sweetly, she looked up at him, "Why, General, what else could I do with it?"

"Let's not go into that!" His expression was one of a

gambler who knew he had to take a chance, even one as great as trusting Tonya.

Most Americans abroad cared little how the taxpayers' money was squandered overseas. Only a few were thoughtful enough to bring some of the Lend-Lease money home. But these few were returning it for their own use.

Shortly after four, Marva returned with the Maharaja. Mahabir Singh found difficulty in paying attention to anything other than Tonya. And vice versa. As her head tilted back to look into the tall Indian's dark eyes, Tonya appeared enthralled.

She guessed him to be about thirty years old. She could see he was over six feet tall, very athletic and extremely handsome.

"I thought a Maharaja wore a turban with a big jewel in the center," she said playfully, raising an arm and rotating long slender fingers around her head.

"The headdress is only worn on special occasions—a formal dinner, or an affair of state."

"I'd love to see you dressed formal," Tonya glanced down at her bosom, "over a dinner table."

The Maharaja turned to include the other two. "General, why don't the four of us fly up to my place for dinner next week? We could show your guest some of the more beautiful parts of our country, and perhaps entice her into staying for a tiger hunt."

"I'd be happy to," Sittel said. He noticed that Marva was beaming all over with acceptance. Turning to Tonya, he added, "The dinner would be in your honor, Tonya."

"But—but—I won't be here," Tonya stammered.

"No?" the Maharaja turned in surprise.

"Tonya has to make an early flight to Kunking Friday," Marva said.

"In that case we must have a farewell celebration tomorrow evening. I'm having a few members of state for dinner at my home here in the city. Will you do me the honor of joining us?"

Although the invitation was all-inclusive, his eyes were upon Tonya alone.

"I'd love to come." Tonya smiled up at him.

"Then it's settled. General, may I expect the three of you for dinner at eight?"

"Fine. Now that's settled, shall we have a drink before the others arrive?" Boliker rubbed his hands together in anticipation of moistening his already dry throat.

Several drinks were consumed before the other foursome arrived and the group moved on to the hotel's private dining room for dinner. During the interim, Tonya had not been idle. Arrangements had been made for the Maharaja to visit 17 Cryer Street after dinner to hear some of Tonya's new French records.

After the last coffee and the final cigarette, the group moved to the bar for one last drink. At the entrance Tonya put a hand to her temple. "It's been such a long day for me. I wonder if I could be excused. Perhaps your driver could take me home, General?"

Before the general could reply, Mahabir Singh spoke. "That won't be necessary. My car was to be here by ten o'clock. It would be on my way to take you. I too must say goodnight."

As the long sleek Bentley rolled into the driveway of 17 Cryer Street, Tonya turned to the Maharaja. "Must your driver wait, or can you call him when you're ready to leave?"

"I'll call him," he replied as he patted her hand.

One small lamp was lit in the spacious living room. Without bothering to turn on more lights, Tonya walked over to the bar.

"I'll fix you a drink, then get the records."

As she handed him the drink, she moved close and whispered up to him, "Take off your coat and make yourself comfortable, I'll be right back."

He reached out an arm to pull her close, but she gracefully eluded him, and moved toward the door.

Mahabir Singh was studying his partially consumed drink when he heard the door open again, and looked up to see a vision. Standing in the doorway, in a sheer gossamer gown of the palest blue, with the hall light behind her like a halo, Tonya left little to his imagination.

Mahabir Singh rose as she approached him. There was no doubt now that this was real and not a vision. And that reality became even more evident when her hands slid up across his chest and locked behind his neck. A warm body pressed close. After a few moments, he released her slightly—to look at what he held. Without a word she moved silently to the cabinet at the far side of the room. Lifting the top, she placed a record on the machine, and as the strains of "*J' attendrai*" softly filled the room, she glided back to him, speaking softly.

"This is my favorite. I already had this record—but it's almost worn out!"

Pulling her close, Mahabir Singh repeatedly pressed his lips against the white throat and face, finally resting them upon the oval parted lips. Then, as one, they sank down upon the soft divan.

Later they heard sounds coming from Marva's rooms at the far end of the hall. They could recognize Boliker Sittel's voice. Neither Tonya nor Mahabir had even been aware of their arrival.

Tonya stretched languidly, still pressing close to Mahabir. He seemed spent—for the moment at least. As his hands wandered searchingly over her, he spoke softly.

"Shall we have a drink and start the phonograph again?"

"Why don't we fix them and take them into my room? I can show you what I brought with me and you can tell me what to wear tomorrow night!"

"Isn't there a song—or a saying, 'Come as you are?' " He looked her over approvingly and laughed. "I like that!"

"Oh, you!"

Drinks in hand, the two entered Tonya's bedroom. She pulled back the sliding doors of the closet to display a row of dresses. A plan was forming in her mind.

Reaching up, she lifted down a straight black dress secured to the hanger by two clothespins.

"This is the only dressy one I have with me—and it's strapless. I didn't bring so much as a strand of pearls or a pin to wear with it. And without jewelry it's nothing! Maybe I can't come after all!"

"Of course you will." Mahabir stepped forward, putting his arms about her. "I have a few things in my safe. I'll send you over something you can wear for the evening—perhaps emeralds to match your eyes."

Tonya melted against him. "I'll take very good care of them!"

"I know you will. You can just leave them with Marva when you depart." He stepped slowly backward as he spoke, pulling her with him until he reached the bed. Then he slipped back upon it, still holding her close.

Late the next afternoon Tonya was sunning on the veranda when she heard a car come into the driveway. A few minutes later Marva brought her a package.

"For you, dear. The Maharaja's driver just brought it."

Tonya was up in an instant. She tore at the package. As she lifted the top of the large flat box, she gasped. There, against the velvet lining, lay a necklace, earrings and bracelet of emeralds and diamonds. She held out the box for Marva to inspect.

"Look, he sent these for me to wear tonight!"

"Whew! I'd say a good night's work, that!" Marva grinned and patted the edge of the lid.

At seven, Tonya stood in the living room awaiting the arrival of the Maharaja. The closeness of the regal jewelry had brought a flush of excitement that intensified her beauty.

General Sittel and Marva had departed a full hour previously in order to stop at his hotel.

Tonya heard the car pull into the driveway, and a few seconds later she heard Sita open the front door. She faced the entrance, and waited.

Mahabir Singh placed his hands upon her bare shoulders. "My beloved, they match your eyes like the white caps on cool green waters. You should always wear emeralds and diamonds."

Tonya smiled to herself. "Maybe I will."

The following morning, Marva sat on the side of the bed watching Tonya pack.

"It's really been wonderful having you here," Marva said sincerely. "A girl can get pretty bored with the social routine here."

"Why don't you avoid it when you get like that?" Tonya placed a neatly folded dress in the suitcase.

"Can't. Business, you know. Besides, occasional new faces break the monotony."

The Indian girl appeared in the doorway, waiting for permission to speak.

"What is it, Sita?" asked Marva as she became aware of the girl's arrival. She always sensed, rather than heard or saw the Indian servant's presence.

"The car is here, Mem-sahib."

The green Buick was outside. Sittel's corporal-chauffeur had been instructed to drop back by the Grand Hotel with his passenger en route to the airport. He didn't know why. But the boss had his reasons: a flat package, containing fifteen thousand rupees, was also making the trip north.

Marva held out her hand. "You won't mind if I say goodbye here, will you Toni?"

"Not in the least. These CNAC planes never leave according to schedule. No telling what time we'll get off. Thanks, Marva, for the wonderful week."

Marva couldn't help wondering at the happiness of her guest at leaving. Despite all the fun she had had in Calcutta, Tonya was evidently happy to be going back home. About an hour later, however, a call from the home of the Maharaja Mahabir Singh explained everything.

Marva informed him that Tonya had left no package for him. Amazed and desperate for fear she might become

271

involved, Marva called CNAC Airlines. "No, the flight has not left yet. . . Yes, we have a reservation for Mrs. Brownfield . . . No, she can't be located. We have tried."

Double trouble weighed heavily on the general's shoulders that morning. Two telephone calls, one from Marva and one from the Maharaja, had enlightened him regarding some "loaned" jewelry. This alone could become an international incident. But as he raced for the airport, the fear of fifteen thousand rupees being confiscated by custom officials was uppermost in his mind.

At the airport a very nervous Tonya Brownfield paced back and forth in front of the gate to the ramp, deliberately ignoring the loudspeaker that was repeatedly broadcasting her name. The DC-3 should be loading any minute. What could be keeping these infernal Chinese!

A few minutes later she saw two custom officers, accompanied by her last night's host, headed in her direction.

Tonya tightened her hold on the black make-up case as the group approached. She looked as if she might be holding a bomb about to explode, not knowing whether to hold it or throw it away and run.

"How nice of you to send me off," she blurted out as they stopped in front of her.

"I'll trouble you for your case, Miss," said one of the customs officers reaching for it. "We'll have to search it."

Tonya stood, pale as a ghost, while the customs man pulled out the velvet-lined box and opened it. He held it out to the Maharaja.

A MAHARAJA MAKES A LOAN

"Is it all here, Your Highness?"

"Yes." Then turning to Tonya: "I'm sorry, but these gems have been in my family for generations." He took the box from the officer. "I do not wish to prefer charges. Mrs. Brownfield is free to go." Then, without even looking at Tonya, the handsome Indian tucked the box under his arm and walked away.

The customs officials, however, were not so willing to drop matters.

"Have you been in India before?"

"Never."

"Do you plan to commute regularly?"

"No." Tonya was beginning to feel desperate, and trapped. She was alone, and it was stark bright daylight. No soft lights and music with which to play her wiles. And the money belt around her waist with the fifteen thousand rupees was getting heavier by the minute.

Then Boliker S. Sittel came puffing up like a steam engine. It took all his powers of persuasion and his military prestige to convince the officers that they should release Tonya to his care and responsibility.

When the delayed CNAC DC-3 finally pulled out of Calcutta, a somewhat humiliated Tonya sat slumped down in her seat. But the fifteen thousand rupees were still intact around her waist!

17 · A Tepid Reception

THE BATTLING BROWNFIELDS screamed at each other for three consecutive days and nights after Tonya's return. Auggie thought he had accused his wife of everything in the book, but he missed a few things Tonya was guilty of that even the book didn't have. After all, she made her own rules.

"This is the thanks I get for picking you out of the slums of Mexico and trying to make a military career for us! Up to now, Stud said I had a good chance to make colonel in the Air Corps."

Auggie stopped ranting long enough to pour a stiff drink.

"What are you talking about? If you had any backbone, you'd be making enough money by now to buy me some jewelry. Then you wouldn't have to worry about other men giving it to me!" Tonya slammed the door and headed for the recreation room.

The bar and the recreation room were unduly crowded with pilots and crew that night. Members from Adobe

A TEPID RECEPTION

Town were there too. All hands had been ordered together after dinner for an important message from their
leader. About the only members absent were Ole Nelson's
Third Pursuit, currently holding down the fort at Rangoon.

Lack of sleep and three days of arguing had taken their
toll of Tonya. As she stepped inside the archway leading
to the bar she appeared tired and haggard. Someone
passed the comment, "She's so pale, her dark circles look
like black eyes!"

"Wonder if Auggie slugged her?" suggested someone
hopefully.

Tonya stood at the entrance for a moment, impatiently
scanning the faces, then turned and left. Echoes from
her high heels resounded down the corridor and the steps
to the main entrance below. Knowing Rusty would be
along any minute, she had decided to wait outside for
him. The cool night air nipped at her bare arms as she
hugged herself to keep warm.

Presently a car drove up and parked. Its lights were
switched off. She wasn't too sure this was Rusty, even as
he drew closer. He had lost weight. His normally deep-
set eyes had sunk even deeper. He walked slowly, almost
painfully.

Neither spoke until Rusty stopped in front of Tonya.

"Rusty!" she exclaimed. "What on earth has happened
to you?"

He stood there for a moment before answering, "I might
ask the same."

275

"I'm serious," she insisted with concern.

"So am I. But, to answer your question, a dengue fever bug bit me before I could get out of Burma."

"You shouldn't be flying." She laid her hand on his arm.

"Nope, not while the Doc's got me full of quinine pills." He moved beyond her reach.

"Why don't you take some time off? We could drive around town and visit some of the Chinese shops."

"No, thanks."

"I get it," she said. "You've heard the gossip and are trying to avoid me!"

"Not exactly."

"What else could it be?"

"Just that I'd like to get back into the Marine Corps when this is over, and I don't want to get mixed up in anything that might involve me in an international incident. So, I've decided to use a little more discretion in my activities." He turned to go, then stopped. "C'mon, let's see what Stud has to say." He offered his arm to her as they started up the rough steps.

His coolness was just because he was ill, she thought. She could bring him around, she was sure. Not that it really mattered to Tonya. She had always been able to get her way before. It was her God-given gift.

"Can you visit me after the meeting?" she asked, assuming everything had blown over.

"Doubt if I could make like a human fly tonight." The

admission caused the corners of Rusty's mouth to turn up into a weak smile. On several occasions, he had scaled the uneven surface of the rock wall in order to gain access to the Historian's suite. Mountain climbing was one of his hobbies that had developed into usefulness.

"Tell you what then . . ." Tonya looked up at him with all the sweetness she could muster.

Rusty wondered what was behind the green eyes.

"I'll be waiting in your car. We'll drive over to Adobe Town after the meeting."

"All right. But let me walk into the meeting alone."

"See you later."

In his quarters Stud was trying to decipher the scribbling on numerous scraps of paper, penciled reminders to himself. On the edge of the bed sat his helpful exec in silence. The air was heavy with smoke. Auggie wiped his watering eyes, and leaned over to knock the dead ash from his cigarette. He would have loved to read the boss's notes, but to do so would entail his putting on his glasses, and this would be too obvious.

"How's the Empress?" he asked in a feeble attempt at making conversation.

"In pretty good spirits today." Stud piled the scraps

of papers together and opened the desk drawer to deposit them.

"Is that so?" Auggie's face relaxed for the first time in days.

"Yeah, Tom Tung sent word that the President has just approved a $500,000,000 loan for China."

"Wow, she should feel good! Most of that is as good as in her pocket!"

Stud glared at him.

"What's the matter?" Auggie inquired weakly.

"Better be careful, that's all."

"Why?"

"Your only chance of getting back into the Air Corps is being inducted on the spot in China. The Empress could have something to say about that!"

"I see." Auggie's face wore a hang-dog expression.

"With your record, you wouldn't stand a chance of getting called back at home," Stud reminded.

"I'm sorry. I thought everyone out here knew how she operated."

"What do you mean by that statement?" Stud demanded sternly.

"Oh, you know . . ." the harrowed man tried to explain.

"Brownfield, if I were you, I'd keep this kind of talk to myself. True or false, we have a job to do." Stud looked at his watch and picked up the case. "Let's get on into the meeting."

"Very well, sir." Auggie was somewhat crestfallen that a subject he knew a little about had to be terminated, thus preventing his elaborating further in his egotistical manner. He followed the leader out of the room.

"Here comes Old Ironsides now," someone alerted the others. "Wonder what he's got up his sleeve tonight!"

"Somehow, I've got a feeling I ain't gonna like it," came another voice.

The general conversation and speculation of the Group was quickly silenced by Auggie yelling, "Atten—*shun!*"

As the members stood, Stud proceeded to a spot near the end of the bar to deliver his address. Auggie shooed the two Chinese bartenders away as if they were flies.

Stud invited his command to be seated.

"Our existence has been approaching a crucial point for some time," he began. "I didn't talk about this earlier, because I didn't know how it was going to work out. This may come as good news to most of you. Others may not agree."

As Stud paused, the members eyed one another uneasily. The leader glanced over the crowd, then stiffening his shoulders, as though for courage of an expected onslaught, he continued.

"The Sharks are going to be inducted into the Air Corps.

279

Each member will be assigned the original rank or rating he held before joining the Group."

A rumble of disapproval came from the audience.

"I know—I know . . ." Stud held up his hands to quiet them. "I told General Sittel that you couldn't live on service pay."

Most of the pilots had been second lieutenants and ensigns when they joined. Such a move would mean they would suffer better than a fifty per cent cut in pay. This was a place where a seven hundred per cent inflation existed; it would be practically an impossibility for them to live on Army pay. Whisky was $50 a bottle. American cigarettes $5 a package. Even a decent toothbrush cost $5. There was no such thing as a post exchange. Luxuries and necessities of life alike were purchased on the black market.

"Don't get excited, this won't take place immediately. I've seen to that. The Air Corps will be flying in logistics personnel in a week or so, but it will be a couple of months before enough supplies arrive to take over completely. Therefore, I was able to forestall General Sittel a while longer.

"When the army officers arrive, I expect you to act and conduct yourselves as military men. Some of these people will be staying here in the hostel.

"Until now, discipline has been fairly lax. From now on, orders will be carried out to the letter. There will be no more asking for volunteers to strafe and support troops. You'll act as military men, or suffer the consequences for failing to obey orders. And let me remind you, this can be death before a firing squad!"

This last statement didn't sit well with Stud's pilots. Most of them had participated in morale missions deep into enemy territory, many times in aircraft that shouldn't have been flown. All this was strictly in violation of their contracts. They had done it for nothing. Now Stud was saying they would face a firing squad if they even so much as complained.

Most of the fellows sat by numbly, not knowing what to say or think. Some were cursing the Chinese. But a resentment for the Air Corps started that could only end in a flame of hate.

The rest of Stud's speech was of little consequence to the Sharks. Noting their lack of interest, he soon brought it to a close. "That's all for now. See you in the morning."

"Just a minute, Colonel," Rusty intercepted Stud as he was leaving.

"What can I do for you, Bush?"

"We don't know everything that's going on out here, but there're a few things we do know!" Rusty looked squarely at the uncomfortable nervous leader.

"I don't know what's got into you lately, Bush."

Other members were collecting about the two, now that they had a spokesman.

281

"We'd like a few answers to some questions, sir." Rusty spoke the "sir" almost with contempt.

"Like what?"

"What gives you the authority to violate the written agreements we have with the United States Government?"

Stud shifted uneasily. "There's a war on—or didn't you know?"

"Yeah, I know. *I've* been in combat. And I also know our agreement states we shall be taken back into our own service without loss of precedence. You're just trying to make a name for yourself, even if you keep us out here until we're all killed!"

Stud spoke angrily. "I'm only doing what's expected of me!"

"Like hell you are," Rusty flung back. "You're sending us out to strafe gorges and jungles, and play sitting ducks patrolling at low altitude and slow speed, for morale missions!"

Before Stud could object, Rusty continued. "Shooting down planes is one thing, but putting on a show for the slopeheads in these beat-up crates is a horse of a different color. We've lost four times as many pilots with your horsing around as we have in combat!"

"That's enough out of you, Bush. You must be drinking." Stud turned to leave.

Auggie stepped from behind Stud, to his side. "Go on, Colonel, I'll handle this."

Rusty stepped menacingly toward the exec. "Brownfield, you'd better stay out of this, or so help me, I'll bend your teeth!"

Auggie quickly placed himself behind the colonel again.

"And all these secret tactics you're supposed to have taught us," Rusty shouted, "what a laugh! We didn't see *you* demonstrate any of these. We found out everything we know the hard way. You want to hog the show so bad you don't even mention who shoots down the planes."

The colonel was almost shouting in his anger. "Bush, I'm warning you for the last time."

"When you sent out your messages on the tactics you taught, there was something missing . . ."

"Meaning?" said Stud defiantly.

"Where you got your info!"

"You don't make sense."

Rusty smiled knowingly. "Let me refresh your memory. You saw the first successful defense tactics used against the Japs drawn on a bed sheet . . ." Rusty waited for this to sink in. "By a fingernail!"

Tonya had bragged to him about teaching the old man tactics, and how her fingernail traced the manner in which two P-40's defended themselves against their more maneuverable foe. She hadn't got the idea across to him too well. In Stud's messages to the states it varied somewhat: "Francis Stud teaches his protégés to fight in pairs. While one is occupied shooting down a bomber, the other keeps the Jap fighters off his tail."

The question of who was going to protect the tail of

the fighter doing the protecting was overlooked! Most readers of newspapers and magazines back home never gave this a thought. But shortly after the first combat, the flyers discovered that by scissoring back and forth, reversing course rapidly, no plane could remain very long on another's tail.

The rest of her clandestine meeting with the Sharks' leader was omitted.

Stud started out of the recreation room. "What bed sheet was he talking about?" Auggie asked.

Infuriated because Rusty had shown him up, Stud stopped just before he reached the door. He turned back to point at Rusty.

"Bush, I just hope you never so much as think about turning down a mission—because it'll make me the happiest man in the world to order you shot!"

In a few minutes, the two Chinese bartenders were back pouring drinks for the members who had attended the meeting. Rusty swallowed one quick drink, and left.

He found Tonya huddled in his car as he climbed in to return to Adobe Town. In silence they traveled along the poorly lighted, gutted roads. Near the center of the city, Rusty shifted into low gear, and the car barely crawled along. The streets were jammed with the peasant masses of China. Their faded blue garments had been mended so many times that now patches were sewn upon patches. They paid about as much attention to an automobile as a herd of sheep back home.

A TEPID RECEPTION

"A horn is useless around here," grunted Rusty after he
had come to a complete stop for the fifth time. "Wonder
where they're going?"

"Going in for their rice," Tonya answered indifferently.
"Mind lighting me a cigarette?"

Rusty tapped the pack on the steering wheel, and held
it up while his lips extracted two cigarettes. He lighted
both, then handed one to Tonya, keeping his eyes on the
road ahead.

"What did Stud mean when he mentioned the *other*
Chinese, tonight?" Rusty said thoughtfully.

"The commies. He's pretending they don't exist, trying
to make you believe they're just another political party in
China."

"Oh."

"Communism," continued Tonya, "is really taking hold
over here. At the rate Mao Tse-tung keeps buying guns
and ammo, they'll take this country over some day."

"Yeah." Rusty shook his head in pity, as he scanned the
surging mass of humanity outside. "I don't imagine you'd
have to promise these poor bastards much to make them
turn in any direction."

As they pushed their way through the crowded streets,
it began to appear as if these folk didn't mind being run
over. Spotting a clear area, Rusty picked up his speed and
started to shift into second. A moment later he jammed
on his brakes.

A Chinese man lay on the ground, contorting his face

285

in pain, and holding his leg. It looked as though he had deliberately walked into the front fender and fallen over backward.

"He isn't hurt," Tonya said impatiently as she saw Rusty open the car door. "Drive on, Rusty."

He looked at her disdainfully. "The least I can do is find out!"

The Chinese was standing by the car window, alternately pointing down at his foot, and holding his hand out for money.

"They do it deliberately to get a few cents," Tonya said in disgust as she saw Rusty hand the man a $50 Chinese national bill, worth about a dollar in American money.

The man accepted the money, but continued to cry out in Chinese, and hold on to the door so that neither window nor door could be closed. Apparently the man wanted more damages. Finally Rusty climbed out, bent over and lighted a match to determine the extent of the injury. He found the big toe on the right foot was crushed and bleeding. The man's open-toed grass sandals had provided little protection.

Thinking it unwise to hang around outside the car any longer, Rusty shoved another note for twice the amount into the Chinaman's hand. Then he jumped into the car, rolled up the window and locked the door.

Soon they were out of the crowd and on their way again.

"They don't do much for the common folk in China, do they?" Rusty mused.

286

"Not unless they're soldiers."

"I can't see that the soldiers are much better off than the others. The other day I was over to a French hospital getting this bullet wound in my leg looked at, and I saw some pretty horrible sights."

"You mean Saint Croix Hospital?"

"That's the one. There were at least twenty Chinese soldiers laying just outside the entrance in the stinkingest litters you ever saw. God, how they smelled! Makes me sick to think about it! I found out they'd been laying there for two weeks, waiting to be admitted. Not so much as a shelter over them. And to think I was admitted with no more'n a scratch!"

"A Chinese life isn't very important out here."

"Now I know what Tex Wong was talking about." Rusty rolled down his window just enough to flip out his cigarette.

"Who's Tex Wong?" Tonya twisted in her seat to face him.

"An American-Chinese from Texas Christian University who came over on the boat with me. Accidentally ran into him a couple days ago. Wouldn't have recognized the boy in his slopehead uniform if he hadn't hollered out in that Texas drawl."

"What's he doing out here?" Tonya crushed the last spark from her cigarette on the sole of her shoe and dropped the butt on the floor of the car.

"Came over to liberate his ancestors. The Empress did

a hell of a public relations job on those second generation Chinese when she toured the States. The poor bastard told me he was getting Chinese army pay—about two bucks a month! Boy, was he in the dumps!" Rusty laughed. "I'll never forget the look on his face, or the way he said it—'If I ever get out of this damn joint, I think I'll go home and shoot my parents for making me Chinese!'"

Inside the hut at Adobe Town, the couple warmed their hands over the charcoal pot next to the bed.

"What'll it be—straight or mixed?" asked Rusty, as he turned to the rickety dresser, upon which were two bottles and glasses.

"Make mine straight scotch," said Tonya as she eyed the crude contents of the room.

Rusty spilled some of the precious scotch on the floor while pouring. "Damn it! If I had a little more light, maybe I could see what I'm doing!"

As she wandered about the room, Tonya had picked up a pair of red dice from the table. Rubbing them between her hands as though to warm them, she walked over to Rusty.

"Here 'tis, m'lady fair," clowned Rusty, handing her the glass. "I'd suggest you perch on the bed, closer to the heat. This room is a bit more drafty than some of your other associates' quarters."

"Now, Rusty!" She sat down, leaning back provocatively. "C'mon," she rolled the dice expertly across the blanket covering the bed, "let's shoot some craps."

A TEPID RECEPTION

"I can't take money from a lady, but I'll play you for fun." He seated himself on the opposite end of the narrow bed, sipping his drink, as he watched the yellow flame flicker in the kerosene lamp.

Tonya rolled the dice and scooped them up with her long slender fingers, keeping her eyes on Rusty. "I made something for you," she said, continuing to pass the dice. "I'll give it to you tomorrow. It's for good luck."

Without removing his eyes from the flickering lamp, Rusty spoke in a dry tone.

"Don't tell me, let me guess. It's a white silk scarf with 'Forever Tonya' embroidered in red on one corner."

"How did you know?"

"By the way, did you give Nelson one before he left?"

"We-e-ll, he asked for it."

"That's two down and one to go. That kinda luck I can do without!"

"Aw, you're not superstitious, are you?" Tonya stretched a slim leg toward him enticingly.

Rusty looked at her thoughtfully. "No, I'm not superstitious," he said slowly. "I just don't like taking gifts from women."

Tonya kicked off her shoes. "I'm not just any woman!"

"Hallelujah! You can say that again!"

"I'll bet you a thousand," she said, playfully rolling the dice out between them. "Want to cover me?"

Rusty looked down at the four and the five eyes on the dice lying on the blanket, and said nothing.

289

The slim fingers retrieved the dice and rolled again. The third roll brought a repeat of the first.

"You owe me a thousand! Double or nothing!"

Without waiting for a reply, she rolled the dice once more and in a few moments, again exclaimed, "I win again! Now you owe me two thousand."

Gleefully, she rolled the dice a third time. This time the dice showed a single spot on each. Quickly she scooped them up.

"Cocked dice," she claimed, implying they were in a ripple on the surface of the blanket. Quickly she rolled again. This time the reading was more satisfactory—a pair of fours.

Rusty watched this one-sided crap game indifferently. After a few more rolls, a seven showed. Quickly Tony scooped the dice up again—with the same comment: "Cocked dice!"

Rusty laughed. "Hope you're enjoying yourself. Doesn't look like I'm gonna get to play!"

He moved over to the soap-box dresser and poured himself another drink. His guest was so engrossed in her own by-play, he didn't bother to offer her another.

As he seated himself again, she cheerfully informed him, "Now you owe me eight thousand! Here we go, double again!"

"Just a minute, sweetheart," said Rusty as she looked up at him, "eight thousand what? You're getting so you sound serious!"

"Rupees, of course! Nothing else is any good around here. You owe me eight thousand rupees. 'Course I'm serious. Want double or nothing?"

"What are you gonna cover with?"

"Oh, I've got it. I collected some gambling debts today."

"Knock off this nonsense," said Rusty, reaching over and pulling her toward him.

"But I . . ." Tonya's words were smothered by his lips as she found herself pressed down upon the bed.

Shortly before eleven, they approached Number One Hostel.

Tonya turned to Rusty. "Let me out here. I'll walk around to the entrance and meet you in the bar."

By the time Rusty had parked the car and walked back into the bar, Tonya was already there, drink in hand. He sensed excitement as he entered.

"Hi, Rusty," called out Truelove, "did you hear the news?"

"Naw. What gives?" Rusty slapped down three rupees to the bartender. "Scotch."

"They had a hot mission over Chiang Mai today!"

"Don't tell me. Another strafing mission? Who got it this time?"

"Nelson and Nichols."

"Lost or shot down?" asked Rusty.

"The message said both were killed is all I know. I happened to be in the shack when it came in!" Bob Truelove shoved his glass to the bartender for a refill. "That ain't all I heard either," he added, not looking at Rusty.

His tone made Rusty take notice. "Well, what else is new?"

"I was in the paymaster's office drawing an advance and our friend Mrs. B. was there too!"

"So what?"

"She was collecting Sandy and Kirk's final pay checks, claiming they were a gambling debt to her!"

Rusty stood motionless. Neither man looked at the other, and neither spoke.

"Well, boys, why so serious?" Tonya sidled up to them cheerily.

Rusty looked at her with unbelieving contempt. "Nelson's dead," he said flatly.

"Oh—" She did not seem too surprised.

"I wonder how much his gambling debt is?"

Rusty brushed rudely past her and strode out of the club.

18 · The End of the Sharks

In Francis Stud's office, a meeting of some importance had just taken place. Paul Eddy was making a last visit from the United States to turn the FEAMCO plants in Calcutta and Toyling over to the Air Corps. Boliker Sittel had flown from India for the occasion.

Francis Stud had been commissioned a major-general in the Air Corps two months prior to the official induction date. This generous portion of rank had been bestowed upon him early, because Sittel anticipated his fullest co-operation.

Although Stud had driven a good bargain with Sittel, he took no chances. Three days after accepting the Air Corps commission, the Empress promoted him to a three star position in the Chinese Air Force, as her aviation advisor. Now, if any of the Air Corps brass tried to transfer him from China, they would be out of luck. Stud had it made. This left only one person to answer to, and he knew too much about the Empress for her to alter his position. The few Americans left in the picture, in any stratum, would be removed, one by one.

Now as Brownfield was helping General Sittel get his baggage into the station wagon parked out front Paul Eddy and Stud had a moment to themselves.

"Well," smirked Stud, "it took a little time, but I finally got you outa my hair."

"So you did, Francis."

"Now that you're out of a job, what'll you do—enlist in the service?"

"You might call it that." Paul was amused at Stud's crude attempt to get his goat. "I'll be leaving for South America shortly. I'm accepting a post as ambassador."

Stud's jaw dropped, and the smug expression on his face slowly disappeared.

"Good God, man, it takes money to be an ambassador!"

"Yes, I know, Francis." Paul winked at his wilted friend, and patted him consolingly on the arm. "I managed to save a few million dollars before closing out the books on FEAMCO."

Before Stud could regain his composure, Paul Eddy had quietly closed the door behind him. Stud sank slowly into his chair.

His exuberant exec brought him rudely back to reality by flinging the door open.

"Well, everything's taken care of, sir," Auggie said cheerfully.

After a moment's hesitation, Stud slowly raised his head. "Sure is," he said, "all but one thing."

"What's that, sir? Something I can do, sir?" Auggie walked up to the desk.

With a sympathetic look at him, Stud nodded, "Take a chair. I've a bit of news for you."

He rose and strode to the window. Staring out across the field, he spoke slowly and precisely.

"Brownfield, you know the honor of our country is at stake in the men who represent her. It looks as though we will all profit well by this induction into the Air Corps."

"Yes, sir." Auggie puffed out his chest in anticipation. "We need experienced men."

"It can lead to a great future, as well as a secured re-tirement," continued the leader. "But, as you well know, the Empress can turn thumbs down on anyone."

The exec nodded.

"Last evening she sent for me, and advised me that Tonya has been making illegal money exchanges here. This is a death penalty for Chinese. Because you are my executive officer, she told me—instead of making an international incident out of it. However, she demands that Tonya be removed from the country. Unless she is, you won't have a Chinaman's chance of getting into the Corps."

The exec's red face twisted in anger.

"Sir," he said, "that is a move I have been contemplating for some time. If my country needs me, no sacrifice is too great. I will take care of it right away."

Before Stud could say more, Auggie was out the door and on his way.

295

TONYA

Shaking his head, as though in pity for the man, Stud said to himself, "Thank God that's one mission *I* don't have to carry out. Guess I better stay away from the hostel if I expect to get any rest before dinner."

Auggie drove to the hostel and dashed breathlessly up the last flight of stairs to the third floor. The exertion did nothing to lesson his rage. He strode down the hall and without knocking flung open the door to Tonya's quarters, and slammed it behind him.

Tonya emerged from the bedroom.

"Well," she said coldly, "I didn't hear you knock."

"I didn't."

"Well, next time do! I like *some* privacy." She started back to the bedroom.

"So you can carry on money negotiations that even your husband doesn't know about, until his career is jeopardized by *it* and *you*?" he screamed after her.

She walked toward him. "And just what business is this of yours?" she demanded, narrowing the green eyes to mere slits.

"You didn't do this alone. Some man had to be in on it—who—where'd you get such quantities of money?"

Noting the intensity of his rage, Tonya's anger somewhat subsided.

Grabbing her by the shoulders, Auggie shoved her back and into a chair. He stood in front of her, his face strained until the veins in his temples stood out like blue lines on a map, and his eyes bulged like an overstuffed toad's.

"None of your business."

THE END OF THE SHARKS

"It's my business you're ruining! My whole career! I'm just about to be made a regular colonel in the Air Corps and you pull something like this!" Auggie gave the Chinese coffee table a resounding kick, scattering its contents across the room.

"Quit kicking my things around," shrieked Tonya, bounding out of the chair.

"*Your* things! Well, you can just pack *your* things because *you're* leaving. We're through!" He picked up a Chinese vase and smashed it against the far wall.

"I'll leave when I'm damn good and ready."

"Oh no, you won't." For once he had the upper hand. "You'll start packing first thing tomorrow if you expect to take this stuff with you—or you'll be escorted out of the country with only the clothes on your back!"

"What are you talking about? You can't force me to leave!" Her voice sounded dubious.

"Maybe not. But the Empress can—and will. She's given the order!" He stood arrogantly in front of her. This was his moment.

"That bitch!" Tonya was like a tigress. "Who does she think she is? All those girls she travels with sure aren't *maids!*"

"Well, she's boss, and it's *her* country!" Auggie kicked a chair aside.

Tonya's reply was a carved wooden head, flying in Auggie's direction.

Ducking, he stepped forward and grabbed her arm as she reached for another.

297

"You no good tramp! Get yourself ready to go. You'll be shipped out with the others we don't want, as soon as the group is inducted. In the meantime, stay out of the city and everybody's way. Those are orders from Stud and the Empress!" He flung her arm down and headed for the door.

"And be sure you get a divorce as soon as you get stateside, or I will!" he screamed as he stormed out.

On the first floor, the small group of pilots looked up the stairway as Ross Dickey said, "First time I ever knew an earthquake could be confined to such a small area!"

A couple of weeks later, a few of the pilots were getting themselves good and drunk in the Number One Hostel bar. This was becoming a nightly occurrence, with the induction less than three weeks away. None of the Sharks wanted to stay a day longer than necessary, regardless of what Stud's plans were.

"Chuck, ol' boy, I didn't see you come in." This greeting from Bob Truelove brought a chuckle from the group because it was doubtful that Bob could see much of anything at this point.

"Just did. Ol' Stud's been giving the crew a heartbreaking talk." Chuck gulped his drink and sighed. "We just got through donating two hundred thousand rupees to the Chinese war orphans."

"Two hundred thousand rupees! Where'n hell did ya' get that kind of dough?" exclaimed Rusty.

Chuck enlightened his friends: "Before Rangoon fell, we loaded a truck apiece full of Springfields, machine guns, mortars, ammunition and medical supplies. We told the slopeheads at the border we was carryin' airplane supplies, and they let us through.

"Toni Brownfield got the contact for the deal, but we didn't know she was sellin' to the commies.

"Anyhow, Stud tried to threaten us at first, saying smuggling carried a death penalty, and all that crap. But when he saw he wasn't getting nowhere, he changed his tactics. The whole matter was forgotten when we agreed to give the Empress the money for her favorite charity."

"Did he tell you her favorite charity was herself?" asked Ross.

"I'll bet Toni didn't cough up her cut," Rusty said, in a nasty tone.

"We didn't say who our contact was," Chuck scratched his head. "I'll be hanged if I know how they found out."

"Why, you stupid chumps!" ridiculed Rusty. "Everybody gets what they want, same as always. The commies get their guns and the Empress gets her dough, and the Sharks can go live with the Chinese war orphans."

Official induction day was over. It had been a gala occasion for Stud. There were many flowery speeches.

The Empress and Stud had monopolized the show. The highlights of China were brought out in eloquent detail, and the shadows were carefully avoided.

The longer the grim-faced Shark leader talked, the more carried away he became with his own words. According to Stud, every man in his command would be staying on in China. They would be accepting their respective ranks and rates as fast as the Air Corps induction board officers could look over their records and sign them up.

So much liquor was consumed that night that in the morning a collective hangover covered the Group like a London fog.

Later in the morning a number of the celebrants were in search of a little hair of the dog. Number One Hostel's bar was closed as tight as on election day. The residents of Adobe Town, however, were carrying on like another county. Their bar had never closed.

"What'sa matter, Chuck?" asked Rusty, noticing him shake his head after a big gulp of bourbon.

"Just thinking about how generous Stud talked yesterday." Chuck tipped up his glass again. "The way he offered us to the Air Corps. First he says there's never gonna be another group like us—then he turns 'round 'n tells this crowd of Air Corps jerks exactly the opposite!"

"How's that?" asked Rusty, refilling his glass from the bottle sitting in front of them.

" 'Remember,' he says. 'The Empress expects the members of the Air Corps to carry on the brave tradition of the

300

THE END OF THE SHARKS

Sharks—so henceforth, you'll be known as the Flying Sharks.' Man, do you know what that means? Every cook, baker and grease monkey that sets foot in China, or sets eyes on Stud, is gonna call himself a Flying Shark!"

"You're about right, Chuck," Rusty said. "That's another reason I'm going over to Number One Hostel and collect my pay—just as soon as I get through talking to the induction board."

"What'll you tell 'em, Rusty?"

"I'll tell 'em where they can stuff their commission first," he snorted. "Then I'm gonna tell 'em I'm going back in the Marines." He took a healthy slug from the bottle between them. "What'll you do, Chuck?"

The unshaven mechanic paused for a moment, his eyes glassy with moisture. He answered slowly, "Going back to Arkansas first, to see my mama and my daddy. Then I'll decide." He brightened up as he added, "I can hear my old daddy saying, 'Charles, we knowed you was a-coming back, 'cuz we never got that ten thousand dollars insurance. You know, son, we could've done a heap of fixing around here with that kinda money!' "

Rusty laughed heartily as Chuck finished with his usual sheepish grin. He was going to miss the old Arkansas traveler.

"Well, are you gonna be one, or buy one?" Chuck said.

"Thanks, hold mine. I'll be right back." He staggered slightly as he moved away from the support of the bar. "I gotta go see the paymaster!"

The door swung closed behind him.

As Rusty emerged from the paymaster's office, he heard familiar steps hurrying after him.

A familiar voice called, "Rusty! Hey, Rusty, wait a minute."

He stopped as Tonya ran up to him.

"Hi, what's the hurry?" she panted.

"No hurry—just have to get back to Adobe Town and finish packing."

"I just heard you were leaving tomorrow. I'm leaving Thursday—catching the boat in Bombay."

"Good, hope you have a nice trip." He turned to leave.

Tonya placed a restraining hand on his arm and moving close, smiled up sweetly. "Why don't you wait for me in Bombay and we'll take the boat together?"

Deliberately, he removed her hand from his arm.

"No thanks, Baby, this is where our trails part. If I'm lucky, they won't cross again. If they do, do me a favor—forget you ever knew me!"

On Thursday morning Tonya boarded the CNAC plane for Calcutta, en route to Bombay. In the few days previous there had been considerable confusion connected with getting her choice belongings shipped out. Even now, she carried more weight than was allowed. But with orders from the Empress, the officials overlooked it in order to expedite the elimination of this personage from the country.

Her departure was without fanfare. Other than the official Air Corps driver, who delivered Tonya and her baggage to the terminal, there were only Chinese.

As Tonya alighted from CNAC in Calcutta to await her departing plane for Bombay, two hours hence, she noticed customs officials eying her. One of them approached her as she was about to enter the bar.

"Do you expect to be with us long, Madam Brownfield?"

"Only until my plane leaves in about two hours," she replied haughtily.

In Bombay crowds had gathered at the pier to see the ship depart. Everyone seemed to have someone bidding him Bon Voyage—that is, everyone except Tonya Brownfield. She stood at the rail alone. At the sound of a familiar voice, she turned to see Ross Dickey heading in her direction. Stepping back from the rail, she smiled and called to him as he started to pass. He saw her—she knew that—but from the look he gave her as he deliberately brushed past she knew she would be traveling alone. She turned back to the rail, hugging the mink coat on her arm tightly to her, as a chill passed over her body.

She became aware of someone standing close. She looked up to see Gil Withcomb smiling smugly at her.

"Having trouble getting a traveling companion?" Obviously he had observed the brush-off from Ross. "Perhaps I can accommodate."

Tonya's face slowly broke into a smile, as she slipped her arm cozily through his in acceptance. After all, he was a man!

The bluff Stud had tried to pull on his volunteers, saying they had to be inducted, had failed. As a body, they stood pat, insisting upon their contractual agreements that they be returned to the United States. Most of them were time-worn men, but Stud would be the last to appreciate this fact. Only the members of his former staff wanted to remain. Stud knew better than to submit their names.

A few weeks later the last of the Group's business was completed. Auggie was still hanging around, expecting a colonel's commission to be forthcoming any day.

"I can't understand it," Auggie had muttered this repeatedly in Stud's presence.

"Can't understand what?" Stud finally asked in self-defense.

"My commission. I wonder what's keeping it. Hope they didn't check my file in Washington."

Stud sat behind his desk watching the frustrated man pace back and forth in front of him. He had intended to talk about this before. It might as well be now.

"Auggie . . ."

"Yes, Colonel," came the submissive response. He

looked like a whipped dog. Apparently he could feel it coming.

"I want you to know that I've done everything possible," Stud said with a straight face. "All I can say is, you can't fight City Hall."

"I suppose so," said Auggie weakly.

"Tell you what I'll do," volunteered Stud. "Let me write you a letter of recommendation to Sittel. You can take it along with you. Undoubtedly there will be some nice civilian jobs in headquarters."

Auggie's shoulders drooped as he said in a low voice: "Thank you, sir, but I think I'll go back to Mexico. Might even do a little prospecting."

Like a man suddenly aged he walked slowly out of the office and closed the door quietly behind him.

Stud sat in silence, thinking. He kind of hated to see Brownfield go. The place wouldn't seem quite the same without him. He would miss him, also the convenience of using his attractive young wife without his finding out— or letting on if he did. But, after all, sentiment might jeopardize his future, so he would have to go.

19 · The Widow On The Hill

A VOLLEY OF RIFLE FIRE rang out from Arlington Cemetery.

On these occasions the sound always seemed to penetrate the wooden buildings of Marine Corps Headquarters located nearby. The echo was exceptionally loud on this August afternoon, or so it seemed to the colonel seated in his office there.

Another volley ripped the air.

"Damn it all," a young private first class exploded as one of his broad fingers hit two keys on his typewriter. Judging by appearance, the lad would have been more at home fighting for the heavyweight championship of the world.

"Never ceases to amaze me," commented the graying colonel, as he watched the Marine reach to clear the tangled letters on his machine.

"What's so amazing?" the young officer in the chair beside the colonel's desk inquired politely.

"Our friend over there," the colonel nodded in the

306

direction of the husky typist. "How do we do it? You always see some Marine that weighs a hundred and thirty pounds, sopping wet, changing tires on a ten ton-truck, and a gorilla like that sweating over a female's printing machine."

A third volley of shots echoed through the room.

"Must be having a military funeral next door," said the colonel, taking another sip of coffee from a white mug. Letters in red nail polish designated its owner: COL. R. A. BUSH, U.S.M.C.

"This morning's paper said General Francis Stud was being buried today. That shooting must be for him," the young officer said.

Suddenly the graying colonel with the deep-set eyes started to laugh, as though the young officer had said something funny.

"I don't get it." The young officer was somewhat awed by this outburst. "I thought you were one of his boys."

"When I left him seventeen years ago, he didn't think the world could get along without him."

"Boy, that certainly must've been a great gang, those Flying Sharks. I was in high school at the time—used to read everything I could lay my hands on about them." He paused thoughtfully. "It seemed odd to me at the time that only two books were written by people who were there. They came out during the war."

Colonel Bush shook his head. "Must've missed those.

After I returned to the Corps, they sent me back to the Pacific for the duration."

"What happened to this good-looking babe, Tonya Brownfield, that wrote *The Shark Woman*?"

"She was no mermaid," sighed the colonel. His eyes rested upon the large pale yellow stone mounted in a massive gold ring on his little finger. It radiated beauty. He held his hand up and blew his moist breath on the ring. Then he sat polishing it until the fire from the stone was more brilliant than ever.

"I didn't think she wrote much of a book," the younger man broke the silence.

"I didn't read it," said the Colonel, "but she had enough material to make *Forever Amber* look like a girl in kindergarten!" He reconstructed the story for the young officer.

Shortly after her arrival in New York, Tonya contacted a publishing firm. With the shortage of paper during the war, they were wary of giving a contract on anything as mediocre as her diary until she mentioned a guaranteed five thousand copies! If she could obtain a written guarantee for these, they would publish it.

Next came Washington, D. C. The Chinese Ambassador, Sam Choy, received a call one day. An appointment was made for lunch. Sam appeared delighted when Tonya showed up in the company of her most recent traveling companion. Gil Withcomb was no stranger to Sam, who had a good idea of what was on Tonya's mind. She couldn't have played into his hands any more perfectly than by bringing Withcomb along.

Tonya went straight to the point. "Mr. Choy, do you recall our conversation in Kunking?"

"Certainly, my dear, I'll be most happy to help you."

"Good, then you won't mind writing my publisher and guaranteeing my first five thousand copies." She reached into her purse and extracted a card. "You'll find the name and address on this."

"Surely you're not going to attempt such a project yourself?" Sam asked as he slipped the card into his pocket.

"I tried to get Mr. Withcomb to help me, but he keeps insisting on a fifty-fifty split straight down the line." She turned to Gil and smiled. "Perhaps I can get someone on the West Coast for a flat fee."

"It's customary for a ghost-writer to get half of everything," said Gil with a hurt expression.

"I should think Mr. Withcomb would be the ideal person," Sam encouraged. "He's been over there. In fact, he's seen it from both sides, being a captive."

"But fifty per cent!" argued Tonya.

"Now—now." Sam was a real diplomat. "Mr. Withcomb could make an exception—" he paused until he could catch Gil's eye—"couldn't you, Mister—Gilbert—Withcomb?"

"All right," he agreed, looking more insipid than ever as he realized this was an order, not a question.

TONYA

In his letter to the publisher, Sam Choy protected himself by explicitly stating that Gil Withcomb would ghostwrite the manuscript in its entirety.

After receiving the completed work, the publishers were more disappointed than ever. But they were stuck. The first printing was five thousand copies. With the subsequent lack of orders, a second printing was not necessary.

The colonel smiled to himself as he continued explaining. "I also heard she signed a year's lease on a plush, completely furnished, two-bedroom apartment. You know, one of those where you pay the first and last month's rent in advance. Toni stayed there the three months it took Gil to complete his work. That first and last month's rent was all the landlord received in rental. And when Toni departed, they found they had an unfurnished vacancy. She had sold every stick of furniture in the place lock, stock and barrel!"

"That woman sounds fantastic!" was the only comment the awed young lieutenant could think of.

"A gal long on looks, and short on morals!"

"Have you seen her since?"

"No," replied Bush, "but I heard she finally got married again."

"To money?"

"Not the way I heard it. Her reputation finally caught up with her."

The young officer sighed. "Not to change the subject, sir, but I'd like a little advice."

The colonel grinned. "I'm probably the last person you should come to for advice, but fire away."

"Well, sir, you know a reserve officer has about as much chance of getting a retirement out of the Corps as a snowball in hell."

"Thinking about getting out?"

"I've had offers thrown at me from a couple of different sources in the Caribbean. I don't know which to take."

"Soldier of fortune, huh? Let me guess. One from Santo Domingo, and the other from Cuba."

"How'd you know?" the lieutenant looked surprised.

"The Caribbean is a second home for Marines. Trujillo hired a bunch of non-coms when their enlistments ran out. That was some years ago when they were chasing bandits in Haiti—Charlemagne Peralte and the like. Last time I was down there was before the war. Most of these non-coms were generals then.

"I asked one of them how he liked it. He told me, 'We all married local girls. The pay is good. We send our children to school in Europe or the States. We live quite comfortably!'

"When I asked him if he'd ever had any regrets he said, 'At first when Trujillo established authority, I came close. He had thousands of Haitians put to death. We had to supervise this. Their heads were chopped off into a long

311

pit. It took nearly three days to get the job done. Sometimes the blood was ankle-deep. By the third day, when
the flies had got to the mess, it was pretty nauseating.'"

He paused, taking a long draw on his cigarette.

"Kinda looks like some old Marines might be losing
their security. The absolute dictatorship is tottering, thousands of rebels have been put in jail. Castro and the people behind him are fostering this move, may even attack
Trujillo openly one of these days." The colonel sounded
concerned.

"Which side do you think will win, Colonel?"

"That's not the important thing," Rusty pointed out. "If
you're interested in making money, then pick the side that
has Uncle Sam's blessing. That's where the money lies."

"I get your point, Colonel. It's well put," the lieutenant
said. "What are you going to do? I understand you're
retiring next month. Get yourself a little turkey ranch on
the West Coast?"

"Not this chicken." A twinkle came into Rusty's eyes.
"I might even go with you. After all, the Empress has
taught me how easily it can be done."

He leaned back in his chair, looking thoughtfully at
the ceiling as he spoke again.

"Next time I won't be so obstinate when I see people
fleecing Uncle Sam, now that I know he doesn't care too
much! I'll keep my big mouth shut and work right along
with the others."

The chair came forward. Rusty rested his elbows on the desk as he looked at the lieutenant smilingly.

"I'd a whole lot rather retire in Acapulco than on a stinking chicken ranch."

In the rural suburbs of Los Angeles, a teenage boy and girl sat in a car parked at the end of a residential street at the top of a hill overlooking the valley below.

They watched the postman stop at a house close by. A brown pekinese dog barked ferociously at him, charging back and forth. The two laughed as they saw the postman kick at the animal, who carefully bounced out of reach, and circled the man to nip playfully at his heels.

"Doesn't seem to like the postman, does he?" laughed the boy.

"He's a stranger. You never see him stop there except about once a year."

"Who lives there?"

"I don't know her name. Here in the neighborhood we call her the 'Shark Woman.'"

"Jeepers, where'd she get a tag like that?"

"I don't know. I've heard her called that all my life. I heard Mom and Dad say something once about her being married to some guy who drank himself to death.

313

She's lived alone ever since." The girl pointed, "Look, there she comes now! I bet she checks that mail box three and four times a day. First time I ever saw the postman stop, though."

"Gee, what a creep! Bet she's eighty if she's a day! Look at the wrinkles! If I didn't know what a prune was, I'd say that's it!"

"She does look pretty dissipated. But I heard my dad say she was only about forty-eight. But he said she'd lived those years twice. Don't know what he meant. I've never seen any visitors there. Her shades are always drawn."

"Who'd want to visit that!" The boy turned in his seat, "C'mon, baby, sit close—you're my type to visit!"

Tonya heard Lucy barking out front. What in the world could it be—the dog barked only when people came near the house. She hurried to the front door, just in time to see the postman walking away. After a moment, when she was sure he had passed, she hurried down the walk to the mail box. As she opened it, her heart fluttered at the sight of the familiar square envelope lying inside. Removing it, she clutched it to her breast, and hurried back up the walk and into the house, closing the door quickly behind her.

THE WIDOW ON THE HILL

Inside, Tonya leaned against the closed door for a moment, as though to catch her breath, still holding the letter close. Then she moved slowly to the teakwood table standing in the hall. A large mirror hung above it.

Looking down at the letter she held, she read the return address in the top left hand corner:

> Ross Dickey, Secretary
> Shark Invitational Banquet
> 10776 Crannon Ave.
> Los Angeles, Calif.

Carefully she placed it, unopened, on top of fourteen other identical envelopes that lay on a silver plate at the end of the table.

She raised her eyes to the mirror. The reflection she saw was not one to be proud of. Wrinkled skin made the faded green eyes look as if they were peering through cobwebs of the past. Auburn hair was dry and lifeless from too many years of dying. Even recent applications of auburn dye failed to help it.

"Well, Tonya," the reflection asked, "what excuse shall we send this year? Shall we be leaving for Rio de Janeiro this time—or have we used that one before?"

315